STOLEN FROM THE DEMON PRINCE

LAUREN CROWNE

ENID BOOKS

1

VERA

"I thought you might be down here."

Wiping the sweat from my forehead, I turned around at the sound of Leo's deep voice. I didn't know how long he'd been watching me train, but he stood on the edge of the pit, his silver eyes staring down. Large even for a demon at more than six feet tall, Leo already towered above me on a normal day, but now, looming over where I stood on the mats covering the pit, his body was even more imposing.

Leo crossed his arms over his broad bare chest, his black wings folded, their silver tips barely visible behind him. His wavy black hair was messy from sleep, and the black sweatpants he always slept in hung low on his hips. I wasn't surprised to see his tail tapping the floor beside him in short staccato beats; it was a dead giveaway that he was pissed.

Despite his scowl, I did my best to smile. "Just getting some extra training in."

"At three in the morning."

"I couldn't sleep."

Leo's wings swung open, and he swooped down into the pit, forcing me a step back when his huge body landed inches away.

So close.

He was so close.

I should have known he would see right through me.

"Couldn't sleep, eh?" Leo tilted his head and examined me, and even as I tried to stand tall under his scrutiny, his intense stare made me hold my breath. Then his scowl shifted into a smirk. "Are you saying I didn't wear you out earlier?"

My cheeks burned as visions of tangling in his sheets flashed through my mind. His hands running through my long brown hair. His hands... everywhere. Flesh and sweat, heat and lust.

We had both fallen asleep quickly tonight, but like most nights since Leo announced that we were going back to Vestia, the demon kingdom, I woke up after a few hours, the warmth of Leo's body next to mine not enough to lull me back to sleep. It was surprising that this was the first night he had noticed that I was gone. There was no use tossing and turning in his bed, cursing my lack of sleep, when I could go sweat for a few hours while I worked on training my fae magic.

Especially tonight. Our last night at Leo's home before we left for the demon kingdom.

"That's not it," I told him. "I thought coming down here to train would help me be stronger. I know you think the demon kingdom isn't a safe place and you're worried about me."

Leo's smirk vanished, and he let out a loud breath, all humor lost from his expression. Accompanying Leo to Vestia had been a source of conflict between the two of us ever since Leo announced that he was going. We both knew he needed to confront his father after Leo's prototype was stolen, but I refused to stay here while he flew across an ocean. By that point, he knew there was no changing my mind and that I was going no matter what he said.

"No, Vera." He shook his head slowly. "I'm not worried about you."

"You're not?"

"No. If something were to happen to you while we're there," he said, eyes meeting mine, their intensity burning into my own, "I don't think I could survive it. I'm worried about myself."

So that was it. I stood up on my tiptoes and gently kissed him on the lips, a mild shock of electricity hitting us both when we touched. "Nothing is going to happen to me." I stared up at him and hoped my words would convince me as well as him.

"My father, his council, my cousins, all of them, they're ruthless, and they maintain their power through fear. To them, fae are only slaves. They wouldn't think twice about hurting you or taking you and selling you back into slavery. I wouldn't put it past any of them to try to use you to get to me."

"I won't let them."

"You can't defend yourself well enough to do that."

"Then *you* won't let them."

"I will do everything I can to protect you, Vera. You know I will."

I knew he was thinking of the night in the yard when Henry, the only human I'd thought was my friend, stabbed me and left me at the point of death for Leo to find. If Leo hadn't been there, if he hadn't been able to link with me and heal most of my injuries, I would have died. Henry was able to almost kill me in Leo's own home, yet now we were about to fly across an ocean to an unfamiliar place with openly hostile demons.

"I'm getting better," I insisted. "That's why I'm down here."

"You don't understand. I don't want you to ever have to defend yourself. What I want is to wrap you up and tuck you under my blankets for safekeeping. I want to know that you're warm in my bed, not down in the pit in the middle of the night training to fight demons."

I let my hand wander up to stroke his face, and we both shivered at the contact. I wasn't wearing any suppression tech since I was down here to work on increasing my strength. I concentrated on the feeling of his skin, the warmth spreading through both of us as my fae magic transferred to him. Sighing at the sensation, Leo leaned into my palm, closing his eyes at my touch.

"As much as I like your bed"—I smirked and tugged gently on his ear before cupping his face—"it sounds more like you want to keep me as a favorite toy, Leo."

With his eyes still closed, cheek pressed into my hand, Leo frowned. "As *my* toy."

"But I'm not a toy. I'm a former slave who has been freed by you. I know this trip is going to be dangerous, but we're a team. You and me. Right?"

Leo opened his eyes. "We are. Otherwise, I'd leave your cute ass here and go without you. But the thought of leaving you without me is even more aggravating, as if all the death threats I've been getting haven't been enough."

"You know you're popular if they care enough to want to kill you."

"I've never given a shit about being popular."

Circling one arm around my waist, Leo pulled me against him, the other pressing on my back as if to keep me as close as possible. I dropped my hand from his face and let him hold me, relishing the warmth our bodies created.

"Vera," he murmured into my hair, "sometimes I look at you and remember what you looked like... that night, bloodied in my arms. You were..." His grip on me tightened. "And it was because of me. Because my father wanted to steal my work."

"It wasn't your fault, Leo."

"It was."

"It wasn't. If I had been less naïve, I would have realized the danger I was in right away. If I'd been stronger, I could have fought him off. That's why I'm down here. I need to increase my magic so that I'm never left powerless again."

"I won't let you blame yourself either. You are incredibly powerful, especially over me."

"Oh yeah?"

Leo let go of me and took a step back, keeping my hands in his. "Vera, you're more powerful than you realize."

"Damn right I am. Let's go back to bed and maybe I can give you a demonstration." I tugged on his hands.

"No. Or at least not yet." Leo gestured to his own body. "I want you to hit me."

"Right now?" I frowned. "What about going back to bed?"

"We will. But I want you to try to hit me first. Everyone in Vestia is going to want to hit me for being gone for so long. You might as well get the first shot." With one hand, Leo patted his bare chest. "Show me what you've been working on down here. I'll judge if it was worth flying around my house in a panic when I woke up and found you were gone."

A smile broke out across my face and warmth filled my heart at the idea that he was worried about me. "You were panicked?"

"Of course I was."

"See? This is why I have to go with you to Vestia. If you're this upset about my training a few floors away, imagine how you'd feel if you left me across the ocean when you went home."

"Vestia is not my home."

"It's where you're from."

Leo's silver eyes narrowed, and his jaw was tense. "But it's not home. You, Vera. You are my home."

"Then right now your home is about to hit you."

Now it was his turn to smile. "We'll see."

"You ready for this?" I dropped into the stance Leo had taught me.

"I guess."

"Ready for a world of pain?"

"Sure."

"You don't sound ready. Okay. Here goes." I took a deep breath and readied myself before punching forward, hitting Leo square in the chest.

He didn't budge. "We're both losing sleep for you to hit me like that? Try again."

I shook out my hand, my knuckles stinging from the impact. "That was a warm-up."

"Of course. Now try again."

This time I focused more of my magic in my arm, imagining bolts of lightning zapping their way through my body, across my shoulder, down my arm, and into my balled-up fist. Reeling my arm back, I punched him in the chest again as hard as I could. He didn't move, but this time he flinched. It was such a small movement that anyone who didn't know him like I did might have missed it, but I didn't. I knew that punch had hurt, at least a little.

"What did you think?" I asked him.

"That was... better." Leo's hand went up to his chest where I had hit him. "Vera." His breathing was getting quicker, and he leaned over, dropping down to one knee on the mat. Oh shit, how hard had I hit him?

"Are you okay?" I crouched down next to him. "I didn't think one hit would hurt that badly. Are you sure—?"

Suddenly my foot was yanked forward, and I fell back onto my butt. In a second, Leo was on his feet, and his tail was wrapped around my ankle.

"You jerk!" I shouted up at him, but he only smiled. I twisted around and tried to drag myself away from him, but his tail held firm. I sat back down and focused on trying to unwrap it from my leg, but he kept it tightly circled around my skin.

"You can't let your mind get distracted, little one."

"I thought you were really hurt!"

"You were too trusting. If the injury is nonfatal, the enemy is still dangerous. I thought I'd taught you that already."

"But you're not my enemy."

"What if I was?"

"But you're not. I thought I'd hit you too hard and was going to make sure you were okay."

Leo exhaled loudly. "Another mistake. A hurt enemy is even more dangerous."

His tail relaxed and let my leg go, but before I could scramble to my feet, it wrapped around both ankles and pulled them together. Leo was suddenly on my back, his heavy body pressing my chest against the floor.

His arms were around me.

"Vera."

With Leo on my back, I could kick my feet, but my face was against the cold mat while he held down both my arms. My arms. My arms where Henry had stabbed me.

"*Vera*," he'd said.

Henry had held me down too. He'd slashed at me with a holo-knife. He'd taken my blood.

"Vera, what's wrong?"

Henry had laughed while stabbing me. He'd smiled when he held me down against the ground. He'd been so proud to be able to take my blood to give to the demon king.

"Vera!"

I'd stopped kicking and was lying flat on the floor, but in less than a second, I was scooped up from the mat and in Leo's arms.

"What did I do?" Leo's words came out in a rush as he cradled me against him. "Was that too much? Talk to me. You're shaking."

"I'm..." I stared down at my hands and was horrified to see that he was right. My hands were shaking, my arms were shaking—all of me was trembling no matter how much I wanted it to stop. There were no more lightning bolts, no more energy zaps, no more magic at all. I tried to say more, to figure out what had just happened, but my words were caught in my throat.

"Vera." Leo's voice sounded a million miles away. "Listen to me. You're okay. It's going to be okay. Take a deep breath."

I tried, but there was just no way. I couldn't. My breaths were coming with difficulty, each escaping with a short, rough gasp. Tears streamed down my face as I shook, but Leo held me tighter.

Damn it. I thought I was past this. I thought I was prepared for everything that was going to happen, no matter how dangerous. I wanted to be strong for Leo, for me, for this trip, but here I was crying in his arms. Tears came faster the more I thought about my own failures, my frustration only adding to my fear.

A comforting hum from Leo and his hand rubbing on my back brought me out of it. Twisting in his lap, I threw my arms around his neck and buried my face against his skin, wanting to feel nothing other than his presence and breathe in his scent for forever. I held on to him, forcing my body to calm down as I hoped desperately that he would anchor me in the present where everything was okay. My shaking slowly subsided as he ran his hands through my hair and let me cry against him.

"That night. When he... I was so *scared*." I sobbed.

"I know. I know, Vera. I know. I was too."

The next day we would be flying to the demon kingdom. We'd be across an ocean in a brand-new place. But that night, at three in the morning, down in the musty pit Leo used as a gym, the overhead lights were too bright, and the ever-present smell of stale sweat hung in the air. And on cold mats on the concrete floor, the two of us held each other, not wanting the warmth between us to end.

If I'd only known how quickly our lives would change.

2

—————

VERA

The plane took off in darkness. Within hours we were over the water, each mile taking us farther from what had been *a* home but never truly *my* home. Even as we flew overnight, the ocean between the human and demon continents felt infinite, its never-ending waves sparkling under the moonlight. I stared out the window at the ocean that separated Vestia from the human continent, and for the first time in my life, I truly felt like I was flying.

Rand slumped into one of the leather seats across from where Leo and I sat, tossing his brown hair back with a flick of his neck. Even though ninety percent of the time Rand seemed allergic to shirts, preferring to have his perfectly chiseled chest exposed, tonight he'd decided on a black button-down—the top buttons undone of course—and black jeans. Even dressed down, he looked like he'd just stepped out of a magazine, his whole demeanor fashionable and chic.

Rand stretched his long legs out into the aisle, crossing his brand-new black boots. He was almost as tall as Leo and just as cramped on this plane, but otherwise, their builds were very different. Rand was slender where Leo was broad, and Rand's adorably shaggy brown hair was effortlessly styled in contrast to Leo's dark, tousled waves.

"Isn't this fun?" Rand asked. "It's like we're in costume."

Costume indeed. Rand had insisted we dress in all black for the plane ride across the ocean, as if we were secret spies sneaking into Vestia. In a way, I guess we were. It would be after midnight by the time we landed, but even at that hour, demons would still be on the streets near Rand's apartment building downtown. He'd even bought black paint to cover the silver tips of Leo's wings since the prince was the only demon with that particular wing coloring. A trait passed to him from his mother and her silver fae wings.

We might have been trying to stay low-key, but the plane was anything but. The interior was all black leather, and everywhere I looked I saw the red Hellfire flame, symbol of the demon kingdom.

"Everything is ready for us at my old apartment." Rand thumbed through his phone.

Leo had been on his phone as well; while I stared out the window, he had been hunched over it, furiously texting and emailing his manufacturers and distributors for Syn. He was really doing it; he was really producing fake Dust without using a drop of fae blood, and I couldn't have been prouder of him. Tonight he didn't look like the wealthy entrepreneur that he was; instead, like Rand, he was dressed head to toe in black, a hooded sweatshirt underneath a leather jacket paired with jeans and boots.

"You kicked that girl out?" Leo didn't look up from his phone. "Hadn't she been living there all year?"

"I let her live there to keep my lease." Rand shrugged, likewise continuing to text. "Jasmine knew it was a temporary thing."

"Isn't it always a temporary thing with you?"

"You wound me, Your Highness. But yes, now it's ours for as long as we need it. There's a car waiting for us once we land, and it will take us all the way to my building. We'll only be on the street for a brief minute, so it's unlikely we'll be recognized unless some of my adoring fans see my incredibly handsome face and realize that I have returned."

"I want to hear more about this Jasmine," I told him. "And the fact that you have fans."

"*Had*," Leo said. "He had fans. I doubt they're still pining over you now that you've moved away."

"You're probably right." Rand sighed dramatically. "My fans have probably moved on to some other trendy young noble. I hear Zell has made quite a name for himself lately."

Leo finally looked up from his phone at that.

"Who's Zell?" I asked.

"A demon I hope you never meet," Leo answered. "And one I would prefer we never talk about again."

"He's a cousin. On the bad side," Rand continued. "I'm on Leo's father's side, which is bad enough, but Zell is on Leo's mother's side, which is a whole other level of awful. I guess they're both bad sides, actually."

"Oh." By *Leo's mother*, Rand meant the woman who had raised him, his stepmother, and not his actual mother who was the fae mistress of the king.

"Last thing I heard was that Zell was working for the king in his lab. Probably developing some new party drug if I had to guess."

"Such a waste of talent. Anyway." Leo put down his phone finally and draped an arm over my shoulders to bring me closer. "We'll get some sleep tonight, and then tomorrow I'll go see the old demon."

Rand didn't look quite as sure. "I still feel like we need a better plan first."

"I have the perfect plan," I told them. "We walk straight into his throne room—does he have a throne? Because I'm picturing an old dude on a throne—and kick his ass."

Leo stared at me like I'd grown three heads. "Vera. No."

"Yeah, no," Rand agreed. "He's a *terrifying* old dude on a throne."

Leo sighed deeply. "We're not even there, and I'm already ready to leave."

"Soon enough," said Rand. "As your strategist, Leo, I recommend a little more stealth here. For example, is the king at his country house or the palace? How much does he really know about Syn and Vera's blood? We need to find out what he knows, what his plans are, and then make a plan of our own."

"I don't care what his plans are. I'm going to tell him that I'm renouncing any claim I have to the kingdom."

Rand grimaced. "Is that really the best idea? Maybe you should think about that some more."

"I don't have to think. I know. As long as he still thinks he has power over me, he'll never leave me alone. I have to sever all connections with him. Once I make that official, he'll have no reason to get in the way of anything that I'm doing any longer."

"Except that he's still your father," Rand said.

"He's never acted like it. I don't think he cares about Syn at all. He only had that human steal it as a way to get me to come back. Well, he's getting his wish." Leo leaned forward in his seat, his eyes dark. "I plan to make him regret it."

"Then let's *plan* to gather information first. I know a guy," Rand told us. "He'll be very discreet. We'll get settled tonight and go there tomorrow."

News had spread quickly, it seemed, that Leo had developed a drug that could rival Dust, a drug that delivered the most expensive and powerful high known to man, made from the blood of fae. Syn, Leo's creation, was a powder that could be made in a lab without the use of fae blood, and it was stronger than regular Dust. Every human distributor wanted to get their hands on it to be the first to sell it, and Leo and Rand had been working around the clock on the details.

Unsurprisingly, Leo's phone rang again, and this time he stood up and went to the back of the plane to take the call.

"With this talk of cousins, I'm curious about something. If Leo doesn't become king next, who does?" I asked Rand.

"Since Leo is an only child, the succession will follow a complex path among various uncles and cousins. Most of the uncles are too old, so it will probably settle on some random cousin of ours. There are a couple of those who would be worse than others, but all are equal parts awful and dangerous."

"Since you're Leo's cousin, could you be the next king?"

Rand made a face as if he had just smelled something awful and shifted uncomfortably in his seat. "No, thank you. Leo's the natural choice, but once he renounces his title, it's going to be a bloodbath. There are simply too many evil relatives in this family who will murder each other if given the chance to hold that much power. Once Leo makes his announcement to the kingdom officially, we'll need to get back on this plane and go home—immediately, if not sooner."

"Even if he renounces the throne, he'd still be in danger?"

"If they think he poses a threat to their own power grab, then yeah. Definitely. This family is crazy. You still sure you want to be here?"

I glanced behind me at Leo, who stopped yelling into his phone when he saw me looking—just long enough for his scowl to turn into a small smile—then went back to the conversation.

"I'm sure."

"Speaking of official, is this whole thing between the two of you"—Rand gestured between me and where Leo was pacing— "official now?"

Suddenly my hands were the most interesting thing in the world. "I think so." I absentmindedly twirled the suppression bracelet around my wrist. "Sometimes it feels like he's keeping me at arm's length, but other times it feels like he'll never let me go."

"I see the way he looks at you. He's bringing you home to meet the family. That has to count for something, right?"

"His murderous, power-hungry family. Can't wait. Anyway, enough about me. What about you?"

"What do you mean, me?"

"Have you talked to Rob?"

With a dramatic sigh, Rand flung his head back against the seat, his wings curling around him to hide his face. "What's the point?"

"Uh, because you like him?"

Slowly, his wings relaxed, and I saw Rand's face. It seemed that just the mere mention of our fae friend was enough to get a reaction. Where normally Rand was all charm and chatter, now his face had fallen, his voice quiet. "It will never work. He's too pure for someone as morally corrupt as me."

I couldn't roll my eyes hard enough. "So that's why you bought him a phone and have been texting him the whole flight?"

Rand's mouth dropped open in surprise. "You little sneak. How did you know that?"

I held up the phone Leo had bought me. "You aren't the only one with Rob's number. Let me see…" I pulled up the texts. "Here's the screenshot he sent me. That message you sent him an hour or so ago was especially juicy. Would you like me to read it aloud?" I cleared my throat.

"That bastard. Is nothing private? Give me that." He snatched my phone away. "Let's see what you and Leo have been texting then, hm? I can't wait to read what cringey love notes he's been sending you."

I laughed, trying to grab the phone back. "He hasn't!"

He looked up from the screen. "And why not?"

"I don't know. Because we don't need to text. We're always around each other."

"Damn right you are. Can you blame him for keeping you close by? After what happened with that idiot human?"

"I guess not. Don't get me wrong. I want to be around him. I don't want to be anywhere else."

"Then what's the problem? Because there's obviously a problem. If you're not happy…"

"No, there's no problem! Everything is fine! We are very happy!"

"Happy people don't try to convince others that they're happy, Vera."

"I…" I sighed and leaned back in the leather seat, not sure what to say. This was the exact conversation I'd had in my own head a thousand times, and each time I only ended up more confused. "He makes me happy. But do I make him happy? I want to be with him, and I know he wants to be with me. But what if that's not enough? You know how long it took to convince him to let me come on this trip. If he wasn't worried about his father sending someone else to try to hurt me, there's no way he would have let me come with you guys. I know Leo and I are better together, and that's one of the reasons I insisted on coming, but I don't want to be another part of his life that's causing him stress."

Rand leaned forward in his seat and took one of my hands in his. "I can't speak for Leo's stress, because the truth is he's under more pressure than ever before to get Syn manufactured and distributed. Marcus and I are helping where we can, but none of us have ever done anything like this before, either. That being said, if you're not..." He waved his other hand around as he searched for the right word. "If you're not *okay* with the way things are, then tell him and change it. Communicate with him. You've never held back what you thought before, Vera, so I'm not sure why you're doing it now."

"It's not that easy."

"I'm Leo's chief communicator. I know what I'm talking about."

I raised an eyebrow. "I saw exactly what type of communication you specialize in when I saw that screenshot, Mr. Chief Communicator."

Rand smirked. "Jealous?"

"As if—Ow!" I yelped as Rand's tail playfully flicked against my leg like he'd snapped a rubber band against me. "You jerk." I rubbed my skin while he snickered. "It's a good thing I like you."

"You're damn right it is. You're stuck with me, my dear. I've hitched myself to that guy back there"—he gestured to Leo—"and I'm going to make sure we get Syn produced so I can be wealthy and never work again."

"Do you actually work now? Rob said you spend so much time texting him that there's no way you're doing any real work."

Rand shot me a glare before rolling his own eyes this time. "I work! It may not look like it, but I do. Someone has to negotiate the deals, you know, or we'll never make any money. Someone has to finesse things since"—both of us flinched at the sound of Leo yelling on the phone—"well, since Leo's like that."

"We both know it's not just about the money for you."

"The truth is I'm lazy." Rand shrugged. "The money doesn't hurt. Don't be too surprised. Not all of us are as noble in our ambitions as you and Leo are, Vera. Once we get the logistics worked out and everyone is buying Syn instead of Dust, I want the dollars to pour in so I can sit back and do whoever and whatever I want."

"How is that different from what you currently do?" Leo collapsed into the seat next to me and tossed his phone at Rand. "Take all my calls until we get there. You," he said, patting his lap, "get over here."

My face breaking out into a big smile, I climbed over and faced Leo while curling up in his lap and letting his big arms circle around me. I rested my head on his shoulder as one of his hands lazily rubbed my arm until he met my bracelet, which he turned off. Instantly I felt warmer as my magic returned, and combined with the warmth from Leo's body, suddenly everything was right in the world.

Surely sensing the return of my magic, Leo held me a little tighter. His tail wound around my ankle and gently caressed my leg while his hand snaked under my shirt and up my back. *This. This is perfect.* I never wanted to move from that exact spot. I shivered as his fingers trailed up my spine to the base of my neck.

"Vera was just sharing some interesting thoughts she had," Rand said.

I twisted my head around to glare at him. If looks could kill, right then there would have been one dead demon.

"Oh, really?" Leo asked me. "Tell me."

"Yeah, Vera. Tell him."

"Rand, I swear—"

"I'll give you two some space to talk. I have some calls to make anyway." Rand's silver eyes met mine. "To a friend. *Just* a friend."

"He's been strange lately," Leo said once Rand left us alone.

"That happens when you fall in love."

"So I've learned. Wait, he's in love? You know what? I don't need to know."

"You really have been in your own little world lately, haven't you?"

Leo closed his eyes. "I have. Once this trip is over and we can go home and live our lives, things will be different. Once I have a better handle on this business—"

"Once, once, once. That's the future, but what about right now?"

"What about right now?"

I ran my fingers through his hair. "Right now's pretty great, don't you think?"

Leo cupped my face in his large hands. "Yes. Yes, it is. Vera, I know I've been busy, but you're important too. You're the most important part of my world. You're what makes everything else bearable."

Hearing those words from him was all the affirmation I needed. "I love you, Leo. I support you one hundred percent. I didn't just fall in love with the demon who freed me, I fell in love with the demon who will help free all fae. I know things are tough right now, but I want you to know how incredibly proud of you I am."

Leo pressed his forehead against mine. "Thank you."

"Now when do I get to meet your dear old dad?"

"Never."

"We'll see about that."

VESTIA WAS unlike anything I had imagined. Before being auctioned on Alliance Island, the fae I'd lived with in the dorms had whispered about the demon kingdom, a place of sin and smoke according to them. Mad demon scientists run terrifying labs, the gossip went, conducting their insane experiments for the sake of progress, not caring at all about their unsuspecting victims. I'd also heard that the demons of Vestia blocked out the sun with their wings and lived in a world of shadow with flames dancing in the streets.

Leo had laughed when I repeated those rumors to him, but in truth, Vestia was louder, brighter, and more chaotic than any of the gossip had suggested. Stepping out onto the sidewalk, I marveled at the night sky that was barely visible between the tall buildings that loomed over us.

It was midnight when we finally landed, and when we got out of the car at Rand's apartment building, I understood why Leo had insisted we all wear sunglasses. The street was as bright as day from the artificial lights around us. Buildings lined the streets and seemed to reach into the air for miles, concrete walls crowded against each other and hovering over the asphalt of the street below. The fluorescent lights from the windows of these enormous buildings were a poor substitute for stars, but they were the only bright spots that I could see.

Rand's own apartment building was one of the tallest in the area, and huge digital screens and signs covered its walls; flashing videos advertised inventions I'd never heard of and created a cacophony of noise and color, all demanding attention from the street below.

Despite the late hour, it was hot. Leo had tried to prepare me for the notorious heat of Vestia, but it was something else entirely to actually feel the steam wafting through the air compounded by the warmth that radiated from the crowded sidewalks. Not that the temperature seemed to bother any of the demons on the street; demons could handle almost any level of heat.

I stood next to the car while our bags were unloaded and demons brushed past all around us. Combined with the nerves I was already feeling being in a new place, I was sweating as we walked into the building. I was so caught up in looking at the skyscrapers that I didn't see Leo stop right in front of me and bumped into him, my face hitting his wings.

He glanced at me over his shoulder and smirked. "Don't forget to look down sometimes."

"Right. Good advice." I nodded before again looking up at the glaring lights of the city. "It's just that I've never seen anything like this before. It's... I don't even have the words to describe this place. I can't stop staring at all the signs and lights and ads and, well, everything."

Leo turned around to face me, studying my expression. "Do you like it?"

I wasn't sure how to answer. This was his home, after all, even though he'd taken great pains to move away and cut off contact with his family.

What would it be like to grow up in a place like this? From where I stood, the city seemed to go on forever. There was no end in sight to the skyscrapers and roads, making me wonder how far the city spread. Were there trees *anywhere*? Or maybe a park of some kind? A field? A lake? Not that I could see. Leo once told me that his mother grew roses, so it was possible that he at least had been able to spend time outside, but all I could see was gray concrete and black roads.

"I'm not sure," I finally answered. "It's a lot to process. There's so much to look at. Everywhere I turn is something new."

The palm of his hand gently guided my face so that I was looking up at him instead. "The only thing I want to look at is right here." He leaned down to press a quick kiss to my lips.

"You're drawing attention to us." Rand's voice rang out in a tense singsong as he appeared beside us. "The whole point was to stay under the radar so no one would know that you're back. Making out on the sidewalk is not staying under the radar. We need to get inside."

"No one is paying any attention to us," I told him. "Even with so many demons everywhere." Demons passed us on both sides, some choosing to fly over our heads instead. No one was talking to anyone; everyone seemingly on their own mission, headed in their own direction, ignoring the demons around them. We were surrounded yet anonymous, cramped but alone, hot but also cold.

Leo let go of my cheek and stared off into the city. "And you wonder why we both left."

"No." I looked around at the concrete and chaos. "I don't wonder that at all."

"Darling!"

None of us had time to react before a blur of neon pink hair and black wings leaped onto Rand, arms and wings curling around him before he could open the door to the apartment the whole way.

"Ja—" Rand stumbled back, but she held on, wrapping her legs around his waist.

Beside me, Leo exhaled loudly, but the demon with pink hair didn't seem to notice. And how could she? Her face was too busy smothering Rand in a thousand kisses.

Finally, Rand managed to untangle her from around him and gently place her on the floor in front of him. "You're... still here?"

Her silver eyes lit up with excitement as she adjusted her dress, a pink minidress not unlike the pink of her hair, the neckline low enough to show off the top of her very large breasts. Everything about her was bright shocking pink: her long hair, her tight dress, her lipstick, her high heels.

"Yep!" she squealed. She moved toward Rand again. "You have no idea how much I've missed you!"

This time he put up a hand, backing away. "You are most likely right about that. I thought you were leaving."

Even though Rand was talking to her, she was already looking past him to where Leo and I stood. Not that she saw Leo. It seemed like I was the only one worthy of the death stare she was sending my way.

"Who are you?" the pink-haired demon asked between gritted teeth, all her earlier excitement gone in an instant.

"Hey." I smiled and gave her a little wave. "Can we come in? It's great to meet a friend of Rand's, but we've been traveling all day, and—"

"You're a friend of his?" She growled at me, eyes narrowing. "Since when?"

"Jasmine." Leo's deep voice was enough for her to stop, and she blinked up at him, as if she had somehow missed the tall demon standing beside me this entire time.

Instantly she bowed her head, muttering apologies.

"Thank you for taking good care of the place for Rand." Leo pushed the door open the rest of the way and walked around her and Rand.

"It was my pleasure, Your Highness!" She kept her head bowed as Leo took my hand and walked by her, pulling me behind him into the apartment.

Right away I smelled sugar, and Jasmine was about to be my new best friend if she'd stocked the house with cookies or cakes.

"Everyone will be so glad to hear that you're home."

"I'm not so sure," Leo told her. "But thank you all the same."

I thought that was going to be the end of that and maybe we'd finally get to go to sleep for the night, but Jasmine trailed behind Leo and me, her words spilling out faster than we could walk away.

"Your room is the last one on the right, Your Highness. Rand and I will sleep in one of the guest rooms, and you will have the master suite. Let me know if you need anything at all! You will hardly notice that I'm here, I promise!"

"That's because you shouldn't be here!" Rand shouted after her.

"Don't be ridiculous," she shouted back. "The prince is here! And you're here! Besides, I had to coordinate with everyone to get the apartment ready."

We'd made it halfway down the hall when Leo stopped. "What did she just say?"

"Coordinate?" Rand groaned. "No one was supposed to know that Leo was coming. I told you to not say anything to anyone."

"I didn't! I only told the housekeeper and the chef since I had to hire a new one because the old one said it was too much pressure to cook for royals and of course the doorman downstairs and the baker since Rand told me to make sure I had sweets ready, Your Highness. Oh, and I called Marcus yesterday."

"Marcus?" Rand's brow knit in confusion. "How did you get his number?"

"From your phone one time when you were asleep, silly, but anyway, it's been over a year since you've been home, Rand, and I wanted to make sure I had all your favorite foods, so Marcus was the only person I knew other than his highness who would know you the best, but then *he* said I should talk to someone named Robinson instead, so I called him—"

"Holy shit." Rand's mouth dropped open. "You did what?"

"—and he was not very nice at first, I'll have you know, but he said you liked anything spicy, so I ordered from that place in midtown we used to go to and—"

"I need to make a call," Rand muttered, taking out his phone.

"I don't know why you're being like this. You should be grateful for everything I did taking care of this place, keeping it clean, taking care of your plants."

"The plants are fake, Jasmine!"

For the first time since we arrived, it seemed the pink-haired demon was speechless. As funny as it was to see Rand flustered for once, that was our cue to go.

"There's food in the kitchen when you get hungry!" I heard her call out to us.

"Thanks!" I shouted over my shoulder before lowering my voice so that only Leo would hear me. "What's the story with those two?"

"They dated a few years ago. When Rand decided to leave Vestia, he asked if she wanted to move into this apartment. Apparently she misunderstood and didn't realize that she'd be living in it alone."

"And you chose him as your communicator?"

"From what he's told me, she can be... challenging. He's been paying the rent this whole time, and apparently Jasmine thought that meant something it didn't."

"She seems nice."

"You think everyone is nice. Right now, I don't care about her."

"Oh? What is it that you do care about, my prince?"

Leo yanked open the bedroom door and tugged me into the room with him.

"You. I want you. Now."

"You have me. All of me."

He sat on the bed, his eyes never leaving mine. "Then show me. I want to see what's mine."

LEO

"And the unicorn and the dragon's eyes watched the same stars and the same moon, heard the same crickets chirping, and felt the same cool nighttime breeze. Because they would always be together, the two knew that from now on—"

"—everyone would live in peace," I finished the sentence for her. Aurora had read the book to me so many times that I could have recited it myself purely from memory, but it was so much better to hear my nanny's voice and cuddle against her warm side before falling asleep. Each night when I was shuffled off to bed, we usually had a few hours alone when the king and queen were too busy to deal with me, their sullen child who preferred taking apart his toys and putting them back together again instead of the parties and dinners of royalty.

Even if my parents weren't there, Aurora always was. I vaguely knew what it meant for her to be a slave, but mostly I assumed it meant she was supposed to play with me no matter what, whenever I wanted, and I took full advantage. Not that it ever seemed like she minded, and I basked in her attention, especially when it meant having her read books to me and tuck me in and stay with me in my large cold bedroom until I fell asleep.

At five or six years old, when I'd slump into bed covered in welts from training with my father's best fighters, she would be there. The general and his demons didn't care if I cried, and they didn't care at all how old I was or how many times I screamed from pain. Their methods were merciless.

Those nights especially I'd ask Aurora to read to me, the same book, over and over, her calm voice bringing a sense of security to my painful world. Sometimes she would put a hand on my head or gently run her fingers through my hair until I was asleep. She'd linger on the bruises if they were visible; her touch was so calming and soothing, and it never failed to make me feel warm and comfortable. It was as if the day's pain and worries washed away with the simple touch of her hand.

But not this night.

The door flew open, banging against the wall, and Mother swept in, her long dark red hair floating behind. Aurora didn't move from her place beside me, her comforting hand resting on my arm.

"Of course you're here." Mother scowled as she landed by my bed, picking up the book and flinging it away in disgust. "Filling his head with nonsense again. Dragons eat unicorns, Leo. Don't forget that." Her silver eyes narrowed as she looked at where the fairy's hand had been on my arm. "Slave," she snapped. "Did you touch the prince?"

Not giving her time to answer, Mother stomped around to the side of the bed where Aurora had been sitting and slapped her hard across the face. The fairy's hand flew to her cheek, but she kept her head down, staring at the floor. Instantly I was up and beside her, shaking in fear as I stared in horror at my mother.

"Why would you—?" Tears welled in my eyes. As if in slow motion, Mother's vicious gaze moved to me.

Aurora spoke up, like she always did for me. "Your Majesty, I was only helping him get to sleep. The pain is making it difficult. The bruising on his arms and legs—"

"Are a sign that he needs more training, not coddling. Maybe you need some bruises of your own to understand." The queen grabbed Aurora's arm, wrenching her away from me and tossing her on the floor. I jolted out of the bed as I watched Aurora fall, not sure what I could do but determined to not sit there and do nothing. The instant I was off the bed, the queen's long, thin tail smacked against my face.

"Leo—" I heard Aurora say, her voice oddly calm.

"*Prince* Leo," my mother snapped.

The fae instantly bowed her head. "My apologies, Your Majesty. Of course. I'm so sorry."

"Actually, it doesn't matter what you call him, because if I have my way, you will never speak to him again. Guards!" Mother yelled. Two demons, members of her guard, appeared in my doorway, shuffling through and grabbing Aurora's hands, pulling her to her feet.

Watching her expression, I couldn't understand why Aurora was so quiet and calm. Why wasn't she fighting back? Was she okay with being taken away? With the idea of never seeing me again? Why was she looking at me like I was the one to be pitied when she was the one with two guards dragging her from my room?

On some level, did I already know the answer?

I'd noticed the looks Mother gave Aurora when the fairy would play with me outside, the way Mother would roll her eyes at anything Aurora said and the way she openly mocked the fae woman whenever my father wasn't around.

Where was he now? There was no way the king would allow this. My father was always kind to Aurora and would even join her sometimes to watch me train. If I could get to him, if I could let him know they were hurting her, that Mother was threatening her...

I started to move, but Mother caught me before I could fly away and held me tight.

"Let me go!" I screamed, thrashing in her arms, trying to get to Aurora, to get out of the room, to run and tell Father, but Mother's hold only tightened. "Let her go!"

But nothing I said mattered. Aurora looked over her shoulder as they held on to her arms and led her away. She gave me a sad smile that would be burned into my memory from that day forward. "Leo. Be strong. I love you."

No matter how loudly I yelled or how hard I thrashed, they didn't stop. Once the door slammed shut behind them, I collapsed into my mother's cold arms, gasping for air as I sobbed.

"You are weak." She scoffed, tossing me down on my bed. "To let a fairy make you think she cared about you. To believe their lies. They only care about themselves."

"That's not true!" I shouted at her. "She is nice! Aurora isn't mean like you!"

While I tried to calm down and catch my breath, Mother sat down on the bed a few feet away from me, even though it now felt like miles. "She is nothing but a slave whore. They are vile creatures who will ruin your life if you give them a chance." Mother reached out to stroke my hair, but her hand was cold, her movements mechanical, and I flinched.

"But now you won't have to worry about her anymore," she said. "It was a mistake for her to ever be here."

"What do you mean?"

She stared at me for a long time, not saying anything, her silver eyes studying me before she let out a breath and looked away. "I thought maybe you would understand, but you're just as dumb as they are." She stood up from the bed and headed for the door, flicking the light off. She stayed in the doorway for just a moment. "And you disgust me just as much."

Jolting upright, I clasped my hand to my heart, as though it might burst right out of my chest. I had to gasp for air, and my whole body was drenched in a cold sweat.

I was in bed. With Vera.

I'd dreamed of my mother. As I thought of her, the muscles in my chest felt like they were being pulled tightly and could snap at any second. My real mother. The fairy woman I had thought my whole life was my father's slave until I learned the truth. But by then it had been too late. The dream had been a memory of the last time I saw her. The next and last time I ever heard her name spoken in the palace was when I heard that she was dead.

"Leo?"

At the sound of Vera's voice, raspy with sleep, my shoulders finally relaxed. I lay back down, wrapping an arm around her as much to ground myself as to comfort her. I brought Vera closer and took a deep breath, sucking in the air as deeply as I could, hoping to calm the rapid beating of my heart. Her small hand gently reached around my waist, seeking my own hand that I locked with hers.

"You okay?"

"Yeah," I whispered. I looked down to see her slightly awake, her brown eyes droopy as she yawned. "Go back to sleep."

"Mm-hmm," she mumbled as I scooted her closer and tucked her against me. I needed her closeness tonight. I hadn't thought of that night in a long time. The memories of the last time I saw my real mother were always there, but normally I kept them locked away in a deep part of my brain. It was too much to bring them forward, the mental and emotional weight better kept far from the surface of my thoughts.

"Too tight," Vera mumbled.

I relaxed my arm, only then realizing how firmly I had been gripping her against me. I was so used to the comforting warmth of her skin that I was seeking it out without even thinking about it.

"Something is wrong," she said. Her hand idly reached up, her fingers delicately touching my face.

Again, I took her hand in mine, kissing the tips of her tiny fingers before threading them with my own. "Everything is fine."

Everything wasn't. I had thought this could work. I thought I could have Vera and still be the demon I needed to be, but being here in this place, this *hell*, it felt impossible. Eventually someone would find out that she was here and connect the dots. Someone would hurt her or use her to hurt me. All I knew was that she was safer here than she was across an ocean from me. Selfishly, I had to have her here.

"Is this about seeing your father? I could go with you to meet him."

"No," I said, firmly squeezing her hand. "I need to deal with him on my own."

She nodded and scooted closer, pressing our bodies together. "But you're not on your own, Leo. Don't you know that?"

"I do."

"And you're sure you're okay?"

No.

"Yes."

Kissing her hair, I held her as she drifted back to sleep, listening to the sounds of her tiny snores in the dark room. How insanely lucky was I to have her here, with me, beside me? Before Vera, I only cared about creating Syn, and the only warmth I felt was when I'd watch the sunrise after a long night in the lab.

But now? Now I wanted nothing more than to close my eyes and fall asleep peacefully next to her. Now *Vera* was what mattered, and that included making a future where she could be safe. Where we could be safe together.

How could I ever save all the fae if I couldn't save just one?

4

VERA

"Good morning, sleepyhead!" Jasmine's chipper voice in the kitchen was way too loud for the early morning. The sun had been up for a few hours at most, and the demon was already fully dressed, this time in a bubblegum-pink top and matching flouncy skirt. "Did you sleep okay? Want some breakfast? Coffee? The chef left some muffins—or at least I thought he did. I don't see them anymore..."

"Leo probably ate them," I chuckled. They were his favorite food.

"That bastard." She must have realized she was talking about the prince, because her hand flew to her mouth. "Of course I didn't mean that! Please don't tell him I said that."

"Don't worry." I laughed. "I won't."

"His Highness seems different. He's always been very serious, but this morning he was even more so than I remember. Rand didn't give me any specifics, but is everything okay?"

"It will be," I told her. "You don't have to do that." I tried stopping her as she poured two cups of coffee. "I can get it myself."

"Nonsense! You are my guest. Or should I say our guest?" She joined me at the table, her bright pink smile fading quickly. "Or maybe I'm actually the guest? Ugh!"

"No. We're the guests. You live here."

"You're too kind."

"No," I told her. "You are for doing all this for Rand."

"It's nothing, really. I would do anything for him. I met Rand during a really tough time, and he helped me out. I was so sad for so long..."

I watched her play with her fingers, each tipped with hot-pink nail polish, and had trouble imagining that this demon in front of me was ever sad.

"Then Rand waltzed into my life in that charming way he does, and everything changed. I couldn't believe someone like him was paying attention to someone like me. I know he doesn't return my feelings." Jasmine sucked in a deep breath before continuing. "But no matter what, I will always be there for him, even if we're not together. I know that might not make sense to you."

"Actually, it does. But I'm starting to think you could do a lot better than Rand."

"I can't help what my heart wants, Vera." Then her big pink smile was back, and Jasmine leaped up from her seat. "I almost forgot; Leo left a gift for you!"

He probably felt bad leaving me alone on our first day in Vestia, but I'd understood when he said he'd only be gone a few hours.

In an instant Jasmine was back, and in her arms was a bouquet of yellow daffodils, my favorite flower, in a tall glass vase that she proudly placed on the table in front of me. It had only been a few months, but it felt like years since the night Leo and I met, when he'd caught me lurking around a garden at night and I'd told him I liked daffodils better than roses. He'd brought me daffodils the night Henry attacked me, and he had kept a fresh bouquet of them in his house ever since. I sniffed the flowers and smiled, knowing this was his way of making me feel at home here.

"I don't know how he found those since I've never seen anything like that flower around here. They look so delicate." Jasmine touched one of the tiny yellow petals carefully.

"They are and they aren't. They don't live long normally, but under the right conditions, they come back every year."

Jasmine flipped her pink hair over her shoulder, her brow furrowing. "Maybe I should get Rand a gift. A welcome-home gift. Last night when we went to bed, I offered—"

"Nope." I held up my hand to stop her from telling me any more details.

Eventually Jasmine left me, and with Rand and Leo also gone for the day, I put on my sunglasses, pulled one of Leo's big hoodies over my head, and ventured downstairs to sit at the windows and demon watch. The building lobby itself was worth wandering around in all on its own; there was a grand marble staircase in the middle of the room, and the stairs led to an upper balcony that overlooked the main lobby below.

Hidden in a corner, I was becoming bored watching demons out the window when I saw a fae enter the lobby and start carrying boxes up that beautiful staircase. He was hard to miss, really, with his blue wings the color of the sky in summertime and white hair. I couldn't take my eyes off him because, even though he was tall, everything about him was graceful, from the purposeful steps he took to the way his sparkling blue wings, much larger than any I'd seen when I lived in the dorms, fluttered gently with each stair he climbed. Without a doubt, I knew that this fae had once been wild, which was why his wings had been able to grow so large.

Sunglasses on, hood over my head, I slowly moved off my couch to the bottom of the stairs so I could see him better. In Vestia, only the royals owned fae slaves, so who did he belong to and why was he here? He seemed to be struggling with the three boxes he was carrying. If he hadn't had suppression tech on, he could have used his magic; he'd easily have enough strength to carry those boxes and more. If his magic wasn't suppressed, he could fly them up to the top of the staircase in seconds. Instead, he was struggling to balance the boxes piled high in his arms.

"Shit." He cursed at the same moment the small box that had sat precariously on top of the others tumbled behind him, down the stairs, and right toward me. Balancing the other two boxes in his arms, he twisted around to watch it bounce down the steps, but then he saw me standing there watching him. His blue eyes, almost the exact color of his wings, were striking, went wide.

The box landed at my feet.

"Shit," he muttered again, quietly this time, but I still heard him.

"Hey! Need some help?" I called up to him, but he didn't respond.

Of course. Since he was a slave, it wouldn't be proper here for him to talk to a human, and it would be even stranger for a human to offer to help. I remembered the punishments I'd received back on the Island from speaking out of turn and shuddered.

Picking up the box, I held it out to him, even though he didn't move from where he stood several stairs higher than me. From that distance I doubt he'd be able to sense that I was also fae.

"Here." I made my voice sound as friendly as possible. I desperately wanted to ask him what it was like to live in the demon kingdom as a fae, but I was supposed to keep my identity a secret.

His blue eyes blinked, watching me. If I hadn't heard him curse earlier, I would have doubted he could speak. Finally, he took one step, then another, but then the second much larger box he was carrying fell off too, rolling directly at me, hitting me and knocking me back on the floor.

"Oh shit! Are you okay?" He ran down the rest of the stairs, leaving the other box behind.

"It's okay! I'm fine!" My butt hurt like hell from hitting the hard floor, but otherwise I wasn't hurt.

"I'm so sorry." He reached out to help me up, his suppression bracelet visible on his bare arm. Mine was hidden underneath the sleeve of my shirt, so I knew he wouldn't see it.

"Thanks." I took his hand, and he pulled me up from the floor, my eyes transfixed on his beautiful blue wings and the way they glittered behind him. The blue reminded me of the reflection of a clear summer sky in a pond, perfect and shimmering with the ripples of the water.

"You!" A voice barked at us from down the hall. "Slave. What are you doing?"

Both of us froze. Immediately we dropped hands, sharing a brief second of eye contact before facing the stranger.

"I'm not a—"

"My apologies, sir."

Beside me, the fae bowed his head. A short demon, closer to my own height than the fae slave's, was stomping angrily in our direction, his chest puffed and heaving as he approached, his brow sweaty. He was dressed in a suit, his dark hair slicked back while his tail furiously swayed behind him. His brow knit in anger, the demon glared at us as he approached, until I realized that he wasn't glaring at me at all. He was staring at the fae slave. The fae who had held my hand.

"He was helping me up," I explained. "These stairs are slippery from the rain."

The demon completely ignored me. "How dare you touch a human, you revolting insect?" He smacked the fae across the face.

"Whoa!" I rushed between the two of them before he could do it again and faced the demon.

"How dare *you*?" I hissed. "I am the only one allowed to touch my slave."

"Your slave?" both the demon and the fae said at the same time.

"Yes," I insisted with all the confidence I could muster. I spun around to face the fae, hoping he could see that I was trying to save his ass. *Play along,* I silently willed him to understand. He was holding one hand to his cheek where the demon had struck him, but I could see the confusion clearly on his face.

He'd been hit because of me, because he was helping me.

I wasn't going to let that happen again.

"This one is my slave. In fact, *slave*, go gather those boxes for me. Right now." I clapped my hands. But instead of moving, the fae simply stared at me. "Why are you taking so long, *slave*?"

"Oh? Uh, of course. Yes, ma'am." The fae nodded seriously, shooting me a sideways glance before gathering up the boxes.

"You shouldn't let your fae be so free with you."

I turned back to the demon. "It is my choice how I handle my own slaves."

"You have to show them who is in control. If you let them talk to you like that, they're going to start to think we actually care what they say."

"I do care what they have to say."

Scrunching up his face, the demon took a long look at me. "A human? I don't remember ever seeing humans in this building before."

Shit. I needed to think of a lie quickly. "I'm… staying with a friend."

"What's their name? I know everyone in this building."

"Jasmine. Her name is Jasmine. You know, pink hair? Loud? We're, like, best friends."

"I saw her yesterday, and she said her boyfriend was staying with her. What exactly is going on here?"

"Nothing!" I insisted. Shit. Shit. Shit. This was not going the way I wanted at all.

"I don't know you. You don't live here. Someone let you in, but you don't belong here." I gasped as he grabbed the front of my shirt in his fist, pulling me toward him. My fingers tried to pry his hand off, but he wouldn't budge. "Tell me exactly what you're trying to do."

"Right now I'm trying to get you to let me go!"

A fist connected with the side of the demon's head and his face swung to the side from the blow. The demon dropped me, but then someone grabbed my hand.

"Come on!" the blue-eyed fae yelled at me, pulling me behind him. "This way!" Following his glittering wings, I ran with him through the lobby, darting under the stairs and racing down the hall, the shouts of the demon fading as we ran. But then a thundering of wings behind us made me stop. Noticing that I was now a few feet behind him, the fae quit running as well, eyeing me with confusion.

"Why you'd stop?" he asked before he saw him too. Leo. Down at the end of the hallway, black wings spread wide as he loomed over the demon who had yelled at us.

"We don't have to run anymore," I told him. "We're fine now."

"Doesn't look like it. Let's get out of here," the fae whispered to me, anxiously glancing back down the hall.

"No, really, it's okay. Follow me this time."

"I think I'll wait back here."

"Suit yourself," I said as I crept closer, the blackness of Leo's wings completely filling the narrow hall and acting as a buffer between the other demon and the two of us. I waited behind Leo, safe and hidden behind his wings. The silver tips of Leo's wings, a trait I had never seen on any demon besides Leo, a trait inherited from the silver wings of his fae mother, were obvious now that the fullness of his wings was on display. The much smaller demon seemed to realize who he was facing in that moment.

"Your Highness!" Immediately the demon was on his knees, hands down on the floor in front of him in a deep bow at Leo's feet. "I had no idea that you were here or that this human and her fae were under your care. My sincerest apologies, Your Highness."

"Yeah, that's right!" I called out from behind Leo. "You *should* be sorry. In fact—" One sharp look from Leo over his shoulder silenced me.

"Leave. Now," he said to the demon, watching with disdain as the much smaller demon scrambled up from the floor and scurried away. Then Leo's eyes switched to me, facing me fully. I couldn't help but squirm under his intense glare. "Are you okay?"

"I am now."

"Good. Then what the hell happened?"

"Leo. You should have heard that demon. He was such an ass. And then he hit him! Just walked right up and hit that fae in the face. He hadn't done anything except help me up off the ground."

"Why were you on the ground?"

"It doesn't matter." I waived my hand in the air dismissively. "But a box hit me, and I fell down."

"That fae threw a box at you?"

"No! The fae was carrying boxes up the stairs and one fell. Well, two fell. And one of them hit me."

As I spoke, I watched Leo's eyes darken. "That was on purpose," he seethed, immediately glaring around the hall as he searched for the fae. "You were alone and an easy target. Where is that fae now?"

"He was right... there." But he wasn't there at all. The fae with the sparkling blue wings and matching blue eyes, the fae with hair as white as frost and ice, was gone. "And no, it wasn't on purpose. He was carrying too much, probably because his owner was making him. It wouldn't have been too much if he'd been able to use his actual strength instead of being suppressed by these damn bracelets."

Leo wasn't even looking at me, his eyes still darting around to find the fae instead. "I don't like it."

"I don't either."

"No, I don't like the fact that a random fae slave was here in this building. No one who lives here has slaves."

A few demons passing by had stopped what they were doing to watch us. "So much for staying under the radar," Leo muttered. "Let's go upstairs."

We rode the elevator in a tense silence that followed us to the apartment and even into the bedroom.

"You can't do this, Vera. You can't go around defending every slave every time you see something happen."

"Yes, I can, Leo. That's exactly what I'm going to do."

"Not if I have any say in it."

"Then it's a good thing you don't. Why are you defending that demon? That asshole hit a powerless fae for the crime of helping *me*. I remember a demon who helped a fae once when she was being abused by a human. At the auction, you killed a man who was going to hurt me. Why is this any different? Is it because this was a demon?"

"It's exactly because it was a demon." Leo sighed and pinched the bridge of his nose in exasperation. "And because of where we are. Things are different here."

"Leo, what that demon did was wrong. And I couldn't stand there and let that fae get hit in front of me without doing something."

"He hit him back, didn't he? If I hadn't shown up, hitting a demon would have meant an immediate punishment or worse for that fae."

"That demon grabbed me!"

"I'm not saying it's right. This is just the way it is right now here."

"Well, I hate the way it is. I thought we were here to change all that."

"I'm working on it, Vera. I know you're impatient for change. I know you are. We both are. But we're making progress with selling Syn to the humans, and we'll do the same here. Once I get my father off my back, we'll leave and never set foot here again."

"Except to free the fae here too. Right?"

"That will come," Leo said. "One step at a time. You don't understand where you are, what it's like here, how dangerous it is here."

"Your own home was dangerous for me unless you've forgotten."

Suddenly, all of Leo's intensity was trained right on me, his body rigid with anger. "I will never forget. That's why I need to protect you here even more than at home. What would have happened if I hadn't shown up? What if he saw your bracelet and realized what you were? What would you have done then?"

"I…" I hung my head. "I don't know." A wave of guilt rolled over me, and on some level, I knew he was right. I hated to admit it, but if Leo hadn't interceded, I wasn't sure what I would have done.

Then his voice was softer, lower, and he reached for my hand, locking our fingers together. "Let me protect you, Vera."

I wanted to give in to the feeling of his large hands holding on to my arms. I wanted to lean against his chest and feel the safety of his body against mine. Even if it was only for a moment, being this close to him did make me feel safe. With him, I felt like I could survive anything.

I nuzzled against his shirt, enjoying the scent of campfire and mint that was so distinctly *him*. "Why don't you tuck me in your pocket and carry me around with you?"

"I wish I could," he said, smoothing down my hair against my back. "But I also don't want anyone here to know that you're mine. If they knew, they'd use you against me."

"Oh, I'm yours now?"

Leo tugged on my hair, pulling my head back slightly so I could see him. His silver eyes narrowed as he stared down at me. "You've always been mine."

Leo let go of my hair and ran his hands up and down my arms as I wiggled into place in his lap, comfortable and warm against him. I relaxed with him holding me like this, but he didn't feel relaxed at all. In fact, his body seemed more rigid and tense than normal.

"Am I doing the right thing?" he asked, and I was struck by the quiet and vulnerable way he sounded, so unlike his normal tone of voice. "I could become king, you know. I could be the king and use that power to free all the fae slaves here. With the power of the Hellfire throne, I could influence the human territories as well. Combined with the distribution of Syn, I could do it. Really do it."

"I know."

"But I want you." He pulled me to him again, burying his face in my hair. "Gods, I want you more than I have ever wanted anything. If I could fly you to another galaxy where it was just the two of us, then everything would be perfect. We could be together, and I could let this whole planet rot."

I pulled back gently. "And everyone in it?"

The silence hung heavy in the air.

"Maybe. I almost lost you once. I can't lose you again. I need to find somewhere else to hide you."

"Leo—"

"It's this city." He squeezed me tighter. "All the memories. There's a reason I left in the first place, and every second we spend here I'm reminded of that."

I leaned back so I could see his face. "There are no good memories here at all?"

He took another deep breath and closed his eyes. "Even the good ones are tainted."

"Can we make some memories of our own then?"

He opened one eye suspiciously. "I'm listening."

"I don't know. I was just thinking..." I maneuvered out of his arms and turned around to face him, dropping one leg on each side of him.

"I have to say it was superhot when you swooped in to rescue me earlier."

"It was super annoying that I had to rescue you."

"Oh, come on." I ran my hands down his face, gently touching his cheek and watching as the tightness of his expression softened. "You're trying to tell me you don't like being my hero, my rescuer, my *prince*?"

"I'd like it a lot more if I didn't have to rescue you at all."

I pinched his cheek playfully, and he instantly clapped down on my wrist to keep me from doing that again, his soft expression becoming more pointed. Leo's hand moved to my suppression bracelet, the metal cracking under his strength, and my magic flooded my body like pure sunshine coursing through my veins. "When I think of someone touching you, hurting you, I lose my mind."

"Aw, my poor prince is having trouble controlling himself?" I asked, grinding my hips down on him.

"I've gotten better at controlling how I take in your magic."

"Yeah? I think we need to practice more."

In answer, Leo wrapped one hand around the back of my head and pulled me down to him, kissing me. With the first touch of our lips, that fire was back, the fire we knew so well, making us wonder how we could ever stand being apart. Those kisses held heat and passion, fueled by the desire to be as close as possible to each other—no, closer; impossibly close. There was an urgency and hint of possessive desperation in the way Leo's hands grabbed on to me, squeezing my flesh, but each eager touch made me know how much he wanted me, and I wanted him just as badly.

Leo rolled us over, but pulled back for a second, and even then, it was only a few inches. "I like how you taste," he breathed as his hand ran up my side. I gasped when it slipped under my shirt and Leo took advantage to deepen the kiss, our tongues tasting each other.

"You're so sweet," he murmured against my skin. "Here." He dotted a kiss on my neck. "And here." Another kiss on my chest as he slid down my body, this time just over my breast before shoving up my shirt to expose my bare stomach. "And also, here."

From my belly he stared up at me, silver eyes twinkling as he traced tiny circles on my bare skin with his fingers, his touch tickling my belly button. Moving lower, he rolled my pants down, taking my panties with them, and then threw them off to the side. Gently pushing my thighs apart, he licked his lips as he stared at my naked sex. His mouth hovered just over me, his hot breath tickling my skin.

A shiver of pleasure rushed through me as he placed tiny, fluttering kisses on my inner thighs. "Fuck. You taste sweet everywhere, in fact," he murmured, his words humming against my skin.

"You're a tease." I squirmed under kisses he kept planting everywhere but where I really wanted them and threw my head back against the bed in frustration as he backed away, leaving me cold without his body touching mine.

"I think you deserve to be teased a little after today." His hands ran up the skin of my sides. "Are you going to be good for me from now on?"

"Come on, Leo." I looked up at him with hooded eyes. "You know how good I can be."

He smirked and came closer, moving his body between my legs. "I do. Do you know what you do to me? Do you have any idea?"

Reaching down, I wrapped my hand around his cock, and it pulsed against my palm. "I have some idea."

Leo swatted my hand away, and I tried so hard to keep the noises I was making low, but it was almost impossible with the way he continued to hit just the right places each time. Finally, I attacked his shoulder with my mouth, hoping that would be enough to muffle my moans.

Leo, however, wasn't making any effort to stifle the sounds he was making, and when he finally stopped teasing and entered me, forcing me to take it inch by inch, not rushing even when I begged, both of us cursed when he was finally fully sheathed inside.

I wrapped my legs around him, wanting him even closer as he started to move, pushing his hips against me. Leo wrapped one arm around my waist, pulling me against him, and then he leaned down, his mouth hovering near my ear. "Yeah? You liked that?" He rolled his hips again, his body rubbing up against my clit, each touch sending shock waves over my whole body.

So overwhelmed by the feeling of him against me, stretching me out inside, all I could do was nod, my agreement coming out as a whimper.

"That's what I thought." He chuckled lowly. The ragged, raspy tone of his voice let me know he was hardly keeping himself in control and was giving in to pleasure just as much as I was.

"Feels so good," I mumbled. "More."

"Don't you worry. I'll give you more."

And he did, there on a strange bed in a strange city, again and again, crashing into me and claiming me as his own.

5

———

VERA

"This is a bad idea." Leo stared out the tinted window of the car while Rand drove us out of the city. I was staring too, watching the changing landscape as the skyscrapers were slowly replaced by smaller buildings, lower and more industrial, a few with windows busted out or in need of dramatic repair. It didn't take long before the city lights were far behind us; these streets were dark, getting darker the longer we drove.

"I never would have agreed to this if you'd told me where we were going," Leo scowled.

"Which is exactly why I didn't tell you."

"Guys?" I chimed in from the back seat. "Talk me through tonight again. The demon who runs this place will have information about Leo's father?"

"He should," Rand said as we turned in to a large parking lot full of cars even at the late hour. "He's the father of a friend. A friend who apparently doesn't answer my phone calls anymore, so we're going in person without her help."

"She's not a friend," Leo grumbled from the front seat, his wings rustling behind him. He had his jacket pulled up over his head, and

Rand had painted the tips of his wings black, hiding that distinct silver that made him so unique.

"She?" Combined with Leo's reaction, I was suddenly more interested than I had been a few seconds ago.

"Her father runs this club," Rand explained, nodding toward the building in front of us, "and knows everyone's business. Always has. He'll be more than happy to see Leo and give him all the gossip, I promise."

As we exited the car, though we'd parked in the back, away from the crowded front doors of the building, the sounds of shouts and cheers and a deep bass rumbled through the walls and seemed to pour out of the windows.

Leo whipped around when he heard my door shut. "Where do you think you're going?"

"With you."

"No, you're not."

"Well, I'm not waiting in the car, so yes, I am."

Leo looked around the crowded parking lot and must have realized that I was right. It was better to go with them than wait by myself in the car in the dark.

"Fine," he said with a jerk of his head. "Come on. Stay beside me."

Lights flashed inside and noise spilled out the warehouse's large double doors as we approached. Several demons milled about in the parking lot. Instead of going in the main entrance, Rand led us around back to a side door. He opened the door, but before we took two steps inside, several demons in dark suits stepped in front of us. One tall demon with broad shoulders and arm muscles the size of my head glared at the three of us but didn't move an inch from where he stood. "Who are you?"

Rand flashed a smile. "Hello, gentlemen. We're here to see the duke."

The tall demon barked a laugh. "Then you're going to be waiting for a long time."

"Is he in?"

"The boss is busy."

"Not too busy to see us, I am sure. I assume his office is up there, right?" Rand pointed to the staircase that led to a door at the top, but as we moved forward, a demon put out his hand to stop us.

"The boss is busy," he repeated.

"Busy watching the matches in the arena?" Rand asked. "I can hear all the fun happening out there. Why don't you let us pass so we can watch them with him?"

"No."

"Why don't you ask the duke about that? I know he's watching us," Rand said, pointing to the corner of the room. My own eyes followed and saw cameras stationed on the walls, high up and aimed in our direction.

The demon touched his earpiece, listening for a moment. "Boss says bets are low tonight."

"What does that have to do with us?"

"We need a new competitor to shake things up. People like to bet on the underdog."

"This might be a waste of time after all," Rand muttered. "Let's go," he said to us. "We'll figure out something else."

"Fuck that," Leo spat out. "We're not going anywhere. The duke is going to see us."

The surrounding demons starting chuckling among themselves, their snide smiles making it seem like they knew a joke we didn't. The first demon we'd talked to touched his earpiece, listening for a moment. "Well, look at that. You're in luck. The boss has agreed to see you after all."

Leo let out a breath. "Fucking finally. Let's go." He moved forward past the bouncer, who put out an arm to stop him.

"Not so fast. There's one condition."

"What is it?"

"She has to win first."

"What?" All three of us exchanged confused looks.

"Her," he said, pointing right at me. "The boss wants to see her fight."

After a stunned silence, Leo was the first to speak. "Absolutely fucking not."

"Then no audience with the boss," the demon said. "Those are the terms."

"What would I have to do?"

At the sound of my voice, Leo's eyes snapped down to meet mine. "It doesn't matter"—he moved between me and the guard, blocking my view— "because you're not doing it."

The guard leaned to the side so I could see him and spoke only to me. "All you need to do is entertain the crowd out there for a few minutes, sweetheart."

I sensed Leo bristle at the nickname, but I had to stay focused. "By fighting someone?"

"You got it." The guard nodded, smiling smugly. "We'll pair you with another girl about your size. Three minutes. That's all."

"No way," Rand interjected. "We'll do it, but not her."

The bouncer crossed his arms over his chest and laughed, a deep throaty laugh that shook his whole chest. "Yeah right. You wouldn't last a second, pretty boy, and quick deaths are boring."

Rand smirked as he sauntered forward, slowly spreading his black wings as he approached the bouncer. "I appreciate the compliment, but I'm not talking about me. I'm talking about him," he said, pointing behind him at Leo.

The bouncer leaned to the side to get a better look before shrugging. "Still boring."

"Tell your boss to come down here then," Leo demanded. "Now."

"Maybe you didn't hear me the first time. No."

Hearing footsteps, I glanced to the side and saw at least five demons I hadn't seen before suddenly crowding in. They were on the other side too, flanking us. All were surrounded by a faint yellow glow, the telltale sign they had recently taken Dust. Depending on how much they'd taken, their strength could be much more than ours. I'd improved my fighting ability over the past few weeks with Leo's assistance, but would the three of us be able to take them on? If

I could kiss Leo, I could boost him as well, but I didn't exactly want to kiss Rand, too.

As if anticipating my next move, Leo shifted, putting out a wing to shield me, but I swatted it away. I needed to see what was happening.

"Guess we aren't so boring," Leo said, letting out a low laugh. "You must realize the kind of threat you're facing if you need this many demons for backup."

"You heard the terms," the demon said. "She fights or you leave."

"And if I do this, we get to talk to your boss?" I asked.

"That's right."

"Even if I lose?" I asked.

"Correct."

Leo looked like he was about to say something. If he revealed who he was and word got back to his father, then he'd know Leo was here and all this secrecy and intelligence gathering would have been for nothing. I had to speak first.

"I'll do it," I said.

Leo's eyes were wilder than normal, his wings starting to spread out behind him. "Like hell you will."

"I said I'll do it," I said directly to the guard, who nodded again before mumbling something into his earpiece. "Tell me how this works."

The corners of his mouth turned up in a leer more than a smile, like the cat who had finally cornered its prey. "One timed match. Ends when one of you is pinned or unconscious. We fight clean. No Dust. No weapons except what you were born with. Got it?"

"Got it."

Still smirking, he pointed down the hall. "Dressing room is that way, kid."

I did my best to not pay attention to my two favorite demons who followed the guard and me down the hall, one raging at my decision-making and the other trying to calm Leo down. The bouncer led us to a small dressing room, more of a closet with a mirror than anything else; inside there was a chair with clothes strewn over it and a dirty mirror hung on the wall. I purposely ignored the dark red stains on the floor.

It was obvious that Leo wasn't ignoring them, however; his tail twitched behind him, careful not to touch the floor. Leo shot Rand a look, and Rand understood the message, backing out of the dressing room, leaving the two of us alone.

Leo scowled as he leaned against the wall, arms crossed over his chest. "What is this really? Are you trying to prove a point to me?"

"No. I'm doing what I can to help."

"Getting beat up for the crowd's entertainment won't help."

"You were ready to fight, Leo. Why can't I do the same?"

"Because you don't know what you're walking into. These fights are usually between veteran fighters paid to kick the ass of their opponent. The idea of you going up against any of them is absurd. You can't fly away, you can hardly control your magic, you—"

"As much as I appreciate this list of things I can't do, if I *can* do this, we'll get to talk to the demon you're looking for, correct?"

"If the duke wants to play games with who gets to speak with him, I'll pull out his tongue the next time I see him. I refuse to stand here and let you get yourself killed."

"And I refuse to stand by and do nothing."

"This is completely absurd, Vera."

"You are the one who taught me how to fight. Don't tell me that you're doubting your own training methods."

"This has nothing to do with my training methods."

"Hey," I said, softer. "What's the worst that could happen?"

"You get killed."

"Unlikely."

"You get hurt."

I kept my voice low so that no one outside the dressing room would hear us. "Then it's a good thing I know someone who can heal any injuries."

We hadn't spoken of that night and what he'd done. The night at his mansion when I'd been stabbed but he linked with me and healed my injuries. The night when he'd revealed to me that he was half-fae.

"You're really going through with this?"

"Yes."

He took my wrist in his hands, turned off the suppression bracelet, and removed it. "Then you need to give them hell."

While I shed my clothes, Leo rattled off various defensive strategies and gave me advice about how to dodge and kick, advice I'd heard him give me countless times. It seemed to make him feel more relaxed to say it one more time, so I half listened while I rummaged through the clothes that had been left out for me.

I found a few things that looked like they'd fit and held them up against me. Costumes, I realized. These were costumes designed for the performance I was about to give the crowd. Overall, they were nicer than what I was expecting; the fabrics felt thin and rough, but the designs were simple, and the clothes seemed well constructed, like they'd survive the fight even if I didn't.

Eventually I found a black sleeveless crop top, red ribbons lacing down the front to add a sexy, feminine feel. I also grabbed a matching pair of black shorts with similar red ribbons lacing up the sides. Holding them against me, I realized the shorts were so tiny my ass was going to be hanging out, no matter how much I tried to pull them down. A costume indeed. It was obvious what the crowd enjoyed. Thankfully, there was also a short silken robe, black on the outside, lined with red on the inside, those same red ribbons used for the tie with large slits in the back for wings. I wrapped that around me and checked myself out in the mirror.

Could I really do this?

I had experience fighting Leo, but my only real-world fighting was limited to the one time I'd been stabbed by Henry. I'd been powerless to do anything to stop him. I'd been too weak, too small, too fragile to do anything, really.

Wrapping the robe's ribbons tighter around my waist, I made myself a promise. That wasn't going to happen tonight. I wasn't as strong as him, and I probably never would be, but I wasn't a weakling either. Tonight I'd show the crowd—and Leo—that I was stronger than I looked. I'd beat my opponent and prove to Leo that he didn't need to be worried about me all the time.

Who *was* my opponent anyway? A demon? A human?

Maybe I should have asked for a few more details before agreeing to this fight.

My back to Leo, not letting him see my nervousness, I folded my own clothes on the chair way slower than I needed to and took a deep breath to regain my courage before turning around to face him.

The door opened, and a demon poked his head in. "Time's up. Let's go."

With one hand, Leo pushed the door shut on his face.

"Leo," I scolded.

"I don't like this."

"I know."

"I know I can heal you, but I don't want you to ever need my healing. Vera, when I saw you that night," he said, closing his eyes for a long second, "when you were in my arms, hardly moving..."

"Hey." I touched his face. "It's going to be okay. I'm going to be okay."

The door opened again, and this time Leo used his tail to push it closed, but it held firm and Rand walked in instead.

"Look at you, little fighter," he said, eyeing my outfit approvingly. "No wonder the duke wanted to see you out there. You look hot." A glance from Leo had Rand putting his hands up in defense. "I just came back here to give you some advice. I've seen a lot of fights here back in the day. Mostly he has humans fighting other humans, with the occasional demon out there as well. If it's a demon, try to grab her tail."

"I was thinking about doing that or going for her wings. I know how sensitive demon wings can be."

"Oh, you do, do you?" Rand asked, raising an eyebrow, a slight smirk on his face as he glanced between me and Leo. "But I don't need to hear your pillow secrets right now. Let's save that for after you kick some weak human's ass, okay?"

"Deal."

Moments later it was time. After tips on how to play to the crowd from Rand and more instructions on defense from Leo than I would ever possibly remember, the demon who had poked his head into the dressing room earlier stood with me in front of two large doors easily three times taller than me. On the other side I could hear the loud booms of music and shouting, sounding more like a war taking place a few feet away than an arena filled with spectators.

He tapped me on the shoulder, and when I looked over, he was holding up a vial of Dust. "Want some?"

I momentarily forgot my nerves as I laughed at the absurdity of a demon offering me Dust. "I thought that wasn't allowed. Wasn't that one of the rules?"

The demon shrugged and downed the Dust himself, tipping the vial back and swallowing it all in one gulp. He shivered, wings twitching behind him. "If you really think anyone follows the rules around here, you might want to rethink your battle strategy."

"Great," I grumbled.

"You ever been in a fight, kid?" the demon asked.

"Kinda?"

He chuckled. "Then good luck. The boss has paired you up with one of the crowd favorites."

"Awesome," I said with no small amount of sarcasm. "Any tips?"

The demon seemed thoughtful for a minute, but then shook his head. "The match only lasts three minutes, so focus on staying upright."

"Stay upright. Okay, I can do that."

A sideways glance from the demon let me know that he wasn't as sure. In front of us, the tall doors opened slowly, and bright spotlights landed right on me while the crowd yelled even louder. I resisted the urge to cover my eyes from the blinding lights and stood tall, staring out into the dark room even though I couldn't see anything. Leo was out there somewhere. I needed to at least pretend to have confidence in what I was doing.

"It's showtime," the demon said, slapping me on the back, the weight of his hand sending me stumbling a few steps forward, and suddenly I was in the arena.

My heart felt like it was going to beat out of my chest as a distorted voice over a loudspeaker shouted something I couldn't understand. Whatever it was, the crowd cheered while the demon and I marched toward the center stage. Now that my eyes had adjusted, I could see rows and rows of demons crammed together around the room on rising levels going all the way up to the ceiling. There must be hundreds here tonight. Thousands, even? So overwhelmed by the sights and sounds, I was hardly aware of the demon beside me, his hand on my elbow guiding me forward. My legs seemed to move on their own, taking me closer to the center stage and up the short staircase to the cage itself.

It really was a cage. An elevated square mat fenced around the edges with a chain link wall that rose high into the air and formed a dome over our heads. Of course. They didn't want anyone flying out.

What had I done? Was Leo right, that this was a huge mistake?

There was hardly time to think about that. The entire room seemed to vibrate, and all around me I could feel the steady thrum of feet stomping and people shouting.

"Hey."

Someone was talking to me, but all I could do was stare out into the blinding lights. Where was Leo? Was he out there somewhere? Everything was a blur of noise, my brain buzzing with the continuous sounds of chaos.

"Hey!"

Finally, I forced myself back to reality. "Yeah?"

The demon who had walked me up was shouting from beside me. "Get in there!" he yelled, pointing to the stage.

Right. Once I was on the mat, I was caged in, literally. The only way in was through two small doors on either side. The demon opened the door closest to me and pushed me inside.

"Your robe!" the demon yelled again from the open door.

Oh yeah. I took a deep breath to try to focus and then slowly untied the ribbons around my waist, letting the robe fall to the floor at my feet. The crowd erupted in cheers, and I managed a smile. Maybe this wouldn't be so bad after all. It was true that they were probably going to be cheering for me to get my ass beat, but at the moment at least, they were cheering for me. Just me.

It was an intoxicating feeling. To have the attention of hundreds, all those silver eyes trained right on me, and I let myself take it all in as I walked with confidence toward the center of the ring when a demon in all red beckoned me forward. By his side, the crowd again let up another roar, this time even louder than before.

Hell yeah.

See, Leo, they're cheering for me.

But then I realized that they weren't cheering for me at all. Even as the crowd shouted louder and louder, I hardly heard them, my mouth falling open in shock when I saw my opponent enter the ring.

Her long white hair.

Her sparkling blue wings.

Shit.

I wasn't fighting a demon.

I was fighting a fae.

A stunning fae in a white top and blue shorts that matched her dazzling blue wings. She seemed to be about my age, with white hair that flowed down her shoulders like liquid ice. She also seemed to enjoy the attention of the crowd; she fluttered a few feet off the mat, waving and smiling like she was having the best day of her life. The crowd screamed even louder when she tossed off her white robe; the demon near her grabbed it and threw it into the crowd for demons to fight over. Her coloring made me think of the fae I'd met earlier, and like him, the size of her wings meant that she hadn't lived in captivity nearly as long as I had.

If she had been wild, that gave me another reason to worry. I remembered the last time I'd encountered wild fae, on the hunt with Leo, and how incredibly strong they'd been, tossing chairs and tables across a room with ease.

I was so screwed.

6

———

VERA

I didn't know what the referee said or what instructions we were given. I didn't know or hear anything at all as the demon nudged me forward and the fae girl and I faced off in the middle of the ring. All I heard was a buzzing sound, loud and clear, startling me back to reality.

And then the fight was on.

The fae girl wasted no time, lunging forward with a punch at my face that I barely dodged followed by a kick, but it only took one bounce to the side for me to get away before her foot connected with my thigh.

"Good one!" she shouted over the noise of the crowd. Even as she readied herself for another attack, the fae smiled at me, her eyes bright and wings glittering under the lights. Her eyes were just as blue as her wings and sparkled just as bright. "This might be fun after all!"

"Fun for who?" I shouted back.

"Me, silly!" She might have been smiling, but her eyes told a different story. Her blue eyes were focused, determined, and confident. In seconds she was airborne, flying directly at me, and all I could think to do was drop to the mat to avoid her like I'd done when

Leo would pull the same trick back home. The crowd cheered as she flew past me, missing me entirely and landing on the other side of the ring.

Unlike the practice fights with Leo, in all those training sessions, he never actually used his full strength, not the strength I'd seen him use when he sparred with Rand or another demon. But this girl... She wasn't holding back. Each move was precise, calculated, as if she had made that same movement hundreds of times before.

"I'm Mia!" she shouted.

"I don't care!" I shouted back as I got to my feet.

"That's not very nice."

Frowning, she flew at me again. *Stay upright.* That had been the advice the demon gave me before the fight. All I needed to do was stay upright and dodge her attacks until the time ran out. I could do that. Sure. Easy. I'd just decided that my new strategy was to avoid Mia at all costs when I saw a flash of silver on a demon's wing out of the corner of my eye.

Leo.

He was there.

I caught Leo's gaze on the other side of the fence surrounding the mat, and in that moment, it felt like time stopped and the noise of the arena silenced. Leo's expression was unreadable, and questions flashed through my mind. Was he proud of me or confident that I'd win? Or was he confident that I'd lose, simply waiting for a chance for him to run to the back and heal me when this was over?

The moment ended when blinding pain shot through my skull as Mia's fist connected with the side of my face. My head jerked to the side from the impact, and I stumbled as the arena erupted with chants of Mia's name.

I didn't care about the crowd. I cared about Leo. I cared about showing him that I wasn't weak. Clenching my fists at my sides, I ducked low, swinging out a leg to kick the back of her knees; I used more force than any human would have been capable of using, causing her to fall back on the mat. The crowd groaned. Mia was on her feet in less than a second, but the fact that I'd made contact gave me a little more courage than I had before.

"You're not bad for a human!" Mia yelled, backing up from me and rubbing her side. "Did you take Dust before you came out here?"

"Something like that."

"Huh?"

Taking advantage of her momentary confusion, I ran straight at her, hoping to tackle her to the floor before she could fly away, but before I could take two steps, Mia was there. A hand on each of my shoulders, she pushed me, shoving me up against the fencing of the cage, and I winced from the impact and from the feel of the metal links digging into my back. I tried to push back, but it hardly seemed to faze her at all. In fact, she seemed completely unbothered and unflinching, even though her face was scrunched with determination, and I could tell her breathing was faster from the effort.

"Two minutes!" the announcer shouted.

Pushing wasn't working, so I relaxed, closing my eyes and sucking in a deep breath. I dropped my hands, letting Mia shove me against the metal cage harder.

"Giving up already?" she shouted.

"You wish."

This close to me, I knew she could feel it. The warmth of my magic slowly spread all over me, but I focused on concentrating the power in my arms and shoulders, particularly where her hands were.

"Wait a second...," she mumbled seemingly to herself as her blue eyes went wide with recognition. "Are you...?"

A second was all I needed.

It was obvious I didn't have Mia's raw strength, so I was never going to win in a shoving match like this. And out in the arena, there was no way I could compete with the ability to fly. There was a way, however, to turn her strength into a weakness.

Mia yelped as I gave the bottom of her wings a fierce pull. Her surprise was just enough to get her to let go of me, giving me a second to duck down and out from her hold, twisting around to get behind her. I knew exactly what to do next.

I might not be able to fly like her, but I could jump.

Leaping onto her back, I wrapped my arms around her neck and my legs around her waist, pulling as hard as I could. Since I was pressing on her wings, she couldn't fly, and her attempt only knocked her more off balance, the two of us falling backward onto the mat. I hit the mat first with a thud, the impact knocking me off.

Mia and I both scrambled to our feet, facing off in the middle of the mat.

"One minute!" the announcer exclaimed.

I was almost there. I'd almost made it without being pinned. I could do this.

We both dropped low in a fighting stance, our hands up in a defensive posture in front of our faces, but then she jumped toward me and her arm shot up, knocking me in the chin. My head flew back from the impact, and the crowd cheered as Mia immediately dropped even lower and grabbed me behind my knees, both of us falling down onto the mat with her on top of me.

I scrunched up as best I could and brought my knee up to hit her in the stomach. It was a desperate move that didn't have much effect, and Mia only shoved me onto the mat, pushing my shoulders down as I tried to punch her sides. No matter what I did, she just wouldn't let up. Was this the end? Was it all over?

"Give up!" she yelled. "You aren't going to win!"

"*You* give up!" I yelled back. "Because I'm not going to!"

"Then I'm ending this right now. Sorry!" she huffed before hitting me in the side of my head with her elbow, the blow making me drop to the mat flat on my back. As her fists pounded into the sides of my head, I had a moment of clarity, a realization that came to me as I tried to roll out from under her as she continued hitting me.

I imagined that I heard Leo's deep voice in the distance, but Mia's wings blocked out the harsh overhead lights, and the crowd was roaring, their shouts and screams forming a steady noise that filled the warehouse and drowned out all other sounds. There was something that I hadn't wanted to admit earlier when my fight with her started, something I was only now realizing.

There had never been a time when I was going to win.

Everything buzzed, the shouts of the crowd blending into a blur of noise that thumped against my skull. The world swam around me. With a final shove, she pushed my shoulders down, and I heard someone counting and then she was off me. The crowd screamed, chanting her name while I lay on the mat, my entire body aching.

It was over.

Had Leo been right after all? I'd lost. I hadn't been strong enough.

I was vaguely aware of her pulling me up from the floor, my body heavy with the disappointment of losing and the pain from my injuries. My vision blurred as she wrapped her arms around me in a hug, and I knew from the air rushing past me that we were flying. As the noise of the arena faded behind us, a familiar warmth pulsed through me, the whole world suddenly brighter, the pain melting away. Blinking back the pain, I saw bright blue eyes still focused on me, but where they once looked like they wanted to murder me, now they were full of concern.

Linking. *We're linking*, I realized. She was healing me.

"Damn, girl." She smiled and shook her head, and with my blurry eyes I could see her skin starting to sparkle in that beautiful way that happened after linking. "You almost had me for a second there."

I coughed, not sure if I was tasting blood or my own saliva in my mouth, or both. "Next time... next time I will."

Mia laughed, blue eyes twinkling. "Hell yeah."

She left me to recover in the dressing room, but I wasn't alone for long.

"Where is she?" a familiar voice shouted in the hallway. Then the door flew open, hitting the wall with a loud thud. As Leo stormed into the room, his eyes went wide, nostrils flaring at the sight of me. Rushing forward, he scooped me up off the chair and into his arms, holding me tight against him. His familiar scent swept over me, and there in his arms, everything felt right in the world again.

"Where are you hurt?" He ran his eyes over me, searching my body for injuries.

"I don't know," I murmured, enjoying the closeness. "I think I'm fine."

"You've got quite a fighter there."

At the sound of the unfamiliar voice, Leo's head snapped up. Twisting around in Leo's lap to see who was at the open door, I saw double, two fae with white hair and blue wings, which didn't make any sense. Maybe Mia hadn't completely healed me if I was still seeing doubles.

Wait. No. That wasn't it at all. There really were two fae in the doorway. One girl, one boy. Mia was there, smiling, but beside her was the fae from the apartment building, the one I'd stood up for when the demon hit him. Why was he here of all places?

When I'd seen him that day in the lobby, I hadn't realized how tall he was, almost as tall as Leo now that the two were standing near each other. He didn't seem at all intimidated or bothered by the presence of a demon in front of him. In fact, the fae's posture—arms crossed over his chest, eyes watching the two of us—seemed to suggest that he was the one who belonged in the room and Leo was the one intruding. He stayed in the doorway while Leo gently put me down and moved in front of me, between the fae and me.

The fae's shock of white hair flopped over his head as he pointedly leaned around Leo to see me. "Hey."

Leo's eyes flitted back and forth between the two of us before finally settling on the fae. "Who the fuck are you?"

"She did great, all things considered," the fae said, not answering Leo's question as he took a look around the room. He picked up one of the discarded costumes and examined it before setting it back down again. "Especially since she was basically just bait for Mia."

While the fae seemed to be making himself at home, I noticed that Leo sucked in a breath, so I put my hand on his arm to get his attention. "Leo, this is the fae I met at the apartment that day."

Instead of turning back to look at me, Leo kept his eyes on him. "Oh, is it?"

"Hey, girl!" Mia waved from the doorway, her tone a million times less tense than Leo's. "Awesome job tonight! Hope you're feeling better!"

Leo ignored her, directing his attention only to the guy. "You didn't answer my question."

"You're right." The blue-eyed fae came closer. He reached a hand around Leo to touch where a bruise had been on my arm before Mia had linked with me, but Leo smacked his hand away.

"Don't touch her."

"I'm just making sure she's—" The fae reached his hand toward me again.

Suddenly Leo had him pinned against the door, his forearm pressed into the fae's throat.

"I said don't touch her," he snarled.

"Leo!" I shouted at him, but he didn't budge. "Stop it! Leo, I'm okay!"

Reluctantly Leo stepped back and released him, and immediately the fae leaned over, coughing as he caught his breath. Leo was at my side again in an instant.

"If you're okay, we're leaving."

"I'm fine too. Thanks for asking," the fae said, still rubbing his throat.

Leo shot him a look of disgust.

"I'm Mia." She extended a hand to Leo. "So...," she said, withdrawing her hand slowly when he didn't take it. "That's fine. I get it. I wanted to come by and make sure you were okay before you left. For what it's worth, you did great out there," she said to me. "The crowd loved it too. I had so many requests for pics of the two of us tonight. We need to do that again!"

I started to tell her thanks, but Leo spoke first. "You hit her."

"Leo..."

"I mean, that was kind of my job though, right?"

"You. Hit. Her."

"And I healed her. I healed your...*fairy*?"

"We're going to go," the other fae said, stepping between Mia and Leo.

"That's probably a good idea," I told him, and the glare on Leo's face told me that he agreed. The two fae seemed to understand, and Leo slammed the door shut behind them as they left.

"You didn't have to act like that, you know. They didn't do anything wrong."

"I don't want to talk about them," he said, giving me all his attention, his intense silver eyes peering down at me. "I want to talk about what happened out there."

"I did okay, I think? At least until I lost."

"Why didn't you kick her ass?"

"I tried!"

Leo crossed his arms over his chest as he stared down at me. "You could have done better. I've seen you do better. Were you distracted?"

I thought about how I'd seen Leo for that brief moment, and that brief moment was all it had taken for Mia to punch me in the face. Yes, I had been distracted. I'd been worried about what he was thinking about me, and that had left me open to her attack.

I started changing back into my regular clothes to buy time before answering. His face unreadable, Leo sat down in the dressing room chair, still waiting for my response. Had he been proud? Disappointed? Did I even want to know?

"What did you think when you were watching me?" I finally asked.

Leo leaned over, his elbows on his knees, his face dead serious. "I was thinking about how all I wanted to do was fly up there and rip the metal cage to pieces."

"Oh, come on. It wasn't at least a little hot?" I smirked, hoping to change the subject. "Seeing me up there fighting a hot fae chick?"

"You mean watching some brat knock you around? No. That wasn't hot. It was terrifying."

"You really thought I was going to lose."

"Vera, you did lose."

"Yeah, but you thought I was going to even before the match started."

"And why wouldn't you lose? Of course you were going to lose. You've never done anything like this before, and without wings—"

That made me pause.

"That's what you thought? That without wings I couldn't do it?"

"Vera. I didn't want you to do it at all. You almost had her when you jumped on her back. When I saw you trying to hold down her wings, I thought that might be the end for her."

"That's what I hoped," I admitted. "One way to defeat an opponent is to turn a strength into a vulnerability. That's what you taught me, right?"

But he didn't answer. "Leo?" I waved a hand in front of his face to get his attention.

"What?" He shook his head as if to wake up. "Yes, turn a strength into a vulnerability." His eyes raked over my form, as if doing a final check to make sure I was in one piece. "Ready?"

I took his hand to pull him up from the chair and looped my arm through his. "I'm ready. Let's go find this duke and get him to pay up."

"Oh." Leo's silver eyes flashed with anger. "He's definitely going to pay."

THE SMELL of stale cigarette smoke and sweat lingered in the air as we marched past the guards to the duke's office. This time no demon dared to stop us or even try. With the scowl on Leo's face as he stormed up the stairs, I wouldn't have tried either. In contrast to the bright and silent arena, not half as daunting with the overhead lights on and the stands clear, Leo was at his most intimidating when he didn't say a word.

He didn't bother knocking. Instead, Leo barged in, swinging the door open while Rand and I shuffled in behind him. I was expecting to see an older man, someone as loud and crazy as the arena itself, but that wasn't the case at all.

There was no word for the demon in front of us other than beautiful. Sitting in a high-back leather chair, blond hair cascading down her slender shoulders in perfect curls, she looked every bit like a queen on a throne. This was the duke? There had to be a mistake.

Her pale hands were folded on the desk in front of her, but she stood up at the sound of the door flying open.

"Where's your father?" Leo asked before she had a chance to say anything.

As she came around her desk, I saw that she wore a short dress of sapphire blue, her black wings relaxed behind her.

To the side of the desk something barked, and I looked down to see a small white dog on a tiny fluffy bed. The dog's paws curled over the edge as it let out another bark at us, obviously displeased by our presence.

"Shut it, Zeus," she snapped before her face quickly transformed into a much more polite expression. "Hello, Leo. Have a seat." She gestured to the couch and low table in her office. I noticed that she didn't bow. Another demon shuffled in, maneuvering around Rand and me, and placed two drinks on the table.

"I'll stand."

She sat.

"Where's your father?" Leo asked again.

"Not here."

"Which means it was all *you*. You're the one who made her fight? It was you?"

"No hello or how are you or thank you for meeting with me, Leo?" She sighed. "I don't know why I expected better manners from you, Your Highness."

"You want to talk about manners after that stunt you just pulled?"

"I prefer to call it entertainment."

"I was not entertained."

"Well, I was, and I think the crowd would agree. I'm glad to see you, Leo, and you too, Rand, I guess. But now I need to know who the hell *this*," she said, waving a hand toward me, "is."

I took a step forward so that I was beside Leo. "Hi, I'm Vera."

She stared at me blankly. "And?"

"And I'm the one who got her ass kicked for your entertainment."

"Vera." When he said my name, Rand's tone was a million times lighter than Leo's had been. "This is the Lady Elise."

"And...?"

Silver eyes glaring at me, the Lady Elise held up her hand. On her ring finger was a bright red stone set in a band of gold, the gem long and deep red against her porcelain skin, as if her own personal flame rested on her finger.

"And?" I repeated, glancing back and forth between the two. Elise did the same, her silver eyes darting between Leo and me, the corners of her mouth turning up in a smirk. "What am I missing?" I asked them.

"Oh, darling." She threw her head back and laughed, her blond curls bouncing as she let out a loud cackle. "You didn't tell her, Leo."

Was this demon calling Leo *darling*? I looked to Leo, but his silver eyes were narrowed, staring down this Lady Elise.

"Elise," Leo growled, her name sounding like a threat.

My blood felt thick as she grinned despite his tone. I swallowed and tried to shove down the uneasy feeling that was slowly taking over me. "Tell me what?"

"That I'm also his fiancée."

7

VERA

y breath caught in my throat. My brain wasn't functioning enough to form words. There was no way this was true. No way.

Fiancée? *His* fiancée?

Leo was *engaged?*

What. The. Hell.

I took a step forward, but Rand's hand lightly touched my arm. My eyes shot up to him, and he shook his head. *Later,* he mouthed silently.

Fuck that. Seething internally, it took every ounce of self-control I possessed to not say something right then when she was obviously trying to upset me. I just fought for the pleasure of merely talking to this bitch, and she wanted to try something like this right now?

Game on.

"A formality." Leo leaned down and picked up a glass from the small table in front of him. "You and I both know that ring means nothing."

Elise watched him closely. "It meant something to your mother."

The glass in Leo's hand went flying across the room and shattered into a million pieces against the wall.

Leo's wings twitched behind him. After the day he told me his mother had been fae, he'd shut down any further discussion of the topic. It was obviously painful for him, so I hadn't pushed the issue.

"Elise." Leo's voice was tight.

"She wore it until the end of her life, didn't she?" Elise held out her hand and examined the ring. She didn't seem at all fazed by the glass strewn about on the floor. "I was just a child when it was given to my parents for me to wear when I came of age. She was such a beautiful demon. I can't wait to be a queen just like her."

She doesn't know he's half-fae. If Elise believed Leo's mother was a demon, maybe it was a secret from everyone else as well. Everything about Elise irritated me, but I felt a certain smugness knowing I might be the only one Leo had told.

The little white dog barked, and Rand bent down to pet it only to quickly draw his hand away when it tried to bite him.

"I'm not here to listen to your hopes and dreams," Leo told her. "Be queen for all I care, but it won't be with me as king."

"You say that, Leo, but we both know that's really why you're here. Once he's dead, it's all yours. The kingdom, the Dust." She smiled, her perfect white teeth shining. "And me."

"I don't want you."

"You wanted me bad enough tonight to let this... *thing...* fight in one of my matches."

I lurched forward, Rand's firm grip on my arm the only thing holding me back.

"Rand," Leo said over his shoulder. "Please take Vera downstairs."

"You heard him." Elise smirked. "Be a good little slave and do as you're told."

"Elise!"

Blood raging, I tried to tear myself away from Rand. "Listen, bitch—"

"Vera!" Leo shouted.

"Excuse me?" Elise stood up from her chair, her wings spreading behind her. "How do you expect to bring a kingdom to heel, Leo, if you can't manage your own slaves?"

Leo held up a hand to stop her from coming closer to me, but I leaned around him and shouted. "I'm not a slave anymore, you piece of—"

"How dare you speak to me like that, slave!" Elise shouted, flying toward me.

Leo caught her wrist. She wrenched away, her little dog barking furiously in the background, but Leo's attention was on me alone as he loomed over me.

"Elise. Sit down." His tone brooked no arguing. She started to say something, but he held up a hand. "I'll deal with you in a minute," he told her.

Then he closed his eyes and let out a deep sigh. When he finally opened his eyes, some of the rage seemed to be gone, but I knew better. He was only holding back to maintain composure in the moment.

"Give me ten minutes," he said to me.

Chest heaving with rage, I tried to focus on him to calm my heart. One of his hands reached up, touching my cheek, and I felt some of the heat inside me melt away. It seemed to have the same effect on him as well.

Leo's eyes softened as he stared down at me. "Give me ten minutes, and then I'll explain everything."

"I'm holding you to that."

His hand never leaving my face, he exhaled. "I know."

Before I could respond, he leaned down, connecting his lips to mine in a gentle kiss. But gentle wasn't what I wanted right then, not after what I'd just heard Elise say, and I sensed him raising an eyebrow in surprise when I leaned into the kiss, melting against him and looping my arms around his neck.

He might have been surprised for a moment, but then he seemed to understand. His hands roamed my back and pressed me closer to his chest. It seemed if I wanted to put on a show, he was going to join me after all. I no longer thought about Elise. I thought only about Leo, his tail twisting around my ankle, his hard chest. As he kissed me, it felt like there was no one else in the universe, like we were alone.

Rand cleared his throat behind me.

Oh yeah. We weren't alone at all. Smiling as we untangled ourselves, Leo and I came back to our senses.

"I'll be quick," he murmured, a hand running through my hair. "Go with Rand."

"Ten minutes, right?"

Leo nodded.

I glanced over my shoulder at Elise. Her surprised expression confirmed that she'd understood the message I'd just sent, and I followed Rand to the door.

I'd be patient for ten minutes. That was nothing. But then I needed to know the truth.

8

———

LEO

Vera walked out of Elise's office behind Rand, and any tiny amount of warmth that might have existed in the room vanished with her. A slow clap began behind me, and it took every ounce of my patience to turn and face Elise.

"Bravo," she said. "That was quite the show. Normally, you have to pay to see something like that around here."

"If you want to talk about putting on a show, you can explain why you felt like showing off that damned ring."

"Aw, is his highness embarrassed by his fiancée?"

"Fuck off, Elise. You can play house with someone else because it will certainly never be with me."

Elise's smile vanished. "Then why are you here?"

"We came to speak to your father. I'm here because he's good at finding out secrets. It had nothing to do with you."

"Hm." She tilted her head, staring at me. "Like this secret I hear the humans are raving about? That there's a new, more powerful Dust? A high unlike any before, they say. Available for a low price direct from the demon prince himself."

I should have known she would have heard of Syn by now. If my father was trying to sabotage the business, he'd want demons to think they were somehow being slighted. It was a shrewd move, and I'd need to keep it in mind when I met with him.

"What of it?"

"You have been gone too long, Leo. You have forgotten the one thing demons care about the most."

"And what's that?"

"Power. Now anyone who can buy Syn can buy power. Real power, if it's as strong as they say. Tell me, Leo, why exactly did you give the humans this new weapon and not your own kind?"

"It's not a weapon. I developed a cheaper alternative to Dust that doesn't require fae."

"You're uprooting the power structure of royal society. Sounds like a weapon to me. A weapon the humans are getting access to first."

"I had to start with the humans because they're the ones with the most fae slaves."

"We have slaves too."

"Yes, you do, but here only the royal families are allowed slaves. The humans sell them off to the highest bidder, no matter how disgusting the person is."

"Humans never did have an understanding of grace or quality."

"Says the demon who runs a fight club."

"It's business, Leo. Blood sells. Whether it's splashed on the mat in the arena or snorted in a powder up their noses, blood makes money. The crowds pay to see it, and who am I to turn them away? I make more money upstairs though." She smirked.

"What's upstairs?"

"Girls. A few guys." She shrugged. "Some costing more than others. Why, are you interested?"

"Not at all."

"Oh, that's right. You already have a little toy. I can't believe you didn't tell her about us."

"There is no *us*."

"There will be. When you're king—"

"I'm not going to go round and round with you on this. I'm not here to talk about the succession. I want to know if my father is in town and if you've heard about his plans. Surely the court talks."

Elise took a long look at me, the silence weighing heavy in the air. "I see," she said. "I don't share information for free, you know."

"I would expect nothing else."

"I want a percentage of Syn."

That made me pause. "What did you just say?"

"A percentage." She held my stare. "Fifteen percent of your profits."

"Why?"

"Twenty."

"I'm not negotiating with you."

"I believe you are," she said. "I want twenty percent."

"Five. At most."

"Twenty."

"Twenty percent of the drug you said was trash?"

"I changed my mind. You forget, Leo, that I understand business better than you. If Syn takes over the market and the fae are freed, it's going to change my business here. I can see the writing on the wall. I need to secure my business's future. Especially if my own fiancé is no longer going to be making the rules. I'm a businesswoman, after all. Fifteen percent."

I understood her point. Once the engagement was called off, her life would change. The special status and recognition she'd enjoyed as the future queen would be gone in an instant. I wasn't completely unsympathetic.

"Five," I repeated.

"That's not enough, Leo. You think that crowd out there will continue to kiss my ass like this if I'm no longer the prince's fiancée? Think again. My whole enterprise could come crashing down. I need insurance. It's the least you owe me for stringing me along all these years."

"I have done no such thing. This engagement was never my idea."

"But you agreed to it. Until you decided to leave." Her voice was suddenly softer. She stared down at the ground. "Why *did* you leave?"

That answer was easy. "I couldn't stand living here any longer."

"Was it because of me? Was it something I did?"

I was about to snap back at her for asking such a stupid question, but then I paused.

Was that how she saw things?

For the first time tonight, I really saw her. Not the boss she wanted everyone else to see. No, I saw the girl I'd known when we were kids, the girl who shyly hid behind her mother's legs the first time we met. "Elise. No. It was never anything you did. You were like me, used by our families."

"I *am* like you, Leo. I just don't know when you're going to finally understand that. No one understands me like you do. No one can ever understand you like I do. You don't need someone you have to constantly protect. You need someone strong who can stand beside you."

Before I knew what she was doing, her hand was cupping my face. Instantly I flinched. "I'm sorry if I gave you the wrong idea just now."

She stared at me blankly for a moment before she chuckled softly. "No," she said, shaking her head. "That was my fault. I've always known where I stood with you. You have always made it very clear how much you hated me."

"I don't hate you. I've never hated you. I hate the situation that we've been put in, and avoiding you was always easier than dealing with it."

"Is that why you're trusting me with your secret? Now that I know you're home, who is to say I won't fly right to the old demon and tell him I saw you?" Her eyes flicked up to meet mine. "And her."

"We both know you aren't going to do that."

"I guarantee he knows you're here too. I did, at least. That girl Rand keeps around likes to talk, doesn't she? We miss Rand around here. I hear he used to be one of our best customers upstairs."

"Take that up with him. Is my father at the palace?"

"He should be. What's your plan exactly? You're not a popular demon right now, Leo. Surely you must realize that. It's not just your father. There are whispers that the Ignitors—"

"Fuck them."

"That the Ignitors are making plans as well. I've heard rumors they're working on something new. The king listens to his councilors, Leo. You should try to get them on your side. You could use Rand. Has Rand seen the general since you arrived?"

"No. Planning to see my father is our focus right now. He'll have to figure out his own father later."

"You could use that angle though, as a way in. The general is a cold demon, but he might listen if his wayward son returns and repents his wicked ways."

"Possibly. What else is going on here? I know there are things I wouldn't hear about across the ocean."

"Since you've been so busy playing house with your little fairy?"

"Elise."

"Your cousin Zell is continuing to make a name for himself. He's been pushing to have a more prominent role at court. He's become known as the king's right-hand demon and seems willing to do anything to show his loyalty."

"You seem to know a lot about him."

"He's hard to miss."

"Just as Zell likes."

"He's here all the time and can't seem to keep his hands or his tail away from my girls. They love him so much it's disgusting. You know, you could learn a thing or two from him."

"I sincerely doubt that."

"I don't know. You come home sulking, hiding even the color of your wings, while Zell becomes more popular by the day. If he were in your shoes, he would have planned a parade celebrating his triumphant return."

"I'm not Zell, and thankfully I never will be."

"That's right." She nodded. "You'll be the king, while he will never be more than another name at court. But he's popular, and the press loves his handsome face. That could really help you gain some goodwill for whatever you want to do. Have him on your side and you'll get some good press, and society here will love you. But if you have him as an enemy, I think you'll find he's going to be the worst."

"I don't need to be popular here."

"You're selling a product, Leo. Of course you do. You're crazy if you think you can convince them to stop having fae slaves. Syn is nothing compared to the power and status that owning a fae slave brings. You really think you can change that?"

"I will change the world, Elise."

Elise leaned back and eyed me suspiciously. "Knowing you, Leo," she said finally, "you just might."

9

VERA

Ten minutes never felt so long.

Standing at the bottom of the stairs, I leaned back against the wall, arms crossed over my chest. Rand stood next to me, and for a long time we waited in silence, my eyes glued to the top of the stairs, waiting for Leo to appear.

In my head, I ran through all the things I wanted to say to him. All the things I wanted to ask him. We had spent months together; how could he have possibly left out this tiny detail about being engaged to someone else?

Finally, Rand nudged me with his elbow. "I know you lost back there, but at least you looked hot doing it. From the comments I heard during the fight, I have a feeling if we had stayed in the arena, you would have had quite the fan club forming."

I turned my head slowly to glare at him. "You're guilty here too, you know."

The demon held up both hands as if surrendering. "Me? What did I do?"

I raised my eyebrows.

"Would it have changed anything if I had told you about the engagement?"

I didn't answer.

"He hasn't seen Elise in months."

"When was the last time?"

Rand sighed and looked to the ceiling for a moment, as if he was expecting an answer there. "The night of the auction. The night he bought you. Elise mentioned buying you first, actually."

I shivered at the idea of being that demon's slave. Her dog was cute, but that was the extent of the things I liked about her. Even knowing she and Leo were alone in her office right then was making every hair on my neck stand on end. Before Leo met me, had they been alone together often? Oh gods, had they been dating? Had they... I had to know. I didn't want to know, but I had to.

"Rand. Did Leo and Elise ever... you know..."

"Did they ever what?"

"You know..." I shrugged, my fingers messing with the suppression bracelet I'd put back on after the fight. "Did they ever...?"

"Fuck?"

"I was going to ask if they ever dated, but okay, yeah, I want to know that too."

Rand snorted. The bastard had the gall to look amused. "Not to my knowledge, but that's a question for Leo, not me. He won't gossip with me like you fae."

"I don't gossip. You're the one always forcing me to listen to you complain about your love life."

"Oh." He considered and then nodded. "Yeah, I guess that's true."

"So, gossip with me about you and Rob right now before I lose my mind thinking of Leo and her up there in her office alone together."

"Well...," he said. "At first I was just really into his muscles, but sometimes really muscular guys—"

I held up a hand to stop him before that went any further. "Never mind. I think I changed my mind."

"Are you sure, because—"

Two demons burst through the door, both dressed in the same black suits and sunglasses as the guards we'd seen earlier. They were loud, their words slurred, no doubt having taken part in some of the post-fight celebrating. I heard them sniffing and watched as one put a packet back into his pocket. Two demons high on Dust then; what could possibly go wrong?

One pointed over at me. "It's that girl from earlier. Hey, sweetheart," the demon called out as they approached, his voice drawing out the nickname. "Want me to show you some moves for next time?"

"Hard pass," I said.

The other demon snickered. "You just got rejected by a human, dude."

"Nah." The first demon's grin was gone, his features tight. "That doesn't happen."

I rolled my eyes, pushing off the wall and standing tall as they came closer. "There's a first time for everything."

The demon only chuckled. "I knew she was feisty when I saw her leap onto that fae girl's back. That fight was so hot. Come on, sweetheart—"

Before they could get closer to me, Rand was between us, black wings spread out to block their path. Then I heard a door shut, and there, finally, was Leo at the top of the stairs.

The two demons heard it too.

"See ya around, sweetheart." The demon sneered, but the two left all the same, passing the packet of Dust back and forth.

Leo gave both of us a quizzical look as he ran down the stairs, but as soon as he was beside me, he placed a hand on my back, signaling with Rand for us to leave.

"That was longer than ten minutes," I muttered as we left.

Leo glanced down at me and swallowed. "Let's get back to the apartment, and then we can talk."

Not a word was said as we walked to the car. Even when Leo opened the door for me, he didn't say a word. He shut it behind me with a thud. Rand started the car, and we were off, driving to the apartment. The longer we were in the car, the more anxious I became.

The buildings grew taller as we drove farther into the city. With every second, I grew closer to exploding.

I leaned forward in my seat. "I'm done waiting. Start talking."

"When we get back to Rand's apartment," Leo said.

"Rand, pull over," I blurted out. "I don't care where."

Leo twisted in the passenger seat to stare at me while Rand cast a quick glance over his shoulder as he drove. "It's late. Why don't we get home, and then you two can—"

"No," I said. "Pull over."

"Vera, we're in the middle of the city."

"Now."

Rand thought for a second and then looked to Leo who nodded. "All right then. Hold on."

The three of us slid to the side as the car screeched around a corner, racing between buildings. I gripped the leather seat as we sped down the alley, finally slamming to a stop that made us jolt forward. We were at the end of the narrow street facing another busy road. Cars zipped in front of us, and a bright beam from something nearby flooded the car.

Leo glared over at Rand. "Here? Really?"

"As good a place as any," Rand offered. "Sort of fitting though, don't you think?"

I didn't know what they were talking about until I was out of the car. After slamming the door, I walked to the end of the alley and looked out at the busy street. Even at the late hour, the street was full, demons passing us on either side, cars racing down the road.

In front of us was a roundabout, a tall statue in the middle. I shielded my eyes to look up at a metal demon several stories high, towering over the living demons and cars going past it. Spotlights were set up on the ground, shining up at the metal, the angles of the statue casting beams of light in every direction.

"Come on." Leo scooped me into his arms and flew over the traffic, then set me down on the sidewalk in front of the statue.

He kept his hand on the small of my back, and together we stared up at the monstrous thing. Standing tall, the giant metal demon looked down on the street below with a frown, its great metal wings spread broadly. One foot was slightly in front of the other, as if he were walking forward, and the demon's long tail curved around the foot in the back. In one hand was a giant hammer held high in the air. From the look on the statue's face to the way he held the hammer, the demon was posed as if he might smash the hammer down on all of us at any moment.

"The bastard has never lifted a hammer in his entire fucking life," Leo muttered.

I looked up again. Of course. How had I missed the crown on the demon's head? The longer I scanned its features, the more I could see remnants of Leo.

"This is your father," I said.

"It is."

"Why is he holding a hammer?"

Leo continued staring up at the demon. "It represents the two sides of Vestia. The hammer is a weapon of destruction, but it is also a tool of creation. Sometimes a thing has to be destroyed before it can be turned into something new."

"Interesting." To me, it looked like the demon was ready to crush anything in his path.

"Personally, I think he just wanted to look like a badass. They put this up not long after the engagement was announced."

Turning to face Leo, I tugged on his sleeve, bringing his attention down to me and away from the statue. "Why didn't you tell me?"

"I didn't say anything to you because it doesn't matter. This engagement means nothing to me."

"It means something to her."

Leo ran a hand through his hair and sighed. "I can't control what delusions she has, Vera. She was only supposed to marry me as a political alliance. She comes from one of the wealthiest families in Vestia. It had nothing to do with love."

"I know that. I know you don't love her, but how long has she been in love with you?"

Leo again stared up at the statue, but he didn't deny it. "We were children when the agreement was made. It wasn't like we asked for it. One day we were both told what was happening, and that was that.

When my... When the *queen* died, that ring was given to Elise as a symbol of the betrothal."

"I see." Knowing that the engagement wasn't something either of them had asked for helped dull the sting slightly. As much as I didn't want to admit it, I could relate to the idea of being a girl whose choices were made for her. "That explains some of her anger then."

"How so?"

"It would be a tough pill to swallow if she thought she was going to be with you forever, only to find out that she won't be with you at all."

Leo's eyes were back on me. "Elise found that out a long time ago."

"That doesn't make it easier. I'm not defending her, because she acted like a total bitch tonight, but maybe I understand her a little better now."

"You don't have to understand her. Once I renounce my claim to the throne, the engagement will be officially dissolved."

"Does she know that?" I asked.

"Of course she knows that. That's why she wants a percentage of Syn."

My mouth dropped open. "She wants *what*? And did you agree?"

"I did. She has contacts here. She can help me—"

"She wants *you*, Leo. She wants to tie herself to you somehow."

Leo waved a hand in the air. "What she wants is to hold on to the little power she currently has."

"Well, she can have whatever power she wants, but she won't have you."

"I have to say"—Leo smirked—"I think I like it when you're jealous."

"I'm not jealous of her."

"Oh yeah you are."

"Of some rich, beautiful demon with perfect hair who is also engaged to the demon I love? What could possibly make you think that I'd be jealous of someone like that?"

Leo chuckled and laced his fingers in mine. He brought ours

hands up to his mouth and kissed my knuckles gently. "Hm. If that isn't why you're upset, then is it because of that gaudy ring she had on?" He kept my hand near his lips as he stared down at me.

"I don't care about rings, Leo."

"Are you sure? Because I think a different sort of ring might look lovely on this hand one day."

I let out a shaky breath, unable to stop the butterflies that suddenly seemed to be throwing a party in my stomach.

"I'm supposed to be mad at you right now," I told him. "But then you go and say something like that."

"I'm sorry." Leo closed his eyes and dotted tiny kisses on my hand. "I love you. Only you."

"And I love you too."

When he opened his eyes, he kept my hand in his but circled his other around my waist, bringing me close. Leo leaned down, his forehead against my own. "It's always been part of my plan to reject all this. The kingdom. Elise. Everything. I don't want any part of this kingdom. I will drive the Dust industry out of business and force my father's. It won't make sense economically to keep fae slaves any longer."

Leo leaned back, still holding me, but again he stared up at the statue. "Three days from now, he'll be in the palace. I'm going to tell him everything."

"And what then?"

"Then we leave and never come back."

10

———

LEO

Today I would walk into the palace as a prince, and I would walk out as just another demon.

Staring into the bedroom mirror, I adjusted my tie and thought of the last time I'd seen my father. It was years ago. I'd spent the day working on holo-tech in the palace lab, fine tuning the mechanisms that would later become the watches worn by thousands. There were so many small things I remembered from that day, like Rand and Zell bickering or the sound of Marcus typing on a keyboard.

How strange that those details stayed in my brain right alongside a memory that was much more important. The last time I saw my father was also the day I found out the fae woman I'd thought was my nanny was actually my mother.

There's really no way to prepare yourself for discovering your entire identity has been a lie.

When confronted, my father didn't deny it. He didn't apologize. He didn't do anything at all other than tell me I should be grateful he'd kept my secret this long.

My secret. As if he had nothing to do with it.

In some ways, he was right. I was the one left holding on to the burden of knowing I was half-fae. My genetics didn't change my father or his life, but they certainly changed mine.

I'd tried to make my departure as secret as possible, but I should have known someone would find out. The general stopped me at the gate leading out of the palace. Hearing him whisper—*him, the general,* the demon who was known for the deep tone of his voice when he shouted at his troops—had been disturbing enough. But then he suggested it was time, past time, for me to take over in Vestia, to move my father out of the picture and become the next king.

What would have happened if I had agreed?

I lived with my choices every day.

I felt Vera's arms around my waist, her head pressing between my wings and resting against my back. Even with the added pressure of her body on mine, I felt some of the weight on my shoulders ease off. Vera squeezed and then let go, coming around to my side where she tilted her head and squinted up at me.

"The offer still stands, you know. Fly me in there, and I'll show that old bastard some of the moves I learned in the arena the other night." Vera punched into the air as if to demonstrate.

Forcing a smile, I finished adjusting my tie, pulling it tight.

"There's no need. This is a simple declaration. I'll sign the forms, and it will be done."

"Why don't you just text him?"

I shook my head. "You can't renounce a title over text message."

"Why not?" She wrinkled her face. "I thought demons were all about technology. Use that fancy demon tech to send a pic of you giving him the middle finger and be done with it."

"If only it were that easy." I wanted him to see my face. I wanted him to see that I wasn't running, that I was facing him head on and wouldn't back down. There would be no secret escape plans. My father had hurt more than one person whom I loved, and I needed to tell him to his face exactly what I thought.

"Hey." Vera was still staring at me. She reached up and touched my face, her hand instantly warming my skin. I shivered, and my heart raced as I realized what she was doing. "I love you," she said, not taking her hand away.

I took her arm in my own hand and kissed the inside of her wrist. "I love you too."

Tugging her against me, I leaned down, kissing her. For Vera, I could do anything.

When we finally broke away, I felt a new energy and a renewed sense of purpose. The glow from Vera's kiss would wear off quickly, but at that moment, it gave me confidence and courage. I took one last look in the mirror, but my own reflection made me pause. Really, at the end of the day, who was I trying to impress? I shrugged off the suit jacket, tossed it on the bed, and then my hands went to the tie to undo the knot before pulling it off my neck.

Vera took one look at the tie I'd thrown on the bed and nodded. We walked together to the apartment door, grateful that we were alone.

"Leo?"

When I looked back, Vera was still in the doorway, one hand on the door. "Yeah?" I asked her.

"Give him hell."

EACH STEP through the palace felt like a mile, my heart thudding in my ear alongside the click of my boot on the floor. The faces of the staff passed by me in a blur.

Elise had a source that tracked the king's schedule, so I knew he was in the palace. Supposedly he had a rare day without meetings, and if my father was still the workaholic he used to be, on his days off he'd be in his office.

My fingernails digging into my palms, I walked the familiar hallways like I'd done so many times years ago.

And then I was there.

Outside his office, I remembered being a child standing in the exact same spot, my ear pressed against the wooden door. I thought of the day I'd stood right here, tears streaming down my face. I had been exhausted from searching the palace grounds for Aurora before I finally decided, as a last resort, to find my father and ask him where she was. That was the day, when I opened the door and saw my father surrounded by his counselors, that I'd heard my mother's name spoken for the last time.

If I hadn't listened in, if they'd noticed me right away instead of continuing their conversation, would anyone have ever told me that she was dead?

Just like that day, I pushed the door open without knocking.

I thought time would have dulled the sharp pain in my gut that came with seeing his face, but no, the pain was still there, just as raw and jagged as it was years ago. I didn't wait for servants to let me in, and when I entered his office, my father was sitting behind his large wooden desk, the same desk he'd sat behind when I told him that I was leaving the first time.

No, not my father. The demon in front of me was no longer my father, and he hadn't been for a long time. From now on he was the King of Vestia, nothing more.

The bastard didn't even look up from his work.

Standing a few feet from his desk, I cleared my throat. Since he wasn't going to speak first, I'd go ahead and say it straight out.

"I'll only be here a moment. I am officially renouncing my title as prince. It's possible I'll come back in the future, but it will be for business. I don't plan on setting foot in this palace again."

He continued writing on his desk the entire time I spoke, finally capping his pen and setting it aside when I'd finished. It was all an act. I'd lived through these little dances many times over the years, and the steps never changed.

He didn't respond right away, and I hadn't expected him to. It was always difficult to tell what he was thinking, never knowing if his silence hid a quiet fury or complete apathy. I wasn't sure which one I preferred, though the fury felt more honest. Quiet anger was more his style, the silence masking his outright cruelty.

The king exhaled loudly and finally his cold silver eyes met mine. "You're here."

"I am."

"Does this mean that you're ready to be a man now? Or are you still a child running away from his problems?"

"I said what I needed to say. I'm going to sign the official documents renouncing my title as soon as I leave this office."

The king grunted. "I didn't know my son was this weak."

I should have walked out right then. I knew he was trying to get a rise out of me, but I couldn't stop myself. The hatred I felt toward him for what he'd done to my mother, to me, to Vera, was impossible to hold back.

"I'm not weak." I spit out each word so he could hear them clearly.

"You ran away from your birthright. You are still trying to run away. That's weakness. It's cowardice."

"Like hell it is." I should have known we wouldn't be able to have an actual conversation. I hadn't come there to argue with him, but I found myself unable to stop. "Instead of staying in this toxic court, I started over. That's *bravery*. My inventions—"

"Are mere toys compared to what you will be creating when you use the Crown's resources. You created a knockoff product, and now you think you're a genius," he huffed. "When you become king, you'll have every scientist and laboratory at your beck and call. Money is no object here."

"You weren't listening. I'm not going to become king, and I definitely don't want your blood money."

"Oh." He nodded smugly. "That's right. You found your own little fountain of fortune, didn't you? You think you can look down on what I have created, boy, when you're using this fae girl's blood as well?"

"The fae girl's blood that you took." I felt the bile rising in my throat with each word. "If you want to talk about cowardice, cowardice is sending some human pawn to do your dirty work. You sent him to attack an innocent girl. And yes, I'll use her blood to create synthetic Dust, and no fae will ever need to be bled again. She's not just some 'fae girl.'"

"I know how that goes. I know how sweet the forbidden fruit can be."

I couldn't listen to him another second. Anger coiled within me, threatening to break out.

"Don't walk away from me, boy," he said the moment I turned to leave.

"I walked away from you a long time ago. I don't mind doing it again."

"If you walk away now, you'll never get to hear about my latest invention."

"Because I don't care," I told him over my shoulder. "All I want is for you to leave me alone. I don't need your help. I don't need your guidance. I don't need anything here. I'm done."

"Then what will you say when I tell you I made this new invention just for you?" I paused, and when I turned around, I saw him holding up a syringe. "I'm glad you invented a synthetic Dust, Leo."

"I don't believe you. What is that?"

"No, truly, I am. If we can still access the power inherent in fae blood without having to have any fae around, it's better for everyone."

As much as my instinct told me to keep walking, to leave and never look back, I had to know. "What's in that syringe?"

"This? This is how we'll finally get rid of those little insects for good."

"Tell me what that is."

"I've refined the suppression bracelet's nanotechnology to get to the core of a fae's powers, learned how it actually suppresses their abilities. Then I isolated those capabilities and created this enhanced serum, capable of much more than merely muting their magic."

"More than muting it?"

"Yes. We no longer have to settle for suppressing fae magic. Now we can end it completely. Once this drug enters a fae's bloodstream, the nanobots in the serum seek and destroy anything resembling fae magic. Permanently. The whole process takes mere seconds."

"How...?" I felt like I was going to throw up at the realization of what he was saying. "How do you know that it will take away all their magic?"

His eyes didn't blink. "Trial and error, of course. Without their magic, my studies indicate that they slowly lose their minds as well and eventually simply die. We'll end fae slavery, my son, just like you want, because no one will need them once they're reduced to humans with useless wings."

I wished I was surprised by his callous disregard for the lives of fae, but I wasn't.

"You're sick," I told him.

"No. You are, and this is your cure. One to cure you of your sentimentalities and attachments. One I made just for you. Only you and I know your secret. For over two decades your... genetics... have driven me to find a solution. The risk of making you king before I had this technology was too great. Now that I can erase your fae side, we have nothing to worry about anymore."

"Ignoring the complete and total insanity in what you just said, we both know this serum isn't just for me. How many fae will you use this on? If you kill your fae, then how will you make your precious Dust?"

"From what I hear, I won't be making Dust for long anyway. If your Syn is cheaper and more powerful, then I have no further need of the fae here. The Crown will take over selling Syn while you rule. Why are you fighting me on this? All the equipment needed to create Syn? Yours. All the lab space? Yours. The warehouses, the manufacturers, anything you need to create your fake Dust is at your fingertips if you stay here."

"I don't want anything of yours. Aren't you listening?"

In a flash, he grabbed me, held me down, stabbed the needle into my arm, and pushed in the plunger. I jerked my arm away, and the syringe clattered onto the floor, bouncing a few feet away.

"What the hell did you just do?" Shooting pain coursed up my arm.

The king simply sat back in his chair. "How do you feel, Leo?"

Sweating, shaking, I clutched my arm where he'd stabbed me. The pain was quickly spreading; I could feel the drug traveling up my arm to my neck and then across my shoulders, shooting down to the rest of my body. Whereas Vera's magic gave me energy as it coursed through my veins and made me feel invincible, this was completely different. The energy rushing through me now was attacking me, like little knives hacking through my nerves one by one. Was this my own fae magic leaving me? Was the drug cutting it out of my body?

"You are insane," I choked out.

"No," the old bastard said calmly. "I'm very sane. This injection will erase any part of you that's still fae. Aren't you ready to denounce that part of you and accept your birthright? You are the demon prince. You *will* be the demon king."

"No." Sweat dripped down my face, stinging my eyes as I fell to my knees. The pain was becoming unbearable. How long would it last? How long could I stay conscious? *I have to get out of this room.* I put a hand on his desk to pull myself up to my feet. Would my wings work the same? I needed to make the pain stop. I needed to tell Vera—

Another surge of pain racked my whole body, blocking out all thoughts as I screamed in agony and fell back against the floor.

"You're feeling the fae parts of your DNA disintegrating one by one, leaving only the demon side of you. The true you. Losing part of yourself must be painful. Most of the fae I used for the trial didn't survive more than a few seconds. I knew you'd be able to handle it though."

Handle it? If I could have laughed, I would have. Writhing in pain, I wasn't handling anything. I couldn't even control the way my tail swished and swatted the floor, and my wings felt like they weighed five times more than normal. My every single fiber was shaking and twitching.

But then... Just when I thought that I couldn't take the pain any longer, when I truly started to fear this was it, that he had killed me, my panic veered sharply in another direction.

Anger.

If the fae side of me was gone, I'd never be able to protect Vera if she needed me. I remembered her helpless body in my arms the night she'd been attacked. If I hadn't been part fae, she would have died. The fae side of me wasn't a curse at all; it was a blessing.

The demon I would never refer to as my father again stood in front of his desk, two guards beside him. My screams must have brought them into the room. Not taking my eyes off the king, I forced myself to my feet and moved toward him, one slow trudging step at a time, like I was walking with cement anchors on each foot.

"You," I managed to say.

"This is the real you, my son. The true prince of the demons. Now you can assume your rightful place and forget all about your little affair. With your fae DNA gone, there is no room for sentiment or emotion in your life any longer."

He was wrong. All I felt was emotion. My emotions consumed me, they blocked my vision and made my feet and arms move on their own toward him. The king barely paid any attention to me, however.

"I've closed off all transportation out of this kingdom."

"What?"

"Once you formally agree to become king, I'll let the fae girl leave. Until then, she'll just have to stay at that little apartment you're hiding in." The king smirked, walking around his guards and back to his desk.

He *knew*. He knew where we were staying. He knew where Vera was.

"If you refuse, you'll leave me no choice." Opening a drawer, he took out another syringe just like the first and held it up for me to see. "I can't wait to see how long your whore lasts after I inject her with this."

"You bastard!" I screamed, every muscle trembling in anger. I lurched forward toward the guards, but they held me back as I lashed out.

"Make your decision quickly, son," he said from his desk as the guards dragged me toward the door. "Take too long, and well, you know what happens then."

Once in the hall, the door slammed shut behind me as I shrugged off the guards.

11

———

LEO

"Leo." Elise's expression twisted in irritation at the sight of me sitting behind her office desk. But just as quickly, her smile was back, and all traces of annoyance were gone. "Are you taking over this business now, too? I know you agreed to give me a percentage of Syn, but I didn't think you were interested in the entertainment industry as well."

"I have zero interest in this place."

"Good, because you wouldn't be half as good at running it as me." She stayed near the door, watching me.

I stood up and came around to the front of her desk. "I need a favor."

"Asking for help is very unlike you. I'm intrigued."

"Do you have a room I can use?"

Elise raised one eyebrow. "I'm even more intrigued now."

"It's not for me."

"Uh-huh."

"I need a place to keep someone."

"Let me guess," she sighed. "Your slave."

"My—" I realized I didn't know what to say. Girlfriend? Lover? It seemed like no matter what I called Vera, it would piss off Elise, and I needed her on my side for this. The king knew Vera was in Vestia, and if I didn't work fast to hide her, he would take her.

"But, yes, her. I know you have other girls who live here."

"Correction—girls who *work* here. Those living arrangements are a financial choice. If I let them live here, I can have them work whenever I want." Elise's heels clicked as she walked over to the window that looked down on the arena below the office. She tapped the glass to get my attention. "I have enough slaves already. Did you see those blue ones? They're darling. And the boy—you wouldn't believe what he can do with his hands."

"I don't care. What sort of deal do we need to make for Vera to live here while I'm in town?"

"Something is off about you," Elise said, raising one eyebrow. "What's going on?"

I'm barely holding it together, my body is revolting against me, and my father wants to murder the love of my life. I'm doing just great, thanks for asking.

"Can she stay here or not?"

"Hm. Okay, first, she'd have to work. She doesn't look like a fairy, so she could do the same work as the humans I have on staff, since she's probably just as useless."

I let that comment slide. "You mean fighting for you."

"Oh, don't worry about that." Elise sniffed, waiving a hand in the air to dismiss my concern. "She won't fight. I already saw how that turned out. A fight against a weakling like her wouldn't bring in any money. There's always the upstairs though..."

"Hell no."

"What's wrong with my club?"

"It's a brothel."

"It's a *club*. We entertain. Some demons like fighting," she said, gesturing down to the arena below, "and some like fucking. I'm happy to make money off both."

"Elise."

"Fine," she said with another wave of her hand. "I'll just have her serve drinks or stock the bar or something. Surely she can manage that, right? What's her name again?"

"Vera."

"Vera," she said, as if testing it out. "Okay. Give me a moment, and I'll see what I can do."

While I waited, I went back to sitting at her desk. I watched out the window from the office as she went down the stairs and called out to several demons who immediately came over to her.

Rolling one of her pens beneath my fingers, I imagined what life must be like for her. With the duke's retirement, taking over her father's business couldn't have been easy, but judging by the way everyone deferred to her, she seemed to have a handle on it. No doubt her connection to the royal family helped, which is why I wasn't surprised she was still spouting this bullshit about being my fiancée.

The pen snapped in my hand, and ink dripped onto her desk.

Cursing under my breath, I opened a drawer to find something to clean up the mess with. A magazine at the bottom caught my eye, and even through the office supplies covering it, I recognized the demon on the cover.

Royals Uncensored read the headline in big red letters, and in smaller font, Lord Zell Tells All.

Yeah, I bet he did—for the right price.

Smirking at me from the glossy cover was Zell. The photo was of him from the waist up, shirtless, because *of course* he was. His black wings were spread out behind him like a damn peacock showing off its feathers, and he wore only a suit jacket, the dark burgundy of the fabric very similar to his red hair. He'd shaved his head on the sides, leaving the top wavy and purposely disheveled.

Nothing about Zell was ever disheveled; if it looked that way, it was because he wanted it to. Everything with Zell, from the multiple piercings on his ears and nose to the silver rings he wore to the tattoos on his neck, was always calculated and intentional. It didn't surprise me in the least that Zell was doing magazine covers now. His reputation had made him the self-styled bad boy of the royal family, but truthfully, he'd always been a narcissistic bastard obsessed with his image, screaming for attention at every turn.

I grabbed a box of tissues from the drawer and wiped the ink off my hands and Elise's desk. I remembered that as kids, while I counted down the minutes until whatever party or dinner we were being forced to attend was over, Zell basked in the conversations, loving the spotlight that came along with being a young royal. But no matter how often our mothers pushed us to interact with each other, and even though we were cousins, we were never friends. Once my engagement to Elise was announced, the difference between us grew even greater. By the time we were teenagers, I split my time between training and working in my father's lab while Zell spent his hours rotating through a list of girls eager for his affection. Because of Zell, I knew the fastest way to sneak out of the palace undetected, even though we wanted to escape for different reasons.

This wasn't the only magazine. Underneath it were several others, all with pictures of Zell on the cover, all promising insider palace gossip. Knowing Elise, she already knew whatever gossip was in these articles before they were printed. Part of me wanted to read them, but another part didn't care about whatever supposed secrets Zell felt like sharing with the press. In the end, I left the magazines where they were, and I had just closed the drawer when the door creaked open.

"All right, she can stay here."

"Perfect," I said, getting up. "I'll bring her over this afternoon."

"Wait. I have one more condition."

"What is it?"

"I'm going to help manage your business."

"Help? We already agreed that you're getting a percentage. Now you want more?"

"I want to be part of running it. All of it. I can make Syn work for you. Who is managing the day-to-day business right now? You? Rand?"

I didn't answer.

"So basically no one."

As much as I dreaded the thought of Elise working with me every day, the idea of having someone else manage the business aspects of Syn was attractive. There was no telling how many hundreds of missed calls and voice mails were currently on my phone. If she planned on staying in Vestia, she could handle the affairs here, and there would be no reason for me to ever have to come back. But could she really handle it? I was hardly able to keep up even now, and we were just getting the business off the ground.

"You're already running this... club. What makes you think you could run your club and my business?"

"This place basically runs without me. Why do you think my father was fine with passing it along to me in the first place? It's a well-oiled machine. I need more of a challenge, and let's face it. You've been gone, Leo. I have the connections here that you don't. Some of my best customers will also be your best customers for Syn."

She had a good point. It was true she would know potential buyers I wouldn't know, and if she could manage the more irritating parts of the business, it would take them off my plate.

"You're not getting a higher percentage of the profits."

"Okay." She nodded.

But there was one piece that still bothered me, and I knew she wouldn't like it.

"And you have to free your slaves."

I watched as her eyes widened.

"Leo..."

"There's no other way."

"Could I keep my blue ones?" she asked. "They're new."

"No. The end of fae slavery is coming. You and I both know that. I'll give you some time to figure out the logistics, but I'm not partnering with a slaver."

"Partners, eh? I do like the sound of that. You are my fiancé, after all."

"Hear me now, Elise, because I need to make sure you understand what I am saying. You and I, we're only business partners," I told her. "That's it. Nothing more."

"Fine. Fine. I hear you." A wry smile formed on her red lips. "I've heard you loud and clear for years, Your Highness." The smile faded as she stared at me, brow furrowed. "What did that couch ever do to you? You're buying me a new one, you know."

I looked down at where my hands held on to the back of her couch while I stood behind it. Shit. Without my even realizing it, my nails had sunk into the leather, tearing the fabric in multiple places. Luckily, this time I had only ripped apart a couch and not someone's throat. I needed to be more careful and more aware of what I was doing until I figured out how to fix the effects of that serum. It was throwing all my emotions out of whack.

"Fine. Whatever. I'll work on the official paperwork and send it over to you." I told her as I headed toward the door. I stopped just before leaving. There was one more thing I needed to say. "And thank you. For allowing Vera to stay here."

"I'm not doing it out of the kindness of my heart, Leo. This is a business arrangement."

"I know that, but still. Thank you."

"Wow." She laughed lightly. "Thanking me? This girl really has changed you."

"Maybe," I admitted. "All I know right now is that I'll do everything in my power to protect her."

"Lucky girl." Elise leaned back in her chair and sighed. "Part of me is glad that you know how it feels, Leo."

"Know how what feels?"

Elise looked up from her desk, our eyes meeting, and in that moment, I was reminded of the little girl I first met all those years ago, the little girl with long blond hair hiding behind her mother's wings.

"How it feels to be scared of losing someone."

12

VERA

"You have no idea how prepared I am for this." Rand flung bags of clothes onto the bed, lace and shimmer and straps and mesh spilling out onto the blankets. "Hurry up and try these on before Leo gets back."

"I don't even want to do this," I told him. "I want to stay here."

"Look. I'm already jealous that you get to live at the club instead of here, so don't rub it in my face that you aren't grateful. Now get dressed."

"We could switch places. You go live there and wear these skimpy outfits, and I'll stay here."

"Don't tempt me."

Plopping onto the bed, Rand leaned back against the headboard and took out his phone while I stared blankly at the outfits he'd picked out, the tiny bras and slinky dresses. All revealing, barely more than small slips of fabric designed to cover as little as possible.

"You went out and bought all these clothes... for me?"

"I stopped in the store on the way back. It's not like I had a bunch of stripper clothes lying around this apartment."

I gave him a pointed look.

"Okay, well, I didn't have these exact ones," he shrugged. "The tags are still on them, so I can take them back if you want. Come on, let's go." He clapped his hands to spur me into action. "Fashion show time."

I'd already thrown the few things I had into my bag and was ready and waiting for Leo to come back. I knew Leo would find a way to protect me, but something told me there were pieces of the story Rand was leaving out.

There was nothing else to do, really. We couldn't return home, and I couldn't stay at the apartment any longer. When Rand first told me I'd be staying somewhere else, I wasn't necessarily expecting... that club. Elise's club. A very private club, with a very exclusive clientele who liked the more sinful things in life.

Clientele like Rand.

"You know I'm only going to be serving drinks, right? I'm not actually going to be dancing at this place."

"Vera." He looked up from his phone. "I know this club better than you, and I know that if you want to blend in, you're going to have to step up your game. Also, if you complain one more time, I'm getting Jasmine in here to do your makeup too, and you better believe I'll ask her to bring the pinkest lipstick she owns."

"I'm going, I'm going," I said, picking up a corset top that I wasn't sure would come close to holding in my boobs. "Who're you texting over there?"

"None of your business."

"Is it a tall fairy with green wings whom you're desperately in love with? The one you refuse to admit your feelings for?"

"Jasmine!" he shouted, but I threw a miniskirt at him, hitting him right in the face to shut him up.

"WHAT DO YOU THINK?" I asked when I finally tried on the first outfit, a lacy black bra top and tight black shorts that had been the longest pair in the pile, which wasn't saying much. With my back to the door, I didn't see it open.

"Vera, are you—" Leo stopped short when he saw me. His eyes

flicked to Rand for only a second before returning to me. "Out," he barked, and Rand and I both knew who he meant. The door hadn't even closed before Leo picked me up, his hands supporting the back of my thighs, and carried me to the bed, flopping onto his back with me on top of him.

His hands gripped the exposed parts of my hip. "I'm not sure if I should be thanking Rand or hitting him for getting you this outfit."

"With you staring at me like that, I'm leaning toward thanking him at the moment."

"Me too."

I leaned over to kiss him, our lips connecting as his hands roamed over my skin and clothes. But something was different. Something felt strange.

"Leo?" I sat back, trying to figure out what it was. He looked the same, but maybe a little more tired than normal, which could be from the stress.

"No talking," he growled, tugging at my shorts. "I want these clothes off you, now."

Ignoring him, I reached my hand out, touching his cheek. Leo was always hot, my own personal heater each night when I snuggled against him, but his skin felt even hotter than normal today.

"Do you have a fever?"

His hand clapped around my wrist, his touch scoring my skin. "I'm giving you four seconds to take your clothes off before I do it for you."

He didn't seem sick. Maybe it was all in my imagination. "And if I want you to do it for me?" I asked, teasing one strap down my shoulder.

"Two seconds."

"Until what? Tell me exactly what you'll do."

In an instant his arms were around my waist, flipping us over, my back on the bed as he hovered over me and leaned down, our foreheads touching.

"I warned you," he whispered. Not wasting another breath, with one hand he broke the straps of my top first, effortlessly ripping the flimsy fabric off my body. There was only a second of cold air on my bare chest before he squeezed one of my breasts, my flesh spilling out between his fingers.

"I'm not sure I'm going to be able to control myself tonight. Can you handle that?"

I nodded, trying to hold back a yelp as he squeezed harder, the heat radiating from him in waves. He let go but only moved to my nipple, tweaking it between two fingers. This time I couldn't help but squeal as he twisted, but he only smirked down at me, like a wolf who knew his prey couldn't escape.

"I might hurt you." He watched my reaction as he tugged on my nipple, rocking his hips against me at the same time. All I could do was whimper in reply. "But right now, you still have too many clothes on."

He was no less delicate with my shorts, and they joined the pile of ripped and discarded clothing on the floor, my panties following quickly behind. His own clothes were gone in an instant, and then his big body was back on the bed. He leaned over me, taking my head in his hands and pulling me toward him for a deep kiss.

One of his hands wandered down to my already dripping core where he used two fingers to open me up. "So wet for me." He pushed his thick fingers in and pulled them back, repeating the motion when he saw how my back arched from his touch. "Good, that will make this easier."

I gasped as he used a third finger, pushing it in and stretching me even more.

"I'm just trying to get you ready." He smirked when he saw me squirming.

"I'm ready, I swear. I want you inside me."

"You know I can never deny you anything."

He moved over on top of me, his breath hot on my neck as he sank his cock into me slowly. Both of us moaned at the sensation, and he leaned even closer, hungrily kissing my neck. His kiss was messy and wet, as if he couldn't get enough.

"You feel so fucking good," he breathed as he entered me, inch by inch, still nipping at the skin under my chin. "I want you so badly."

"You have me." I desperately pulled him closer even as I tried to relax as he stretched me out.

"You're right, I do." Leo didn't give me any more time to adjust, his hips slamming against mine as he buried his whole length in one rough lunge. Our kisses were fast and feverish, each thrust hot and rough, as if we both knew that this wouldn't last.

"Look at me," he grunted, his hand forcing my chin up so that I was staring at him. The intensity in his silver eyes was enough to make my body shudder, and under his gaze my cunt clenched down as I came around him. Even as the wave of pleasure started to die down, he kept fucking me through it, not slowing the pace at all as he chased his own pleasure. "I need you," he groaned as he shoved his dick inside me, deeper each time. "Need you so badly. Always need you."

From that moment onward, there was nothing gentle about his touch, not an ounce of kindness in the way his hands groped and pawed, the way his mouth bit and sucked. Tonight he was greedy, taking all of me and then some, forcing me to stay right on the line between pleasure and pain.

But I was greedy too. I needed to soak in every touch and kiss, to remember the sound of every moan and whisper so that I could keep them safe in my memory while we were apart. After tonight, we'd be staying in separate places, but for how long? Neither of us knew.

So I let the heat envelop me, giving myself completely to him. Both of us let ourselves give in to the pleasure of the moment, because the moment might be all we had.

13

VERA

I had thought the hard part was going to be saying goodbye when Leo left me at my new, temporary home. I thought the hard part would be knowing we were going to be sleeping across the city from each other, especially when I was already suspicious that something was going on that he wasn't telling me.

While I was right that both those things hurt, there was the unexpected pain of watching the two of them side by side, determining the details of my temporary living situation at the club. Standing next to each other, Leo and Elise looked like they belonged together. With her curvy, hour-glass figure accentuated by her formfitting dress and high heels, Elise was breathtaking no matter how much I wished she wasn't. Her heels gave her even more height than she already had, and she spoke with an easy confidence that came from knowing her status and beauty.

In other words, Elise looked and acted like a queen.

After Leo left, I did my best to push away feelings of jealousy while I sat at a table off to the side and watched the women dancing on the stage. The outfits Rand had picked out for me were tame compared to what they were wearing. Or weren't wearing.

Hearing a noise, I spun around in my chair, but no one was

behind me. Odd. Then there it was again, that same hiss I'd heard before.

"Psst, Vera!" someone whispered. "Over here."

Beside the main room was a small hallway with doors on each side. Private rooms, I realized. Taking careful steps down the hall, I saw a door cracked open. The voice had to have come from there. Slowly, I opened the door a few more inches when suddenly a blur of white and blue pulled me into the room and shut the door behind us.

When I saw her face, I understood how she knew my name. The white hair and blue wings were impossible to forget.

"Mia?"

"I thought that was you!" she squealed. "It is Vera, right?" Her eyes wide with excitement, she grabbed both my hands. Before I could yank them back, her eyes went even wider.

"So the rumors *are* true! You're the wingless fae who's here with the prince! I knew it had to be you because what else would explain why that sexy demon was all macho and possessive over you?"

"He's not *that* possessive."

"Yeah." She quirked up her lips in a smirk. "Okay. Sure. Whatever you say. He was ready to murder anyone who even looked at you. That's how I knew the rumors were true."

"There are rumors? About me?"

She was hardly listening, instead flying in circles around me, eying me up and down. "Oh, come on. Among the fae there are! All the fae here are talking about the girl that came here with the prince. A wingless fae! How cool is that? Did you really live with the humans?"

"I don't know about it being cool, but yeah. Yeah, I did."

"And you were auctioned off? What was that like? Do you know how much he paid for you? Why did he pick you? Were you guys already dating? Are you in love?"

An endless supply of questions seemed to roll out of her mouth.

"What is this about? Why are you looking at me like I'm an animal in a cage?"

With a whoosh of air, she quickly landed right in front of me.

"I'm so sorry, Vera! It's just that I've never known anyone who was a slave for the humans. What are they like? Is it true that they don't let you wear shoes? Did you just one day put on shoes and were like, 'what are these weird things on my feet? I can't walk ahhhhh'?"

"Actually, sort of? Honestly, I don't really want to talk about back then."

"Ah! I'm sorry, again! I'm being so rude, aren't I?"

It was hard to be mad at her when she was so excited and genuine. She was so different from other fae slaves I'd met, and not just because her beautiful blue wings were larger than most. Mia exuded confidence and, surprisingly for a slave, happiness. What had slave life been like for her if she acted with this amount of independence?

"I'm sorry about everything that happened in the fight. I hope I healed you enough afterward. It's all just a show I have to put on for my owner. As soon as that bitchy demon lady found out I could fight, she figured out a new way to earn money from me."

"You're Elise's slave."

"Yes. She's gotten even crazier recently, probably because your man is about to become king. Wait, how is that going to work? Isn't she engaged to the prince? Oh wow. Is he cheating on you?" She gasped. "Are you his *side chick*? I am so sorry. Do you want me to kick his ass? I'll kick his ass. You know I could."

"Mia. Stop. Slow down."

Before I could explain, there was a knock on the door, and in an instant Mia was in front of me, her blue wings spread wide. I'd seen a stance like that before, back when Leo was teaching me to spar with him in the pit. A fighting stance.

"I've got this!" Mia said over her shoulder. "Stay back."

"Got what?" I whispered. "Who is at the door?"

Another knock.

"I don't know."

I'd seen her fight firsthand that day in the ring, so I didn't doubt her abilities, but I was more concerned about why she was so nervous. If she was nervous, then it seemed likely that I *really* needed to be concerned.

"Just stay back!" she whispered.

Just as she finished the last word, the door opened and Mia charged forward, a blur of blue as she leaped with the obvious skill of someone who had trained extensively in hand-to-hand combat.

"Good gods, what the hell were you thinking?"

It was him. The fae rubbing his shoulder where Mia had hit him was the same fae with blue wings that I'd seen at the apartment building and then again after our match. His hair was just as white as hers, their wings an identical shade of bright cerulean. Once she saw him, Mia was no longer concerned. If anything, she looked exasperated and rolled her eyes.

"You wouldn't have gotten hurt if you'd done the knock right," she told him, crossing her arms over her chest in frustration.

"There are no wrong ways to knock."

"Apparently there are."

"Well, a bad guy wouldn't knock at all."

"Maybe," she admitted, "but you are supposed to use the secret knock."

"We haven't used that in years."

"So?"

"Um," I cleared my throat. "Hi?"

Two sets of bright blue eyes flashed toward me.

"Oh. I thought you two met the other night, but I guess that sexy demon got in the way. Lawrence, this is Vera. Vera, this is Lawrence."

"Hey," I said, giving him a little wave, but his blue eyes only seemed confused, as if he hadn't even seen me there.

Mia nudged him in the side. "Pick your mouth up off the floor, dude, or else she's going to think you're a creep."

He shook his head. "I'm sorry," he said, holding out his hand. "It's a pleasure to finally meet you officially, Vera."

"You too, Lawrence." I shook his hand, and he held mine there, for just a moment. It was as if he was watching me, trying to determine how I was reacting to his touch. Then he released mine.

"You can call me Laurie."

"Laurie it is."

"Vera is the wingless fae we've heard about," Mia explained. "She used to be a slave, but now she's free. Now she wears *shoes*."

"I'm not really sure what shoes have to do with anything, but—"

"A freed slave?" Laurie asked, raising an eyebrow. "How is that possible?"

"Leo freed me."

"The demon prince, you mean? The demon who turned feral when all I did was speak to you?"

I nodded. "That's the one."

"What is he to you?" Laurie asked, his blue eyes never breaking their stare. Did he blink... ever?

"He's my..." I wasn't sure what to say. Boyfriend? Lover?

"He was your owner," Laurie said. "We've heard that the demon prince has owned many slaves."

"Well, yes, that's true, but not anymore."

Laurie huffed out a breath. "Doubtful. They're all the same. Why are you here with him?"

"It's a long story," I said, not sure how much I could trust these two yet. "Family drama."

"So let me repeat. Why are *you* here? Did he make you come here with him?"

"Laurie," Mia said, her voice a low rumble of a threat.

"It's okay, Mia. He's right to be confused by our situation. Leo owned slaves," I admitted, "but he freed all of them, including me. He's working really hard to get an alternative to Dust manufactured, and when he does, it's going to lead to the end of slavery for all fae."

"A demon who wants to free the fae. I'll believe it when I see it. You know they're the ones who created these." Laurie held up his hand, a metal bracelet circling his wrist. "Suppression tech didn't exist before the war. We would have won if it wasn't for the demons."

"I'm not here to argue about something that happened before I was born. All I know is that I believe in Leo. His intentions are good. Are you and your girlfriend both—?"

Mia burst into laughter, but Laurie only scowled.

"What did I say?"

"Nothing. We're not dating, Vera," she giggled.

Oh.

Oh.

Why hadn't I seen it before? The same white hair, the same blue eyes and blue wings.

"You're brother and sister."

"Twins," Mia smiled.

"I'm older."

Mia rolled her eyes. "By four minutes."

"Still older," he insisted.

I couldn't help but smile watching the two of them, yet something strange and painful still tugged at my heart at the idea that they were siblings. They were *family*. Families were normally split up when fae were caught, so it was very rare that sibling sets were housed in the dorms on Alliance. It was strange and fascinating to see these two together, twins no less, and even stranger that they were slaves at the same place. There had to be a story here.

With promises to talk more later, I hurried back to the main room, knowing they were probably wondering where I'd gone.

"I didn't know the hag hired somebody new," a voice said as soon as I turned the corner, and when I looked to my left, I saw a human standing next to me, a dancer with long dark hair I'd seen on the stage earlier. "You are auditioning?" she asked.

I glanced nervously over to where I saw Elise talking with someone and then back to her. "Oh. No, sorry."

Her eyes gave me a quick once-over. "You could make good money here."

Another human girl appeared on the other side of me, and before I knew what was happening, one arm was draped over my shoulder and another one around my waist, and we were walking toward the stage. Fast.

"Whoa, whoa," I tried to pull back. "I'm waiting—"

"Let's see how you do. It's only fair that the new girl takes a turn so we can get a break."

"She's a new hire?" the second human asked. "Then why haven't I seen her stage work yet? Get up there and let's see what you can do."

"I'm sorry, you have the wrong idea. I'm not a dancer!" I yelled as they tried to shuffle me up the stairs near the stage.

"Boss lady," she called out to Elise. "Does she work here?" She pointed at me.

The blond demon saw us, and her red lips turned up in a smile. "You bet she does."

This bitch.

"I'll take it from here, girls."

"Oh hey, Laurie!" Both immediately ignored me in favor of fawning all over the white-haired fae. I was ready to use his appearance as the perfect distraction to get away when he held out his arm.

"Good thing I stuck around, huh?" he asked.

"You do seem to have a way of showing up at interesting moments."

We had barely taken two steps away when the sound of heels clicked behind us. "Stop!" I heard a voice shout, and I already knew who was behind us. The tall blond demon scowled as she stomped in our direction.

"You." Elise snapped her fingers at Laurie. "Sparkly blue one."

Beside me, Laurie's wings twitched, and I could sense his irritation. The two of us looked at her expectantly, and I dreaded why she wanted to talk to him.

"New girl needs a costume. She can't work here wearing... that." She sniffed, gesturing to my clothes.

I stared down at my black pants and tank top. They weren't the sexy clothes Rand had bought, but I still thought I looked okay. "What's wrong with my clothes?"

"You're questioning me?" Elise asked, her black wings slowly spreading out behind her. "Frankly I'm surprised Rand let one of the prince's slaves out of the house in those rags."

"I'm not a slave." Then I thought of the tight, skimpy black outfits

Rand had stashed in my bag. "And Rand doesn't pick out my clothes."

Elise raised one eyebrow.

"Okay, so he doesn't pick out *all* my clothes," I admitted. "Anymore."

"That's obvious." She rolled her eyes and pointed to Laurie. "Blue one, find something that at least vaguely fits her. What about that one fae who died? She was probably a similar size; she could wear her dresses."

"The one..." Laurie stuttered over the words, his jaw clenched in frustration. "You mean Alexandra?"

"Did she have red wings?"

"Yellow." The word sounded like a growl in his throat.

"Whatever." With a wave of her hand, Elise brushed past us, her heels clicking on the floor. "Her stuff will probably fit," she called over her shoulder. "Hurry up with it. I need her out on the floor tonight."

The two of us watched her leave, and next to me I could feel Laurie's obvious anger rolling off him in waves.

"Fuck her. Seriously, fuck her," Laurie muttered, walking off ahead of me.

Catching up, I let him fume for a few feet before I said, "This yellow... Alexandra? What happened to her?"

Laurie kept his head down, his eyes never leaving the floor. "She didn't even remember her name. That bitch didn't even remember her name."

"She was your friend?"

"Yes. I hadn't known her very long since it happened right when I got here. I heard she'd been assigned to entertain the same demon every night. A young royal, supposedly. This isn't an easy place to work, Vera. Some of the demons have... twisted... desires. For the right price, they get what they want."

"Elise allowed someone to kill one of her slaves?"

"No. She hardly pays attention to any of us until we're needed." Laurie took a deep breath as he stared straight ahead. "Vera. She killed herself."

14

VERA

"One day...," Laurie muttered as I followed him. Watching him, his tense stance, his clenched jaw, I recognized what he was feeling, that feeling of wanting desperately to change things combined with the frustration of not knowing how. "One day they will pay. Elise might not have hurt Alexandra herself, but she is just as guilty for ignoring what her clients are doing and letting them treat the girls like dirt."

"I'm so sorry about your friend," was all I could say.

"Those assholes." Laurie stopped walking and pointed back down the hall. "Our lives are meaningless to every single one of those demons."

"Not all of them..."

"Don't be naïve," Laurie snapped. "Of course it's all of them."

I blinked, surprised by his sharp tone.

"I'm sorry," he said. Falling back against the wall, Laurie sighed and ran his hand through his white hair. "Fuck. I'm sorry. It's just that you... Why is the demon prince's girlfriend even here?"

"Trust me, I wish I wasn't. Believe it or not, it seems this place is safer than where I was before."

"So you're here because you want to be?"

"Something like that."

Suddenly Laurie burst into laughter, his head dropping to his chest, his shoulders shaking.

"What? Why are you laughing at me?"

"Because"—he shook his head, still chuckling—"I'm trying to decide if you are brave or just crazy."

"Maybe a little of both?"

"They say the same of me. Come on, I'll show you the club's dressing room, and you can choose which uniform you want to wear."

I followed Laurie to the back where he opened a door and led me down another hallway that ended in a large dressing room. Tall lockers lined one wall, and he opened one of them and rummaged through the hanging clothes, pulling out a shimmery silver minidress, the front open in a deep *V* cut that would have revealed almost everything down to my navel.

"Uh." I raised my eyebrows in alarm when he held it up. "What else is there?"

He squinted at me. "You don't like it."

"Surely there's something with more, oh, I don't know, fabric?" I touched the dress, imagining myself wearing something revealing like this. If it was what I had to do, then I'd do it, but I had a feeling Leo would lose his mind if I wore this around other demons. "It feels surprisingly soft, but I don't know about showing that much skin."

"You want to blend in, right?"

"Yeah..."

"Then this is part of blending in. White, black, or red, those are your options. There is another one a lot of girls wear," he said, hanging that dress back in the locker and searching for a second one. "Here it is."

He held out a one-piece outfit. It had long black mesh sleeves, and the bodysuit was mostly mesh as well, with thin strips of black at the chest and waist and tiny black shorts. Even though more than half of it was mesh, this one covered more of me than the minidress, at least.

"That seems okay."

"I'm glad you like it. I've got boots for it too. Fair warning, that mesh is always a huge pain in the ass."

"What do you mean?"

"It rips every time a girl decides she's an acrobat instead of a dancer. I keep telling Elise I need better materials, but she's too cheap to let me do anything other than fix it and move on."

"Elise has you fixing the girls' dresses?"

"Fixing them?" He wrinkled his face like I'd just insulted him. "I made them. I don't want anyone else messing with my work, and I certainly don't want some amateur's hands touching them now that the girls finally have some decent clothes."

"I'm impressed. I've never known anyone who could do something like this. How did you learn to sew?" The idea of the humans giving us needles back on Alliance Island was unimaginable. We'd been taught just enough to not appear completely ignorant for our new masters, but never anything like sewing.

"I wasn't always a slave," he said.

Right. I'd noticed his wings were larger than most fae I'd known, their blue a more vibrant cerulean than the wings of fae who had grown up as slaves. Was this an opening to ask about his past?

"How long have you been a slave?"

"Long enough. So which one do you want to wear?" he asked, obviously wanting to change the subject.

"I don't know. You're very talented," I told him. "I'm sure any of them would be fine."

"Those are nothing," he scoffed at the line of outfits. "Come with me."

Laurie nodded toward a door beside the lockers. Inside was a small workroom, about half the size of the dressing room. Several dresses hung on a metal bar on one side of the room. On the other was a small table and stool, with scraps of fabric hanging over both and more piled on the floor beside them. A sewing machine and pencils and scissors crowded the table.

I thumbed through the hanging dresses, admiring the fabrics and colors. "These are beautiful. Do you make Elise's gowns?"

"Unfortunately." Then Laurie grinned, blue eyes sparkling. "Lately I've been making her dresses just a little too small so I can ask her if she's gained weight recently. You should see the look on her face."

"I would say that's mean, but in her case, I approve. These really are amazing, Laurie."

The mischief in his eyes was gone, and he didn't look as sure, frowning at the rows of fabric. "You think so? You should see some of the dresses my aunt can make back home."

"And where is home?"

"Rowan, of course. The fae city. Back there my aunt's a legend. I'm nowhere near as talented as her. If a fae is getting married, she's the one they want making their bridal gowns."

"That's who taught you to sew?"

"Yes."

"Does Mia sew too, then?"

Laurie snorted as he flipped through the hanging dresses. "Yeah, right. She is the last person you want anywhere near this stuff. She'd rather be in the gym than in a dressing room."

"For twins, you're both so different."

"I guess. We both care about our art in different ways. The physical body is an art form as well."

I stopped sorting through the clothes when I realized he was staring at me. "Here. Try these on," he said before I could say anything else, gathering a few of the dresses in his hands and shoving them into my arms. "These should fit. Go try them on, and I'll wait here."

All of them fit, more or less, and I hoped I wouldn't be here long enough to need more than a couple of uniforms anyway. They all looked short and tight, showing a ridiculous amount of skin. When I returned them all to Laurie, he took one more off the shelf.

"Try this one too," he said, piling on a dress that was obviously not made for this club. It was long and heavy, made of much finer fabrics than the others. Laurie didn't look me in the eye as he handed it to me. "I was making it for Mia as a surprise with extra fabric I had, but I haven't decided on a final color yet. You're close in size, so you can help me see how it fits."

The fabric was a basic linen, obviously just an underlayer that would later have something else on top, but even so, the shape of the dress was there, and I knew I would like it before I even stepped into it. The A-line skirt flowed out from the waist, down and then some, gently pooling on the floor, and the linen of the skirt was covered with a layer of soft, white tulle. The dress had felt heavy when I carried it, but once I had it on, it looked light and airy; the white tulle gave it an ethereal quality that shimmered in the light.

The top was cut straight across the chest, with small straps over my shoulders, and that same soft tulle was draped down from the shoulder straps, flowing over the long sleeves to make them look like they were surrounded in a delicate mist. The back was open, dipping all the way down to almost my waist to allow for wings, so I was able to zip it up myself. Mia was a similar size to me, so it fit almost perfectly. Staring at myself in the dressing room mirror, even in this half-finished dress, it was easy to see that the finished product had the potential to be magnificent.

Even though it fit so well, I thought about taking the dress off and not showing it to him at all. It was simple but elegant, and I wasn't sure I should be the one wearing it. Laurie said it was a dress made for Mia, but this was truly a dress for a princess, and what was I? Not too long ago, I was a barefoot fae living in the dorms on Alliance Island. Now I was a supposedly free slave hiding in a dark nightclub for an unspecified amount of time.

I was definitely not the girl in this dress.

The girl in this dress was elegant. She was graceful. She was beauty and poise, and she was nothing like me. But what would it feel like if I *was* her? Twirling in the mirror, I imagined myself as a lady of the Vestian court, waltzing into a large ballroom on Leo's arm, all eyes on the two of us with envy. Especially the eyes of one blond demon. Leo would walk beside me slowly, careful not to step on the dress, and when we took our places at the pair of thrones, the entire demon kingdom would bow, their wings and tails unfurled in deference. In a dress like this, at his side, I'd belong there just as much as Leo did.

Laurie didn't hear me when I opened the door. He was seated at the sewing machine, busy with rulers and scissors and some other, unfamiliar tools. For a moment I watched him, impressed by the quickness and skill of his hands as he worked. This view felt familiar; I'd watched Leo work in his lab multiple times, and there was something so intriguing about watching someone pursue their passion.

Finally I cleared my throat to let him know I was there.

"One second," he muttered behind the pencil in his mouth. Laurie shuffled some of the fabrics on the desk and then spun around in his chair to see me.

The pencil fell out of his mouth onto the floor.

With Laurie looking like he was either shocked or horrified or both, I suddenly felt even more self-conscious about wearing this dress than I had before. I played with the sleeves simply to have something to do other than look at him.

"It's not me, right?" I slowly turned around in place, letting him see how the whole costume fit, but Laurie still only stared, mouth open. "It's a beautiful dress though! Mia will love it once it's finished!"

Laurie picked the pencil up from the floor, his eyes never leaving me as they raked up from the hem of the dress to the top, taking it all in. He swallowed and opened his mouth to speak, but then closed it again. He repeated that motion, obviously trying to figure out what to say, until he finally said, "Um..."

"Should I go change back?" I asked, squirming under his intense gaze.

"No!"

"Then can you please say something? Anything," I begged. "Please put me out of my awkward misery."

"It's just... I don't mean to stare but...," he muttered.

"I'll go change."

"No!" Suddenly Laurie was alive again, jumping to his feet and running over to me. Stopping right in front of me, he reached out and touched the strap on my arm before his hand drifted to the thin, filmy material that draped down from my shoulder.

"Don't change. I know we only recently met, but the way it looks on you... It's like this dress was made for you."

Brow furrowed, I glanced from his hand on the sleeve back up to his blue eyes, but he was still staring at the gown. Finally, his blue eyes met mine.

"You're perfect," he breathed more than said.

"What?"

Laurie's fingers let go of the sleeve like the fabric had bitten him, and he shook his head as if he was surprised he'd said that out loud. "I mean, it's perfect. The dress. The fit is perfect. That's what I meant. It fits you perfectly."

Even more uneasy than I'd felt before, I took a step back, putting a few feet between us, and he was immediately back at his stool, his back to me as he shuffled things around on the desk.

"Sorry," he muttered, head down as he rummaged through various fabric scraps in front of him. "I just realized that the sleeves might need to be longer. I'll fix them."

"Okay. I'm going to change."

"Good idea." He nodded, not turning around.

When the dressing room door closed behind me, I leaned my back against the door, closed my eyes, and let out the breath I'd been holding. I'd seen myself as a princess in the dress, but it appeared that Laurie saw me as something else entirely.

It was possible that I was overthinking things, that I'd misjudged his reaction, that he'd just been thinking about how well the dress fit and not thinking about wanting to take it off me as the look in his eyes suggested. All that aside, the truth was that I never wanted to take this dress off. Even as it was, unfinished, with details missing and hems that needed sewing, it really did fit perfectly.

But it wasn't meant for me. Reluctantly, I unzipped the dress and stepped out of it, careful not to hurt the fabric in any way before I put my own clothes back on. I put the dress on its hanger. Tonight I would be working my first shift in a bar, bringing drinks to horny demons who came to watch girls dance on stage.

I wasn't the girl in the dress right now, but one day. . . could that be me?

15

LEO

"You have to fix me. I don't know what he did, but that bastard injected me with something. I need an antidote or a cure or *something*. Talk to me, Marcus. Tell me how to fix this."

If I trusted anyone to come up with a solution here, it was him. Marcus was the one and only human I felt I could trust or had ever trusted. As much as I would have loved taking all the credit, Marcus had been an essential part of our initial trials for Syn. He had been by my side for years, literally at the lab table next to me, and I was regretting leaving him at my house to watch over the place now that this had happened.

"Slow down," the scientist said on the other line. "What I'm hearing is that your father injected you with something, a drug? Why? What was in it?"

Marcus didn't know that my mother was fae, and this wasn't the time to share that piece of my past, not when we were on the phone. I wouldn't put it past my father to have somehow bugged my phone or Rand's apartment or both. I couldn't take any chances.

"All I know is that ever since the injection I feel like a different demon completely. I'm more aggressive, my sense of time is off, I have blanks in my memory, I... I don't know what I'm capable of doing."

"It could have been a toxin that targeted your hormones and interacted with some of the receptors, or maybe its target is at the cellular level or possibly—"

"Marcus. Stop muttering and tell me what you think."

"Did he say how long the side effects would last? I still don't understand why your father would do this without reason. I can't imagine that he wants to permanently hurt you, not if he's going to try to convince you to stay in Vestia."

"I don't want to get into it."

"Will he tell you what's in it at least? Other than asking him, the only other way to know what's going on with you is to run a blood test. Do you have access to the palace lab? Or is there someone in the lab you trust who could do it for you?"

"No."

"Then I'm afraid you're going to have to do it yourself. You could mail me a sample, but that might take too long. You'll need to run a full panel and see if there's anything suspicious. At the bare minimum, it will give you a place to start."

"I should have thought of that already. It's this drug." I paced back and forth, my heart thumping harder and harder with each step. "I can't think straight. I'm on edge. It's like I have a hole in my chest, Marcus, and the only thing I can fill the hole with is anger."

"Take a deep breath and try to be calm, Leo."

"I am calm!" I roared. The other end of the phone was silent, and I took a deep breath to steady myself. "I'm sorry, Marcus. I'm not angry with you."

"You don't have to apologize. Frankly, I'm not used to you apologizing at all. Text me your results when you get them, and I'll compare with the data I already have on you, okay? I'm sure it's nothing we can't fix. Everything is fine at home, by the way. Lydia has been working on some defensive training, and Rob hasn't left for the fae colony yet. For so long it was just you, me, and Rand, but now with only half our group here, the house is oddly quiet. I'm not sure I like it."

I was glad he was taking care of the house because at the moment it was the furthest thing from my mind.

"Lydia does this cute thing when she concentrates," he continued, and I heard him chuckling on the other end, "where she squishes her nose up like a rabbit, sort of like the Sylvilagus genus but closer to how the Nesolagus rabbit—"

"Marcus."

"Right. Sorry. I'm just saying that everything is fine here, so you can focus on figuring out what's going on with you. What does Vera think?"

A long silence answered that question.

"You haven't told her."

"I only barely trust myself around her or anyone right now."

As much as I loathed the idea, I knew I needed to go back to the palace. The king had most likely made the drug in the palace lab, so that was where I needed to start. If I could bribe or interrogate some of the lab workers, I might be able to get even more information about how it was made and how to counteract it, and I could use the equipment to run a blood sample while I was there.

"Jasmine!" I called out, and in an instant the pink-haired demon was in front of me. "If you wanted to talk to someone about drugs, who is currently the best person at the palace to talk to?"

Eyebrows raised, Jasmine stared at me with big silver eyes full of surprise. "Drugs, Your Highness?"

"Yes. Drugs."

"Is everything okay, Your Highness?"

If she kept looking at me with that worried expression, everything was most definitely not going to be okay because I was going to lose my shit.

"I just need a name. I've been away too long to know the right people."

"Oh. Then in that case, I believe Lord Zell would be the resident expert. Mostly the expert on the type used at all the parties he throws, but I'm sure he'd be happy to see his cousin and help you with whatever you need."

"Zell, huh?" His name alone made me clench my teeth. I thought about the magazine cover I'd seen in Elise's office. Judging by the fact that he'd given a magazine a tell-all interview, I was fairly sure that he wouldn't be discrete if I approached him. I'd have to be careful.

It was time to pay my cousin a visit.

16

VERA

Laurie had been right about the mesh on the costume being a pain in the ass. Not that any of the demons who frequented Elise's club cared; from the looks the men gave me as I carried drinks through the busy club while wearing the black mesh bodysuit with only tiny straps of leather covering the important parts, it seemed like most of the customers would have been just fine with me not wearing anything at all.

After adjusting my sleeves for at least the hundredth time that night, I leaned back onto the bar, watching the girls on stage as they danced, a crowd of demons practically drooling at their feet. As much as the demons of Vestia seemed to pride themselves on being scientific innovators, beacons of progress, clinical experts, and blah blah blah, business was booming at this club that catered to a demon's baser pleasures of fighting, drinking, and sex.

"Vera." Liz, the bartender working that night, a human with dark curly hair, smacked the bar to get my attention. "You're working, not watching."

"I know, I know. What's up?"

"If there was anyone else available, I'd ask them, but I need someone to take this to room 2 right now." She handed me a tray with a bottle of champagne and a few glasses. "And be nice about it."

"I'm always nice."

The look she gave me said she wasn't quite as sure. "Then be extra nice. He's a VIP. Nobility."

"A noble who's a VIP at a brothel. Sounds like a loser," I said, holding the tray with one hand like they'd taught me to do.

"Let me remind you that we work at a *club*, and this particular demon spends a lot of money at this club. He's here almost every weekend."

"As I was saying, sounds like a loser."

"I'll let you be the judge of that. Now go before he gets mad. He's chatty when he's drunk, but he has a violent temper. Bow a bunch, and you should be fine."

Carrying my tray and wondering how it was possible to bow while holding glasses and a bottle of champagne, I quickly found room 2. There was a long hallway with the private rooms on either side, and it was not unusual for all of them to be occupied at night.

In the dark space, a demon sat by himself on the long, plush couch that lined the back wall of the room. In the dim light, he seemed to blend in with the darkness, wearing a black button-down shirt, black pants, and boots. A noble, she'd said. I wondered how well he knew Leo.

When I got closer, I could see his dark red hair, slightly wavy on top but shaved on both sides. And his piercings, several in his ears, and a tongue piercing I only saw because he kept rolling the silver bar around on his lips. His wings folded behind him so he could sit comfortably against the couch, one long arm was stretched out over the back cushions, and his fingers, several of which were decorated with rings, tapped along to the music.

"Hello." I smiled at him, trying to ignore the way his eyes followed my every move. "I'm dropping these off for you. Is there anything else you need?"

The demon didn't say anything, and he didn't smile back. Instead, he watched me as I took the drinks off the tray and lined them up on the small low table in front of him.

Well, fine. My job would go a lot faster if he didn't talk anyway.

"You're new," he finally said, and his voice sounded like it had been raked over gravel.

"Is it that obvious? You're right. I am." I was almost finished setting out the drinks, but when I leaned over to place the last glass on the table, he reached for it at the same time, knocking my hand and sending the glass onto the floor right in front of him, where it shattered.

"Oops," the demon said, not sounding at all sorry.

"It's fine," I muttered, squatting down to pick up the pieces of broken glass. I'd have to get a towel later to clean up the wet carpet. Unfortunately, all the glass shards were right beside his boots, and I had to maneuver around the table in front of him to get to them. "Excuse me," I said, kneeling down to pick them up. Unsurprisingly, the redheaded demon didn't move an inch or even make the smallest effort to help.

Not that I expected him to. It seemed my initial assessment of him being a loser had been right.

I'd just picked up the last piece of glass, proud of myself for not getting cut, since this demon around my blood was the very last thing I wanted and placed a hand on the table to stand up when one of his long legs shot out in front of me, stopping me.

"Looks like some of that drink got on my boot," he said.

"Sorry about that. I'll get you a towel and a new drink after I clean this up."

"Lick it off."

"Excuse me?" Backing up to avoid his leg, I stood up from the floor, not wanting to spend another second with this demon.

"You heard me."

"I was hoping I hadn't. Now if you don't mind—" I turned around and walked the other way. Noble or not, this demon was a jerk.

"I do mind, actually. Normally I get better service here. You haven't even complimented me a single time."

And I wasn't about to start now. Before I could get even a few steps away, he was up and grabbed my wrist to stop me. I spun around but saw his eyes widen as he shoved up my sleeve, revealing my suppression bracelet.

"Why are you wearing this?"

"It's just a piece of jewelry. Nice, isn't it?" I pretended to chuckle and tried to pull away with no success.

"Elise hasn't let fae work these rooms in weeks, or I would have had them by now. Yet here you are."

"And here is where I don't want to be." With a strong tug, I tried again to yank my arm back, but he kept it in his grip.

"If you're fae, where are your wings?"

"Let. Go."

"Did someone cut your wings off? That's extra kinky, even for me."

"No," I growled, giving my arm one final yank back.

He let go, sending me stumbling back a few steps while he threw his head back laughing. "Fascinating. I want to know more."

I didn't want to know a single thing more about this demon or be around him a second longer than necessary. I turned around and headed for the door, but he was up in an instant, his wings carrying him across the room until he landed right behind me, one hand on either of my arms to stop me in place.

He leaned down and whispered in my ear. "I didn't say you could leave yet."

"I don't need your permission."

He clicked his tongue, his tongue piercing clinking against his teeth. "A slave has to do what I say, don't you?"

My whole body shivered as he ran his hands down my arms until one hand connected with the bracelet.

"What if we take this little device off, hm? What then?"

"Don't touch me."

"Says the fae working in a brothel."

"It's a *club*. Just because a girl works here doesn't mean you get to touch her whenever you want."

"I disagree." His fingers curled around the bracelet, and he pressed, hard, the metal cracking in his hand and falling to the floor. Despite myself, I closed my eyes, all my strength returning to me and filling me with that welcome warm feeling that only my magic gave me. With this added burst of strength, I darted away from him, but again he grabbed on to my arms.

"I'll go get one of the other girls. I'm sure I can find one more to your taste."

"Funny you should say taste. I have fae slaves of my own, but I've never tasted one without wings. Do you think you taste different?"

"Don't know and don't care."

Could I hit him and get away with it? How would Leo react if he found out I hit a demon noble? If he was here right now, he would do a lot more than hit this asshole, but I also didn't want Leo to worry about me. I needed to handle this myself without making a scene.

"What do you want?" I asked over my shoulder.

"I want you to dance for me," he said, using his hands to make my hips sway slightly. So close behind me, I could feel the heat radiating from him, warming my back.

"I promise you don't want that. I'm a terrible dancer."

He laughed and gripped my hips so hard that I had to stifle a yelp. Leaning forward, he whispered in my ear. "I'm not interested in how well you know ballet, princess."

Fuck. If I didn't do something fast, this was going to get even more out of hand.

"Mm," he murmured. "You smell so good."

It was so hot in the room, and everything about this was making me nervous and sweaty. *Oh shit.* If he got some of my sweat on him, he'd probably—

He licked a long stripe up my neck.

"Holy shit," he muttered, his hushed words sounding like a prayer.

That was enough. Swinging one elbow back, I hit him as hard as I could in the face. He flinched, and I saw him grabbing his nose in pain, but I also saw a faint yellow glow starting to surround him.

"Get back here, slave," he shouted at me from behind the hand holding his nose at the same moment I grabbed the doorknob. I didn't have time to turn it before his arms were around my waist, lifting me in the air, and we were flying backward, landing on the couch.

"Now I've got you. You just punched a noble, you little shit. Do you know what happens to slaves who attack demons?"

I tried flinging an arm back and kicking, not that it made any difference. "Do you know that you're a total dick?"

"My dick's right here if you want to find out. On second thought, it doesn't matter if you want to find out or not, does it, slave? I am definitely not letting you go now, not when I know you can make me feel like this."

I felt his lips touch my neck, but mercifully, thankfully, as if all the gods were on my side at that moment, the door swung open and two dancers sauntered in.

"Finally!" I shouted, and he was just distracted enough to let me jump up.

The two female demons ignored me as they squealed and flew over to him on the couch, their tails happily curling around him as they started showering him with praise.

I didn't look back. I went straight to the bar and told them I was done for the night and going back to my room.

"Next time warn me, Liz," I said to the bartender. "That guy was a creep. Someone needs to tell Elise to kick him out."

She simply shrugged and continued washing the glasses behind the bar. "Good luck with that, but it will be your own funeral. When you're the nephew to the king, you get to do what you want."

"When you're the *what*?"

"The king's nephew. I'm surprised you didn't recognize Lord Zell. He has been on a thousand magazine covers lately. Every week there's some new article or scandal or something that has to do with him. I don't know why Elise tolerates him, but she won't stand for anyone saying anything bad about him."

Lord Zell. His name was Zell, and he was the king's nephew. He was Leo's cousin, and he was also a total asshole.

And I'd just hit him in the face.

17

LEO

"If you're not going to let me into the lab, then tell Zell to get his ass here right now."

"We're so sorry, Your Highness, but Lord Zell does not allow anyone to have access to his laboratory. I'm sure he'll be back late tonight. If you wouldn't mind, it would be best to come back tomorrow."

"I do mind. I am the prince." For once, I didn't mind using that title. "You can either let me in, or I can force my way in. You get to pick, but I know one way will end in a lot less bloodshed."

The two demons guarding the lab shared an anxious glance before stepping aside, just as I'd known they would. With every hour that passed, I felt the hole inside me growing larger. Was this the fae side of me disappearing, piece by piece? Or was this the demon side of me, growing stronger as the minutes passed?

After finding supplies, I took a few samples of my blood, wrapping one tube and placing it in an envelope that I addressed to Marcus. I gave it to one of the guards to mail, and the others I carried over to the centrifuge and started a few different tests so that I could get a complete picture of what was going on. While I waited on the results, I used those hours to examine the lab's equipment, all of it much newer and more advanced than what I had at home. With a lab this large, with this level of technology, there was no limit to what I could create.

No doubt, I could... I tried thinking of new ideas, imagining new machines I could build, but... Nothing. There was nothing. My mind was completely blank. Was I too stressed to be creative, or was this something else?

I had to find out more about that injection. No matter where I looked, I didn't see any clues that might relate to the serum in the king's syringe. There were various projects set up around the lab, all of them looking fairly normal, and nothing to suggest any were creating a serum to destroy fae magic.

Metal boxes were stacked on the side of the room up against the wall, and when I opened the first case on top, inside were several suppression bracelets, a collar, and two other devices I didn't recognize that looked like small clips. While the devices all looked familiar, there was something different in the metals, and the bracelets had more buttons than I had seen on one before. Was this something new? I slipped one of the bracelets into my pocket so I could take it apart later.

The machine beeped, letting me know the test was completed, so I printed the results and cleared the files off the computer. Running my eyes over the numbers, everything seemed to fall within normal limits except for a few values that I knew from our trials with Syn were related to fae blood. I'd seen these levels in reverse when I'd run tests on fae blood in the past. The levels on Vera's blood in particular had been hundreds of times higher, but here my results were showing that my numbers were next to nothing. Did that mean that the serum really had taken away all the parts of me that were fae?

If that was actually possible, if the king could use this serum on full-blooded fae and take away their magic...

I heard the lab door open, and I quickly folded the paper, slipping it into my pocket.

"They told me there had been a break-in." Zell strode into the room. "Imagine my surprise to hear it was the prince himself."

The redheaded demon had more piercings and tattoos than the last time I'd seen him, but otherwise, that smug grin was exactly as I remembered. His clothes were wrinkled, his shirt unbuttoned at the top, and as he came closer, I realized that he reeked of alcohol.

"You look like hell."

Zell's grin didn't fade. "I could say the same for you. I've had a long night. A fun night, but a long one. Can you say the same? I would guess not if you're here crashing in my lab."

"Your lab? This is the king's lab."

"Right. And you're not the king. Yet, at least. So it isn't yours either." Zell's eyes flicked to where the centrifuge had been spinning. "What have you been in here doing?"

"As you said, it's not my lab yet. I wanted to see what kind of improvements I'm going to have to make once I'm in charge."

Zell barked a laugh. "None then. Everything here is the best, or I wouldn't have it. It's been a while, cousin. I heard about this drug you created. Are you trying to put me out of a job?"

"You actually have a job?"

"Sort of." He shrugged, rolling that stupid tongue piercing around as he smirked at me. "The king asked me to work on projects other than Dust. Instead, we've been tweaking suppression devices lately to see what new tricks we could do with them."

I thought of the one in my pocket, and the cases of them lined against the wall. "And?"

"Like I'd tell you. How's your fiancée?"

Why was he asking about Elise? Did he know that Vera was staying at her club? If I denied that Elise was my fiancée, then I'd also have to say that I wasn't going to be the next king. If I said that, I'd be putting Vera's life in danger.

"Do you care?" I asked instead.

"Of course I do. We all used to be friends, remember? I see Elise sometimes at her club now that she's running it. I always knew she would be a boss. A girl like that is wasted on someone like you, Leo."

I froze at the mention of the club, steeling my face and hoping he couldn't see a reaction.

"I was there tonight actually," he continued, hopping up on one of the lab tables. He scratched at the tattoos on his neck as he pretended to think. "You should have seen the two girls I had all over me tonight."

Was he baiting me? Was he simply bragging about his night out, or was this code that he knew where Vera was? I didn't know but didn't want to stay to find out.

"I've seen enough here," I said, walking toward the door.

"You're not staying at the palace?" He jumped down from the table and flew in front of me, blocking my path.

"No." I tried to take a step around him, but he moved with me, keeping me there.

"Then you must be shacking up with your fiancée while you're in town?"

"No, I'm not."

"Is she staying with you?"

"No. Now move! I'm leaving."

Seemingly satisfied with my answer, he nodded, stepping out of the way, and dramatically gesturing toward the door. Storming past him, I swung open the door to the lab, but was met with a crowd of guards, many of whom I recognized as belonging to the king.

Zell came up from behind me and clapped a hand on my shoulder. "No, you're not. I have orders to keep you here until further notice."

"Orders?" I brushed his hand off. "From who?"

Zell chuckled and held up my phone. He must have taken it out of my jacket pocket without me realizing it.

"Do you really think I wouldn't tell the king you were here before coming to talk to you? Sorry, Cousin. I know who I'm loyal to, and right now it isn't you."

I took a step toward the guards, but they only moved closer, blocking my path.

Zell moved past me, and they let him by. "They're going to escort you to your rooms," he said, waving to me as he walked away. "Looks like you'll be staying at the palace after all."

I had no phone. No way to contact anyone. I couldn't call Rand to tell him what had happened or call Elise to warn her about Zell. They also took my watch before taking me to one of the guest rooms, and the guards made sure I knew I would not be allowed to leave. All I could do was wait as the hours ticked by, waiting for the inevitable moment when the king would come.

The morning came and went. Then the afternoon. I knew it was all part of his psychological game, but as the minutes passed, I felt more and more like a cat trapped in that room. All I could do was pace back and forth until the king finally decided to grace me with his presence.

Judging by the sun setting outside my window, it was almost evening by the time he made an appearance. I was sitting by the window, debating the strength of the security system, when he finally showed up. The king walked in unhurried; in fact, he seemed relaxed, sitting down comfortably in the chair opposite me, his long black cloak draping onto the floor. He was alone, which most likely meant his guards were outside the room.

I didn't wait to hear what he had to say.

"What did you do to me?" I demanded. "I knew you hated me, but I had no idea how much."

The king pursed his lips and drummed his fingers on the armrest of the chair.

"Do you have an answer for me yet?" he asked. "Are you ready to become king, or is it time to kill the fae girl?"

"Fuck you."

"That's no way to talk to your father."

"You lost that title a long time ago. Fathers are supposed to protect their families, not threaten them. When can I leave?"

There was no way I was going to sit there and listen to him for one second longer than I had to. I stood up, but then he was up as well, standing almost as tall as I was. Staring me down, he reached out a hand, pushing against my chest with his index finger.

"Sit down," he said.

My eyes fell to his finger, and there I saw he was wearing a gold band with a tiny red gem in the middle. A Hellfire ruby, as they were called, the same type of stone on Elise's engagement ring, only this one was much, much smaller. The rubies were made by a secret technique known only to demons, a complex and disgusting procedure that used the actual hearts of fae to condense power into a gemstone. I knew this ring.

I smacked his hand away. "I can't believe you'd wear that."

His features shifted momentarily as he realized what I was talking about, as if he had forgotten he'd been wearing the ring at all. He took it off and held it out for me. When I didn't take it, he placed it on the small table between us. "It's yours, you know. It was always going to be yours. She would have wanted you to have it."

"I don't understand how you can wear it like some trophy for what you did."

Gone was the mask of calm from earlier. Now I saw the demon I remembered him to be, glaring at me with a silent anger. "Don't talk about things you don't understand."

"What I understand is that you killed my mother and wear her heart as jewelry."

His hand came up to hit me, but I grabbed his wrist, stopping him. With a grunt he yanked his hand back and took a step away.

"There's the spirit I knew you had," he said. "She had a spirit like that too. In fact, when you speak, I can almost hear her voice."

My hands were shaking at my side as I tried to take a breath. But I couldn't. As my tail slapped against the floor in a rhythmic beat, I felt like I could drown from the pain that filled my lungs. There was no air in the room to breathe; there was only frustration and anguish.

"I thought you might need some more encouragement. I was apparently correct. I want you to see something," he said.

The king pushed a button on his watch, and a holo-screen appeared, showing a black-and-white video feed of a dark room. It was obviously a camera stationed in the corner of the room. There was no sound, but the place looked busy as demons moved about the space and some humans, too.

"What is this?"

"Look closer."

I took a cautious step toward him, leaning in slightly to figure out what he wanted me to see. It looked like a restaurant. No, a bar. Now that I looked closely, I noticed that was a long bar visible on the side of the screen, with several demons seated on stools around it. It was familiar. It was—

My heart was pounding against my chest. Could he hear it?

"Why are you showing me this?" That was Elise's club. That was the bar area where Vera would be working.

"Because you thought you could hide your little toy from me. You were wrong."

He knew where she was. Had Elise told him? No, she wouldn't have. Zell said he was there last night, so it could have been him. Or maybe the king's reach really was this far stretching, and he had multiple places under constant surveillance.

"You can't outsmart me, Leo. You need to stop trying. I had Zell bring a shipment of new suppression devices to the Lady Elise's business." He tapped his watch, and a second screen appeared beside the first. With his other hand, he tapped a few buttons on the screen, making the camera zoom in.

My breath caught in my throat.

Vera was standing beside the bar.

"Let's see what happens when I do this." He tapped another button on the second screen, and speechless, I watched, terrified of what I was about to see.

The Vera on the screen grabbed the bar next to her.

"These bracelets have more than just suppression abilities," he explained. "I can remotely adjust the level of suppression, but I can go beyond that, suppressing not just fae magic, but regular biology as well."

"Turn the bracelet off," I whispered, not wanting to believe what I was seeing.

She looked like she was having trouble standing. The bartender seemed to notice that something was wrong. Then a fae, one I recognized as the blue one we'd met that night, came over to Vera as well.

"Wouldn't it be interesting," the king mused, "to distribute these new bracelets to all fae and see what happens?"

"Turn. It. Off."

Vera grabbed her wrist, holding on to the suppression bracelet.

"I could," the king considered.

Then she slumped over.

"Do it. Now!"

"You're going to stay here. We're going to announce you as king tomorrow night. If you try anything while you're here, I will use this again."

That fae caught her and helped her up.

"Fine! Turn it off!" I shouted.

"Are we in agreement?"

"As if you care! Turn it off!"

"Say it, Leo."

"Fine!" I shouted again. "I'll take your throne. I'll take this whole fucking kingdom. Now turn it off!"

He pressed a button on the second screen, and then both turned off, the holo-screens disappearing into his watch. Seething with rage, I clenched my fists at my side.

"The announcement will be made tomorrow night."

The bastard walked toward the door as if nothing had happened. As if he hadn't just threatened the life of the one person I cared about the most.

He wanted me to be king? Fine. If I were king, I could destroy all Dust production. I could destroy the entire lab. The entire palace.

I could destroy him.

18

VERA

"What's wrong?" Sera, one of the bartenders working the shift, stopped washing glasses to shoot me a look of concern.

"I don't know." I gripped the bar top to steady myself. "I don't feel well. I feel... weak?"

"Want me to help you to your room?"

I doubted I could get there on my own, since my legs suddenly felt like dead weight. The weakness was strongest on the arm with the suppression bracelet. Could it be malfunctioning? Pushing up my sleeve, I tried pressing the normal buttons to turn it off, but nothing worked. This was a new bracelet I'd been given tonight, an upgrade supposedly that was more comfortable than the ones before, but right now I just wanted it off.

I slumped over, but someone caught me before I fell onto the floor. Looking up, I saw white and blue and knew who it was.

"Laurie?"

"Get that thing off her," I heard Laurie say, but before Sera could get to me, I heard a crack and my bracelet was broken, the pieces clattering to the floor. Immediately I felt better as my magic returned.

"Are you okay?"

"I think so? What the hell was that?" I asked, trying to catch my breath.

"Good thing I was here. Those demons would still be standing around watching that device suck the life out of you if I hadn't been close by."

"It was the bracelet? That's why I felt like that?"

"Since you seem fine now, that's my best guess. It must be broken or something, because as soon as I got it off you, you started to look better. It's possible you were suddenly sick and the suppression tech was preventing your magic from helping you."

"I can do that? Heal myself?"

"You've got to stop hanging out with only demons. Let's get you to your room, and then we can talk." He held out his arms for me.

"Are you... Are you going to carry me?" I asked, unsure what he was trying to do.

"Do you want me to carry you?"

"No," I said. "I just..." It seemed like something Leo would do.

Leo. Leo who I hadn't heard from in over a day. Where was he? Why wasn't he answering any of my calls? Rand hadn't answered mine either, which made me think that he was avoiding me as well. Was something happening that they didn't want me to know about?

Laurie helped me to my room and stayed by the door as I sat down on the bed. Even though it had been brief, those seconds before Laurie broke the bracelet had been exhausting.

"I'm positive it was the bracelet," he said. "I'm not surprised it would do something like that. Suppression tech was first created by demons during the Blood War as a way to stop the power of the fae."

"I know this story. Without the creation of the suppression devices they bought from the demons, humans never would have won the war."

"You're correct. Imagine that, demons being traitorous bastards. Who would have thought? But those original devices had to be incredibly powerful, since all fae were wild at the time. This meant they were also expensive, and most slave owners today could never afford something so powerful. The bracelets and collars you see today are much cheaper and thankfully less effective versions."

"That's why Mia can still fly with hers on."

"Exactly. Her natural magic—and my own—is much stronger than these piece-of-shit bracelets that Elise probably bought on sale somewhere. We just pretend like they keep us from flying when she's around so she doesn't know any different."

Something about his words made me uncomfortable. When I first met Laurie, he'd been struggling to carry boxes up the stairs at Rand's apartment building. If he could override the power of the suppression bracelets, why had he had any trouble at all?

I filed that question away for another time.

"If you're able to break these bracelets so easily, why don't you break yours and Mia's and fly away? Or break everyone's and escape all together?"

"Don't think I haven't considered it, but we need a solid plan first. Without a plan, we'd just end up captured again—or worse, sold to someone else who isn't quite as hands-off as Elise. I want to make sure the timing is right, and all the pieces are in place before we get everyone out."

After Laurie left, I lay back on my bed, thinking about how I could help when we finally left Vestia. There had to be a way to bring them with us. Could we sneak them on the plane? Was there another option? If Rand or Leo would just return my calls, I would ask them.

The more time that passed without hearing from them, the more worried I felt. I couldn't shake the feeling something was wrong, that something had happened, and when another day was almost over and I still hadn't heard from Leo, I was more concerned than ever. I had just finished a shift in the club and was one second away from asking Elise what was going on when Laurie came over to talk to me.

"Aren't you done for the day? Why the sad face? You're not still feeling sick from yesterday, are you?"

"No. That's not it."

"Let me guess," he said, hopping up on the barstool next to me. "Something is wrong with your demon boyfriend."

"The last time I talked to Leo, he said he was going to the palace. I thought for sure I'd wake up to a call or text, but... Nothing. Nothing yesterday. Nothing today. I'm worried."

"Worried about the mighty prince of the demons?"

"He's not invincible. So yes, I am."

"You know," Laurie said, leaning back against the bar next to me, tapping his fingers on the wood, "if you really want to go to the palace, we can go to the palace."

"How?" I eyed him suspiciously.

He gestured to his large blue wings. "We fly. I'll make up some excuse for Elise, and then we'll go. I know all the back alleys we can take to avoid being seen. I do this all the time."

"Why?" I had to ask. Why would one of Elise's slaves sneak out to go to the palace at all?

"It's less boring than staying here," Laurie shrugged. "Once we get there, we're golden. Elise has brought me with her so many times that the servants already know me. I'll say you're Elise's assistant and we are on an errand from my owner."

I had an idea. "We could say you're bringing the prince new clothes!"

Laurie's bright blue eyes lit up at the idea. "I like the way you think. See what a good team we make?"

"I'll answer that after you sneak us in."

It was shockingly easy to get through the back gate of the palace. Since only nobility were allowed slaves in Vestia, it was assumed that Laurie belonged to someone important, and he was let in with hardly a second glance. I kept my head bowed and carried two back-packs full of random pieces of fabric to look like I was only there as help. We entered through the kitchen, and instantly we were swarmed by the palace servants. The kitchen seemed completely staffed by humans, and every single one of them was delighted to see Laurie again, the guys giving him the tall fae high-fives and the girls asking excitedly to see what dresses Laurie had brought with him this time.

"Everyone loves you," I said once we'd finally made it out.

He glanced over at me for only a second. "Not everyone. Let's find your prince."

Laurie knew where the prince's rooms were upstairs, so we went there next. We crept down the hall, listening for sounds of anyone. We made it only a few feet before we heard the sound of footsteps.

"Quick, in here," Laurie said under his breath, opening a door near us. We slipped inside what appeared to be a small linen closet, the room barely big enough for the two of us, made even smaller by Laurie's wings brushing against everything inside. Rows of shelves were on either side of us, each one lined with sheets and towels, the smell of fresh laundry in the air. As my eyes adjusted to the dark closet, I realized how close we were, the two of us facing each other as we listened to footsteps approach.

"Laurie...," I whispered.

"Shh," he murmured, placing a hand over my mouth.

Seriously? I immediately gripped his wrist and pulled his hand off, but he only smiled down at me.

Before I had the chance to complain, the footsteps got louder, coming closer to our closet, and we froze, staying still as statues. The footsteps came to an abrupt stop. I held my breath, not wanting to make even the smallest sound and attract the attention of whoever was out there.

Seconds passed like hours.

If we were caught, what would happen? Neither of us was supposed to be there, and there was no way to know what a demon would do to us before we could get in touch with Leo. Would our excuses still work? Or did hiding in this closet make us look even more suspicious?

The tiny space. The approaching footsteps. The anxiety of the moment was starting to make me sweat, and I could feel my hands start to tremble. But then I felt something at my side, only to realize it was Laurie's hand, nudging mine. He hooked his pinky finger around mine, and I didn't move, our fingers pressing into each other as we waited. The small comfort was enough to ground me in the moment.

Eventually, the footsteps continued past us, and both of us let out the breath we'd been holding in. I tried to listen for anyone who might still be out there, but it was all silence. I closed my eyes and took another deep breath.

"My heart was racing," I whispered, trying to calm myself.

"Mine still is," I heard Laurie whisper back. My eyes shot open when he took my whole hand in his, my mouth dropping open in surprise when he placed my hand on his chest. "Do you feel it?"

Laurie curled his fingers around my hand, holding it against him.

"Yeah," was all I could whisper as I tried to take my hand away. But he didn't let me, keeping it firm against his shirt. "We should go, Laurie. They're probably gone."

"Maybe," he said in a hushed tone, but the hand on mine didn't move, nor did he make any movement to leave where the two of us stood together.

This close to him, the tiny closet was starting to feel even tinier, the air getting warmer by the second. "We should go," I repeated.

"Not yet."

His hand let go of mine, and I immediately took a step back, but I was stopped by his hand on my lower back.

"Laurie..."

"It's just that there could be more demons out there. Waiting to catch us."

"I don't hear anyone."

His blue eyes didn't blink. "Doesn't mean they're not out there. We should stay here." He held my stare, as if he were daring me to look away as he spoke in a low whisper. "Until it's safe."

"I think it's safe now," I whispered back.

"No. Vera. I don't think it's safe at all."

"What...? What do you mean?"

"With you, here, this close. I don't trust myself around you."

Letting his words sink in, I felt more and more uncomfortable. "We need to go." I carefully opened the door and peeked down the hall. Thankful for the cooler air, I stepped out, with Laurie right behind me.

"Look, Vera...," he said.

"Let's focus on finding Leo and then getting out of here. We can talk about... that... later."

Laurie said nothing as we slowly crept down the hall, hoping to avoid notice. But then I heard the sound of wings coming up behind us, heavy demon wings, and I knew we were in trouble. Laurie moved to stand in front of me, but when I turned around and saw who it was, I instantly relaxed.

"What the hell are you doing here?" Rand hissed as he landed in front of us. "And hello," he said to Laurie, looking him up and down with a scowl that was very uncharacteristic of Rand. "I don't know you, but what is going on here?"

"It's okay," I told Laurie. "Hey, Rand."

The demon did not look happy to see me. Or Laurie. "Let me repeat myself, what the hell are you doing here?"

"I was looking for Leo."

"Are you insane? Coming here when you know the threats the king has made? And you," he said to Laurie. "Who the hell are you? You know what? I don't care. We are getting out of here right now."

He started to shuffle us toward the stairwell, but Laurie whispered in my ear, "Can we trust him? He's a demon."

"Yes," I told him, but Laurie still didn't look sure. We made it down the stairs to the kitchen, and once again Laurie seemed to be the most popular person to ever set foot in the room, though the laughter only seemed to make Rand more irritated.

"I don't care if you're some kind of fae celebrity around here. You brought her to an incredibly dangerous place," he seethed as he escorted us out the kitchen entrance, thankfully avoiding notice as we got in Rand's car and drove away.

"Laurie was only trying to help, Rand," I said once we had left the palace grounds. "Leo is here. In the palace."

"No shit," he grumbled. "I already knew that. I would have told you that too, but for some reason my phone isn't working. It's like they've cut off signals in the palace."

"Have you seen him? Is Leo being held prisoner here? What is going on?"

"No, I haven't seen him. It seems like they're keeping him under lock and key until this party."

"A party would explain the large kitchen staff," Laurie added from the back seat. His large blue wings took up most of the back all by themselves. "Vera, we should plan on—"

Suddenly the car swerved to the side and screeched to a halt. Rand put the car in park and twisted around to Laurie. "The plan? The plan is for you to not bring my darling Vera into the pit of hell again. Got it?"

"Rand, he was only trying to help. And no one saw us. We were able to get in pretty easily, actually."

"Yes, you were." After a long stare at Laurie, Rand started the car again, but I saw him glancing in the rearview mirror occasionally. "Your wings are impressive. How long have you been Elise's slave?"

"Awhile."

"You must be able to fly despite suppression or else you wouldn't have been able to travel this far."

"Rand, what's up with the interrogation?" I asked him as Laurie reluctantly told him it was true.

"It's nothing," he said, but it certainly didn't seem like nothing. "Forget I said anything."

Later after we got back and Rand left us, the crowds at the club were gone for the night. The club and arena downstairs were empty. The lights in the bar were still low, but now the atmosphere seemed completely different than when it had been flooded with demons. Liz, one of the human bartenders who worked there, was sitting on the other side of the bar with a fae dancer, the two women laughing as they downed shots. A few of the human kitchen staff were seated around a table with two fae men I'd seen down in the arena, all of them hunched over their beers, swapping stories. Someone had turned on music, and a few humans and fae were near the speakers, dancing.

Was I dreaming? How had this bar somehow turned into a little utopia where humans and fae could coexist? When I lived on Alliance Island, we'd hated the humans, but here it was completely different. These humans were social outcasts in Vestia; the demons only held humans in slightly higher regard than us fae.

While I watched everyone mingle, drink, and laugh, Laurie flew up on the bar top. As if on cue, the music quieted, and everyone turned to stare at him. How could we not? With his huge blue wings shining in the low light of the bar, his tall form, and bright white hair, Laurie stood out wherever he went.

"Thanks for coming, everyone!" he shouted. "I know you've been working hard, but the night is still young, and so are we!" There were a few grumbles from around the room. "Well, most of us are!" he said, laughing. Laurie glanced down again, and Liz handed him a small glass filled with a brown drink. The ice clinked in his glass as he raised his hand high.

Looking around, I saw that everyone in the room was watching him, hanging on his every word. Even though he'd only spoken a few words, he'd captivated all of them. No one seemed surprised to see him standing on the bar; in fact, it almost seemed like they expected this of him.

"To those we've loved!" Laurie shouted, and a boisterous cheer rang out in the room. "To those we've lost!" Another clambering of voices and claps, much more somber this time. "And"—Laurie looked down from where he stood on the bar, his blue eyes flicking briefly to mine before once again looking out into the crowd—"to those we've found!" A final shout rang out, and then everyone in the bar took a drink. "Now let's get drunk!"

The music instantly cranked up, the room springing into life as Laurie swiftly flew down off the bar. Before he could take two more steps, he was hounded by several girls, both fae and human; it didn't seem to matter which they were because they were all interested in him. Laurie's tall figure stood over them, and he shot me an apologetic smile before one of the girls grabbed his attention.

"Looks like your brother has quite the fan club," I said to Mia. She wasn't drinking, I noticed.

"Always." Mia smiled, shaking her head as we both watched the girls crowd around him. "He can't help it. He's too nice."

"And Elise doesn't care about these parties?"

"Better to ask for forgiveness than permission, I guess." She shrugged. "Mostly the boss lady pretends like we don't exist until she needs us. When Laurie first had the idea for getting everyone together, he just spread the word. We didn't know if anyone would come at first. But now it's a weekly tradition!"

"So this was Laurie's idea."

"Of course it was," Mia said. "Now I want girl talk. What's going on with you and the big, scary demon?"

"He's not that scary."

"If you say so. You've seemed sad lately. What's the deal with you two?"

"I love him," I said simply. "But it's complicated right now."

"Love always is." She smiled. "Speaking of love…"

Before she could finish her sentence, Laurie flew over, and Mia got up, giving Laurie her seat. "I'll leave you two alone." She winked. "I have some friends I want to go talk to. Over there. Far away from here."

"Subtlety is not her strength." Laurie chuckled as he sat next to me.

"I'm not sure it's yours either."

"That's fair." He nodded. "You know what one of the best parts of being fae is?" he asked me as he climbed over the bar, grabbing two glasses and a bottle of something dark.

"What is that?"

He poured a tiny amount in both glasses before handing me one. "How easy it is to get drunk."

I eyed the drink suspiciously and then him as well. "But you're not drunk at all, are you?"

"Neither are you."

"But I'm not pretending to be."

"If I pretend like I'm drunk, then I'll have an excuse for my behavior if I get rejected when I ask a pretty girl to dance."

I laughed, thinking of the groups of girls that had crowded him all night. "I don't think you're going to get rejected, Laurie."

He suddenly sat up straight, his expression much more serious than it had been earlier. "You don't think so?"

Seeing his hopeful face, I realized the implications of what he had just said. "Oh. No. Um... Maybe you're right. Maybe she will say no after all."

Laurie snorted and turned back to his drink. "I figured."

"You said you lived in the fae city when you learned to sew. What's it like, the fae capital?"

Laurie stared up ceiling as he thought about it. "Rowan? It's nothing like Vestia, nothing like anywhere in the demon kingdom. Pretty much the opposite of everything here."

"How so?"

"Instead of these skyscrapers," he said, a dreamy quality filling his voice, "imagine forests so dense you can't see through them. Instead of parking lots, imagine fields and flowers. Rivers instead of roads, the smell of honeysuckle instead of smoke and machines. The air is clean, and the water is pure."

"Sounds like heaven."

"It could be. For some. Your demon boyfriend would hate it."

"Why do you think that?"

"A veil of magic conceals the entire city, making it invisible to anyone who isn't fae, and because of that veil, regular technology doesn't work in Rowan. Our magic distorts it too much. Devices like suppression bracelets or collars can't exist there."

"Then why did you leave?"

"Mia and I had to find out the truth. One night we managed to sneak out together."

"And then you were captured and made slaves. Your parents must be really worried about both of you."

"Probably. I bet they are more worried about how it looks to all their friends than about our actual safety." Laurie gave me a sideways look. "You know, maybe the magic of Rowan would be enough to draw out some wing power in you."

"Wings?" My ears perked up at that. I'd given up on the idea of getting wings, resigning myself to the idea that I was simply defective and would never have them. "You really think so? Do you think it's possible being there could trigger my wings developing?"

"Anything is possible," he shrugged. "The magic of the original fae queen is what shields the city from outsiders. If it's strong enough to do that, maybe all you need is a little of this magic for yourself."

"Magic, huh? This," I said, waving a hand around at the bar to change the subject, "feels sort of magical. Like it isn't real. Seeing humans and fae together, having fun as equals, isn't something I ever thought I'd see."

"Are you okay with it? After everything you've been through?"

"Strangely enough, yeah. I am. It's comforting to know that there are humans out there who aren't like the ones I knew. I like seeing everyone together."

Laurie nodded in agreement. "There's something about working in a stressful environment that can bring people together, I think. Those two for example." He pointed to a human guy and girl standing at the end of the bar. "This was the only bar that would hire them both. It's hard for humans to find work here because a lot of demons won't hire them. They send most of their tips back home to her sick parents."

The two humans leaned into each other, and I watched as she smiled up at the man. "I had no idea."

"And that guy." Laurie pointed to one of the booths where a human woman cuddled up next to a fae man. "I heard that he used to be owned by Elise's father until she took over this place. His sister too."

"His sister works here?"

"No." Laurie's jaw clenched, and his hand gripped the glass tighter. "She died. They wouldn't let him see her. He was just told that she died, and that was it."

"That's awful."

"They are awful, Vera. Demons are awful."

"And the humans aren't? You haven't seen what I've seen."

"Since none of them own slaves, as I see it, *these* humans, at least, are not my enemy."

"And demons are?"

"Yes."

The two of us sat in silence, watching the rest of the room. Would Laurie ever be able to see someone like Leo as an ally? Would any fae?

A few minutes later, Mia came to fetch Laurie for something, and when he returned, he asked me to come with him to the back, down the hallway toward the manager's office. I hesitated; it didn't seem like a good idea to go back there with just him.

"I don't know, Laurie…"

He put up his hands to surrender. "You've already shot me down once, so I won't try anything else. Tonight at least," he grinned. "I want you to meet some friends. Come on."

When we walked into the manager's office, I was surprised to see the small group gathered in the tiny room. Mia sat in one of the two chairs in the room, and beside her stood a fae woman close to our age, a purple with sharp eyes and dark hair pulled back in a slick high ponytail. While Mia looked adorable at all times, but I knew she could kill me if she wanted to, this fae looked like she could kill me and like she wanted to right then.

What was this? Why did they all look like they wished I would turn and walk out?

Mia jumped up out of her chair and rushed over to me, grabbing my hands. "Vera is our guest tonight," Mia said to the group. "Vera, this is Ava." She pointed to the purple before signaling to the other two. "And the big guy is Jones, and that grumpy cat over there is Seth. They work with me in the arena mostly."

The large fae man with green wings, Jones, leaned against the opposite wall, and the smaller fae with identically colored green wings, Seth, sat in the chair next to Mia.

Aside from having similar wing colors, the two men looked like total opposites. Jones looked a few years older than the green seated by Mia; Seth, much smaller, thinner, and closer to the same height as me, had brown hair and darker skin. The latter sank down into his chair but didn't take his eyes off me.

Jones smiled a big toothy grin, puffing out his chest. "Surely you've heard of me. I never lose a match."

"I haven't, but I'm new here," I added on quickly when I saw his grin fade.

"Back home his family used to guard the Willow Gate, the main entrance into Rowan," Mia explained.

"Our strength is legendary," he said, his proud smile back.

"Unless someone has suppression bullets," the other green, Seth, mumbled.

"Seth, introduce yourself," Mia insisted.

"Do I have to?"

"Yes."

"Fine." He sighed, turning back around in his chair so that he wasn't facing me anymore. "I run the books, take the bets for the fights, handle the cash."

"Seth is a genius with numbers," Mia boasted. "I've never met anyone whose mind works as fast as his. And Ava works the crowd. She's a Dust girl."

"That's not all I do," the purple huffed, crossing her arms over her chest. "I'm Elise's eyes and ears in the crowd. I let her know if someone is getting too drunk or is high out of their mind. I listen. I learn. I report."

Mia's long white hair bounced as she nodded in agreement. "Ava's so pretty they don't even know what hit them until they're spilling all the secrets. Demons will tell her anything."

"It's nice to meet all of you." I looked around at the group in front of me. Laurie signaled for me to sit in the one empty chair behind the manager's desk, but I hesitated, starting to put it all together. While outside in the bar everyone was drinking and having a good time, back here no one was drinking, and everyone other than Mia seemed much more somber than the joyful crowd out there.

"We're not just hanging out back here, are we?"

"Well..." Mia played with her fingers and gave me an apologetic look. "Not really."

"I didn't know we'd have visitors tonight," Seth grumbled.

Laurie stepped forward to answer, but Ava interrupted him. "Now tell us why she's here."

"Ava," Jones's big, deep voice boomed across the small room.

"What?" She shrugged. "I thought this was a closed meeting. But now we're bringing guests?"

"You know it is not up to us to tell—"

"It's all right, Jones." Laurie held up a hand to stop him from speaking further. "I can understand why all of you would be hesitant about me bringing in someone new to our... circle. But I am confident Vera can be an ally."

"A human ally?" Ava asked.

"She's fae," Mia explained. "She just doesn't have wings."

All three of the fae turned to look at me then, not even bothering to hide their surprise.

Jones spoke first. "I'm sorry, but without wings, I'm not sure how the little lady here can be of help to us."

Slowly, all the pieces clicked together.

"You're escaping," I blurted out. It was the only logical explanation for why they were gathered like this in secret, why they would need help, why they were so suspicious of me.

Mia and Laurie exchanged a look. "Yes," Laurie said. "Eventually."

"So what is this, a planning meeting?"

Seth glanced over his shoulder. "I've seen you before. In the arena."

"Yes!" Mia exclaimed. "She fought me one time."

"You were terrible. Most of the bets were against you."

"Shocker." I rolled my eyes. "Anyway, back to the escape—"

"I said most. Not all. One demon placed an incredibly high bet that you'd win."

"Really?" I was surprised to hear that.

"Why would I lie about that?"

I didn't think he was lying, but why would anyone have bet in my favor? Of course, if I had won, that demon would have made a lot of money, but it would have been a risky bet since they wouldn't have known what I was capable of doing.

Seth shrugged and turned away from me again. "Don't get too excited. It was one bet, and he made sure to place it when no one else was around to see him, which wasn't easy since he was so big."

"Every demon is big to you, Seth," Ava scoffed.

"There's some truth to that. Guess he had a big bank account too, to waste money on a wingless fairy."

"Vera!" Mia's eyes were wide. "I bet it was your demon!"

"Your demon?" All eyes were on me again, with Ava's looking particularly displeased. "Your owner?"

"Oh. Well. No." I suddenly felt awkward with all of them staring at me. "I don't have an owner."

Questions started to pour out of their mouths, but I held up my hands to stop them.

"I was freed by Prince Leo. He owned me and other fae, but all of them have been freed as well."

There, in the tiny office, I told them the whole story of living on the Island, the auction, moving to Leo's mansion, and the creation of Syn. They listened intently—and suspiciously in a few cases—asking questions to make sure they understood what I meant when I told them about Syn in particular. The idea of Dust no longer being used, of a demon actually wanting to help fae, seemed too unusual and strange for them to grasp.

When we finally parted ways for the night, I felt a small amount of hope for the future. If these fae really did organize an escape, I wanted to help, and I knew Leo would too.

19

VERA

That night I had the most wonderful dream. We were back home, in Leo's big bed, and everything was warm and comfortable, especially with Leo's strong arms wrapped around me. It was like he was there with me, his hot body keeping me safe and protected. I rolled over, half-awake but keeping my eyes closed to make the feeling last longer, when I bumped up against something.

Or someone.

My eyes flashed open, and I instantly jumped up, scrambling out of the bed.

The redheaded demon simply propped himself up on his elbows and smiled, his shiny white teeth visible even in my dark bedroom. The bastard had the gall to be under my blankets. How long had he been there? Had the comforting warmth I felt earlier actually been him?

"About time you woke up, sleepyhead," the demon grinned. "I was starting to wonder if you were going to sleep the whole day away."

"Get out." I ran to my door to put some distance between us and turned on the lights. I pulled down Leo's big T-shirt to cover myself while Zell leered at me from my bed, his gaze not so subtly shifting down to my bare thighs.

"Maybe in a minute. Don't you want to know where Leo is? Or were you happier snuggling up to me instead? Oh, and cute panties." He smirked.

Not justifying that with a response, I snatched the shorts I had on the night before and pulled them on, continuing to glare at him while the redheaded demon stood up and came closer. His tall form towered over me as he rolled his tongue piercing around in his mouth, but I forced myself to meet his gaze. I was not going to let him intimidate me, no matter what.

"I know who you are now," he finally said. "You are the prince's whore, are you not?"

"Excuse me?"

"His whore. Mistress. The one he's fucking. Whatever name you want to give yourself. It doesn't matter to me. I'm just surprised, truthfully. I didn't think he had it in him. I thought Leo was too self-righteous, but it's good to know he's still got some balls."

"Are you here to chat, or will you tell me about Leo?"

"We can do more than just chat if you want."

"I don't."

"That's a shame." He walked around me, circling me like a cat who has just trapped a mouse, waiting for the right moment to pounce. "What's so special about you, anyway?"

"Nothing. Can you stop doing that?"

"And yet my morally superior cousin likes his whore enough to bring her home with him."

"I'm not his whore, and just so you know, he didn't want me to come here. This was my idea. I'm the one who convinced him to bring me."

"Even better!" Zell laughed loudly, as if that was the best joke he'd heard in a while. "Then he's pussy whipped, eh? Happens to the best of us."

"I don't care what you have to say anymore. Get out," I said through clenched teeth.

"I don't take orders from a slave."

"I'm not a slave."

"Sure. Whatever you say. I want to know why Leo has suddenly decided to come home."

"I don't have to tell you shit."

He laughed. "I'm assuming it's because he is finally ready to become king. He'll get married and make a whole pack of brats to run around the palace. Oh, but where does that leave poor little you?"

"He is not going to become king, and I'm not going anywhere."

"You will. You will when he no longer has time for you. When you get tired of being second best to the true queen. Yet you say he's not going to become king. Tell me what he's planning."

"I don't know. Now leave."

"I've heard rumors about you, you know. I did some digging after our last encounter. Rumors about your blood. I'd like to know if those rumors are true."

A holo-knife appeared in his hand. My mind flashed to that night with Henry weeks ago, and my hands started to tremble. No. Not again. This couldn't happen again.

"Back up."

Zell shook his head. "I told you before that I don't take orders from slaves."

"And I don't give a fuck. Back up. Now." I couldn't let that knife get any closer. My voice was trembling, and I had to force my lip to stop quivering.

"Why should I? When you're so cute and tasty as well? I had that one taste before, but I didn't get your blood. Let's change that."

Right then, my door flew open, hitting the wall with a heavy thunk as Mia flew in.

"Mia!" I shouted, slipping away from Zell and darting over toward her. She moved in front of me protectively, sizing up the situation quickly.

"You. Leave," she said with a sense of authority.

"Too bad. You seem like you'd be fun too." Holo-knife vanishing, Zell sighed. "Guess our playtime is over, princess. See you next time."

"I don't have to tell you what Leo will do if he finds out you were here."

"Leo isn't going to do shit." Zell walked past us out of the room.

"What the hell was that?" Mia exclaimed the second he was gone. "I swear I've seen that guy at the club before."

Before I could answer, Laurie slipped into my room as well. "Why was a demon back here? I just passed one in the hall."

"Laurie, that demon—"

"Let's talk about something else." I stopped Mia. I didn't need to give either of them another reason to hate demons, especially ones related to Leo.

"Okay," Mia said, not looking very sure. "You've been asleep all morning and missed lunch. I was starting to get worried after what happened with the bracelet. We wanted to talk to you about the party."

"What party?"

"That party at the palace," Laurie explained. "Elise wants me there in case there are any issues with her dress. I'll have to stay up in the balcony with the press and spectators, but I don't think anyone would notice another human. There will be plenty there already. Everyone wants to hear the king's big announcement."

How were they going to react when they heard that Leo was officially abdicating his title? Would his father immediately announce someone else as his successor?

"Mia, are you going too?"

"No. With so many demons in town for the party, we're going to be busy here. I'm going to stay and rest up for this weekend's matches."

"I'll sneak you in, we'll watch for a while, and then I'll sneak you out. I have the pass Elise gave me, so no one will question it. You can pretend you're my owner again," Laurie said, grinning, "if it makes you feel better."

It would make me feel better if I could see Leo.

A few hours later, I joined the twins in the dressing room. It had only taken one complaint about not having anything to wear to this party before Laurie was holding out a black garment bag.

Laurie nodded, indicating for me to take the bag. "It belongs to you."

Cautiously, I took the bag and unzipped it a few inches, knowing instantly what was inside. The dress I had tried on, looking just as beautiful as I remembered, except even more so now that it was finished.

"You added the top layer. I like the color."

Watching me carefully, Laurie shifted back and forth on his feet, his wings fluttering behind him. He was nervous, I realized. Was he that nervous about me seeing the dress completed? *Artists are weird*, I decided.

"Yes," he finally said. "Will you try it on?"

"Try it on! Try it on!" Mia chanted.

When they left me alone, I unzipped the bag and took out the dress. The new fabric was a dazzling, vibrant azure, the color of a robin's egg and almost a perfect match to the blue of the twins' eyes and wings. The details on the top layer of fabric were incredibly intricate and must have taken forever to sew. Laurie had sewn tiny, embossed leaves across the bust that trailed down the side of the dress, each leaf delicate and beautiful.

When I let them back in my room, Mia gasped at the sight of me, clasping her hand over her mouth.

"What do you think?" Before I could spin around, Mia was airborne, flying in a circle around me to see the dress at all angles.

"It's phenomenal!" she exclaimed. "Laurie, when did you have the time to make this?"

"Here and there. The machines here are so fast and—"

"Wait. Laurie," Mia growled at her brother as she landed and stomped toward him.

"I made it for you, Mia," Laurie said, holding his hands up in defense and backing up into the door. "It just happens to also fit her."

"Yeah, right," she said. "If you designed it for me, you did a shitty job. I can't kick ass in a dress like that."

Landing beside me, Mia gently touched the skirt, feeling the fabric in her fingers. "You really had to go with this blue, huh?" She gave her brother a pointed look. He immediately blushed and looked away.

"It's just like your wings." I smiled. "Now I can match the two of you in color at least."

"That's exactly what I mean. You look beautiful, Vera. But you. What were you thinking?" she shouted at her brother. "No, don't answer that. I know exactly what you were thinking *with*, you big dummy!" she shouted before smacking him in the head.

He threw up an arm to block her from hitting him again. "What the hell?"

"You deserved that! And more!"

"Is this about the dress?" I asked them.

"Yes," Mia said at the same time Laurie said, "No."

"Well, that clears things up."

"I'm sorry, Vera." Mia turned to me and spoke gently. "This isn't about you exactly. You look lovely, like a dream, like a *princess*. I'm irritated with my brother because he made you—"

"A very beautiful gown." Laurie practically pushed Mia away from me.

Hands on her hips, Mia gave her brother a look. "I'm going to need you to tell her right now, or I will."

"Tell me what?"

"There's nothing to tell, Mia. And—" He stopped short, clenching and unclenching his fists at his sides. "Even if there *was* something, it wouldn't matter."

"Yes, it would!" she insisted. "It might, at least. You never know unless you try."

"Someone fill me in here. What are you two talking about?"

Laurie gathered up the garment bag in a hurry, heading for the door. "We're talking about absolutely nothing. The dress is yours. Do what you want with it."

"Laurie," I said, hoping he'd stop, but he didn't.

"If you want to go with me, meet me at the back staircase in fifteen minutes." He shut the door behind him before either of us could say anything else.

"What was all that about?" I asked Mia once we were alone.

With a deep sigh, she leaned back against the door as if everything that had just happened was completely exhausting. "It's a replica. The dress is a replica."

"Okay? You mean that this dress is inspired by another dress? That doesn't seem like anything bad."

"Yes, but not just any dress." With a flutter of her wings Mia was in front of me, making a big show of kneeling before me on the ground, bowing her head dramatically.

"What are you doing? Get up off the floor!"

When she brought her head back up, Mia grinned. "This dress, my darling beautiful friend, is a replica of the one worn in the portraits of Morgana, the mythical queen of the fae, the founder and original protector of Rowan. She's still worshipped at the Darach Tor festival each year at springtime. Unmarried fae gather at that tree to dance and hopefully meet a future spouse."

"This Darach Tor—that's a tree, right?"

"It's not *just* a tree, Vera. It is the origin tree. See the leaf pattern on the side?" Mia pointed to the delicately shaped leaves sewn into the fabric that trailed down the skirt of the dress. "That's a reference to the motto of Rowan. 'Though many leaves, one tree.'"

"That's beautiful."

"Hell yeah, it is. Fae aren't like these demon assholes. The fae of Rowan believe in art and beauty. And"—she smiled mischievously—"love."

Frowning, I tried to figure out what any of this had to do with the dress. "I don't see anything wrong with having a dress like a queen though," I told her. "It sounds like a lovely tradition."

"Oh, it is! It's just that on the last night of the festival, at the Dance of Darach Tor, it is customary to wear the colors of the person you are hoping to court."

I blinked, too stunned to speak. Almost. "Say what?"

"It's super cute. Kinda like you're giving that fae a little hint," Mia explained. "To let the fae you're crushing on know that you're interested. If your colors match, then you have the unspoken green light to get together and dance the night away. How sweet is that?"

"What if more than one person has the same color wings? How do they know that you're interested in them in particular?"

"Good question." Mia scrunched up her face as she thought, as if this was the first time she'd ever considered such a thing. "I don't know."

"Or what if two girls wore the same color because they were interested in the same guy, but the guy wore a completely different color?"

"Yeah, that would be awkward."

"And if you aren't interested in anyone yet, what color do you wear?"

"I don't know." She waived her hands in the air as if none of this mattered. "Stop overthinking it! All I'm saying is that it's an adorable tradition and now you're wearing a dress like the Queen that matches Laurie's wings." She squealed and grabbed my hands, spinning me around until I was able to stop her.

"He was making this dress for you, not me. That's what Laurie said."

"He said a lot of bullshit, in other words. Eeek!" She fluttered up into the air and squealed again, this time even more high pitched than before. "I knew he liked you! Would you date him? You could date him. You're way out of his league, though. Oh wow, what if you were one day my sister-in-law?"

"Mia. Stop. No."

She landed with a thud. "Oh yeah. You have a boyfriend already. This is bad, right?"

"You're just now realizing this?" I needed to give the dress back to Laurie immediately, if not sooner. I reached behind me to start to unzip the dress and felt a wave of sadness at the idea of taking it off, but there was no way I could keep it now. Not if he meant it as some sort of gift because he was interested in dating me.

"Don't take it off. You need a dress for tonight, right?"

"I do, but I don't think this is appropriate."

"Who cares? You look like a queen."

A queen?

"Laurie will get over his crush eventually," she said, "so ignore him. Just pretend you're playing dress-up as the queen of the fae tonight. You can even surprise your prince after the party since you'll be there. Imagine what your actual boyfriend will think when he sees you in this beautiful dress!"

I watched myself in the mirror, admiring the way the blue fabric pooled delicately on the floor.

Tonight I was not going to be Vera, former slave.

Tonight I was going to be Vera, a queen.

LAURIE'S PASS got us both into the palace and upstairs to the balcony overlooking the Grand Hall. While he went off to check on Elise, I joined the flow of humans and demons pouring into the building, all of us herded through the doors and up the stairs.

It was easier to move in the dress than I'd thought it would be, or maybe I simply felt more confident in it than I normally did. Humans and demons alike seemed to part when I walked through the crowd. I heard a few whispers from the humans around me, but I did my best to ignore them.

"Which noble let their fae wear that?"

"I need to get that designer's name."

"That fae chick is hot. Who owns her?"

Finally, I found a spot near the press with their cameras where I could see over the railing and watch the show below.

As I looked for familiar faces from my place on the balcony, I estimated about one hundred demons milled about the Great Hall, waiting for the night's festivities to begin. I saw Rand chatting with two very pretty demons, both women throwing their heads back and laughing at whatever ridiculous thing Rand had told them.

I felt hands on my shoulders, and I flinched at the unexpected touch.

"Relax." Laurie leaned down and whispered in my ear, his breath warm on my neck. He rubbed his palms on my shoulders. "It's just me. Are we snooping? I love snooping."

"I'm watching. And listening."

Laurie let go of my shoulders and came to stand beside me. He was dressed like the other fae slaves I'd seen tonight. A black tuxedo and matching jacket, a white button shirt and black tie. Even though his clothing was neat and formal, his white hair was as wild as ever. Just as I'd heard whispers about me as I walked through the room, more than one woman was openly staring at Laurie.

He seemed to be oblivious to the attention he was drawing. Leaning over the railing, he grunted.

"What is it?" I asked him.

"Looks like the gang's all here. At least someone from every branch of the royal family."

"Tell me about them."

Laurie gave me a sideways look, blue eyes confused. "Your demon boyfriend hasn't already filled you in on his family?"

"I mean..." I struggled with what to say. Leo hadn't told me much of anything about the royal family. "Sure he has," I lied. "I was just testing you."

Chuckling under his breath, Laurie shook his head and took a step back, coming to stand behind me.

Feeling him close against my back, I started to complain. "You don't need to—"

"Look over there." He leaned over me to point across the Great Hall. Following his finger, I saw a tall, elderly demon in one of the corners of the room. His wings were noticeably thinner than those of the younger demons there tonight. As he leaned against the wall, it was hard to tell if he was asleep or just really, really still.

"Is he... alive?"

"Unfortunately, he's not dead yet"—Laurie laughed softly, his breath tickling my ear—"but probably getting there. He is one of the king's uncles. As old as he is, you just know that demon's seen some shit. Over there." Laurie pointed again, stooping closer to my level so he could see what I was seeing. "That old guy with the pendant around his neck was a general in the Blood War. His daughter is fucking one of the chefs, by the way."

I tilted my head up to look at him, but when I realized how close our faces were, I quickly went back to looking out at the crowd. "How do you know that?"

"There's a lot you can find out when they think you're invisible."

I wasn't sure how someone who looked like Laurie could ever be invisible, but he was right that the fae here in the demon kingdom seemed to be given more freedom than what I had imagined. Demons were so confident about everything, including that their fae would never dare risk trying to escape.

"I don't see your prince."

"I don't either." I frowned, looking for his silver-tipped wings in the crowd. I didn't like it. He was supposed to be down there in the Great Hall tonight, but where was he?

"But I do see your other favorite demon." With one hand planted on the railing on either side of me, Laurie leaned even closer, his cheek right next to mine. "Look to the right of the throne."

She was hard to miss. Her beautiful blond hair, her perfectly styled curls, and her tall, statuesque figure were recognizable anywhere. In a sea of black wings, Elise's sparkling red dress stood out like a bright jewel, matching the red gem on her ring finger. I watched as she smiled at something someone said, never moving from where she stood at one end of the room.

"Acting like she owns the place as usual," Laurie said.

"Her dress looks great though."

"Thanks. I chose a pretty scratchy fabric for the lining. Her skin will be irritated for days."

"Won't you get in trouble?"

"No way. She'll get so many compliments tonight she won't care."

He was right about the compliments. I watched as demon after demon approached her, each one gesturing to her dress. The longer I watched her, the more my irritation grew. I couldn't tear my eyes away from that damn sparkling ring, shining like a beacon even as far away as I was. A low growl was forming deep down in my chest, threatening to rumble to the surface at the sight of Elise.

Laurie huffed behind me. "Easy there. Look closer. Could she be any more desperate? Standing right beside the throne like that, as if she was already the queen."

"She *is* technically his fiancée," I said through clenched teeth.

"It feels hardly fair that your prince gets both a fiancée *and* a girl-friend if you're asking me."

"Good thing I wasn't." I ducked out from under his arms and inched down the balcony. Not that I could go far; we were squeezed in pretty tight.

"I'm sorry, Vera." Laurie came closer despite my attempt to put distance between us. "But if you're so important to him, why is she down there and you're up here hiding?"

I spun around, my hands balled into tight fists, and stared defi-antly up at him. His blue eyes didn't have an ounce of the anger I was feeling. If anything, he seemed amused by how irritated I was. "You'd rather me be down there in that viper den? Why? So Leo could prove to everyone that our relationship is real? I don't need him to do that."

"You don't?"

"I don't."

"Don't you want someone who wouldn't hide you? Who would proudly show you off for the strong, beautiful fae you are?"

Despite my growing frustration, Laurie stayed still in front of me. Calm, even. Irritatingly calm. Didn't he see there weren't easy answers here? I'd known this was going to be complicated when I decided to join Leo here. I'd known they wouldn't accept me, wouldn't see me as anything worthy of the prince himself.

Gently, the palm of his hand rested against my cheek. "I don't want you anywhere near them. I care about you. Ugh," he groaned, tossing his head back in frustration. "I'm trying to get it through your thick skull that you deserve more than—"

Thankfully, he was interrupted by the sound of a trumpet, the whole crowd turning one way in anticipation. We did the same, both of us staring at the two large wooden doors at the end of the ballroom.

"We're not finished with this conversation, Vera," he whispered.

"Yes, we are," I whispered back. Especially now that it seemed like the main event was happening.

Where *was* Leo?

When the creaked doors opened, a tall demon stood in the middle.

So this was him.

The demon Leo had crossed an ocean to escape.

The demon who had convinced Henry to use me to get some of my blood.

Leo's father. The demon king.

Watching the king slowly walk toward the throne, I searched his features for signs of Leo. It was more obvious now that he was there in the flesh than it had been when I'd seen his statue. Leo and his father had the same wavy black hair—though the king's hair had the faintest traces of gray—and the same determined expression, but that was where the similarities stopped.

Draped in a long ruby-red cape, the king walked slowly into the room. Even from where I was standing high up in the balcony, I could tell he was larger than Leo, taller too, physically imposing in every way. His silver eyes never looked anywhere other than at the throne as he progressed through the room, the red cape trailing behind him, so long that it covered his tail completely. Unlike Leo's silver-tipped wings, the king's wings were massive; they were folded against his back, but their sheer size was impressive even so. Normally, demons spread their wings as a show of dominance, but the king didn't need any kind of showy displays to prove his power in the room.

"That is the king?" I squinted to try to get a better look. "He's..."

"Terrifying."

On his head sat a low golden crown, and even as far away as I was from him, I could see rubies encased all around it. Something about the crown, something about the rubies, made me shiver.

"The jewels on his crown look like the one on Elise's ring. They're all that same deep red."

Laurie nodded in agreement. "The color of blood. Those are all Hellfire rubies."

"Hellfire rubies." I let the words linger in my mouth. The name sounded so ominous. "The large one in the middle, is it glowing?"

"Yes," Laurie said, the anger in his voice raw and chilling. His eyes were narrowed, jaw tense as he spoke solemnly. "There are several similar jewels owned by different members of the royal family. If you look around the room, you'll notice them on necklaces or rings. It's a way for royalty to distinguish themselves. They say that the hearts of a hundred fae were used to create each of those rubies. Fewer for the smaller ones, more for the larger."

"One hundred hearts," I whispered, unable to process the horror of what he was saying. As I glanced around, I saw others with the same jewels. Laurie was right. I felt sick.

"And that larger one in the middle of his crown?" I asked, scared to know the answer. The ruby set in the gold crown was easily five times as large as the tiny rubies that decorated the rest of it. "How many fairies were used to create that one?"

Laurie's blue eyes were cold. "Thousands."

Thousands.

Thousands of dead fae. Their blood worn proudly by the king.

"How?"

"The ruby is made with the Dust created from their hearts. Demons wear them like trophies. Brag about how many fae they've murdered. Do you see it now, Vera? They are monsters."

The king certainly looked like one.

As the heavy doors creaked shut behind him, the king walked with obvious authority toward the throne on a red carpet, all the demons parting in the middle to allow him room. They knelt down on the floor as he passed, their heads bowed. Even as far away as Laurie and I were, the king's oppressive aura was clear to everyone.

And that crown. That ruby. The death and pain it represented. My heart ached at the sight of it.

The king stopped at the throne, turning slowly to face the room of kneeling demons. He sat down on the throne, and the demons took that as the signal to stand again.

"Tonight is a special night. My son has returned to me."

A murmur ran through the crowd as they all applauded. His voice was a low rumble, but the room was quiet, and he was loud enough that everyone could hear. The demon king spoke clearly and slowly, each word weighed down by the heaviness of his authority and presence.

Where *was* Leo? I tried again to find him in the sea of demons, looking for the silver on his wings.

Then the large wooden doors opened again, and there he was.

The crowd parted as Leo, in his black tux, strode up that same red carpet toward his father. As the demons knelt again, and I could see him clearly, I knew that it *was* Leo walking through the ballroom, and yet the demon I saw before me didn't seem like the Leo I knew at all. This Leo didn't look like the Leo who would pepper me with warm kisses in the morning or squeeze me in his arms. No, there was no warmth in the demon I saw in the ballroom. There was only cold, a terrifying cold. I could sense that same terrifying aura coming from him that I felt from his father.

My eyes darted back and forth between the two demons, and then I saw what was in his father's hands.

"No. He's..." I could hardly speak, the words getting caught in my throat as I saw the crown in the king's hands. A crown that looked eerily like the one on the king's head, with only a slightly smaller Hellfire ruby. A lump formed in my stomach.

"No way," I said, more to myself than to Laurie, horrified at what I was seeing.

Leo took his place standing next to his father's throne, and the demons in the room all stood again, a murmur running through the crowd.

"What the hell is going on?" I seethed. "What is he doing down there?"

"We have much to celebrate." The king's voice rang out from the throne. "I want to announce that I am pleased my son has decided to make the demon kingdom his permanent home once again."

His *what*? That wasn't what we planned.

"And I have decided it is time to pass the torch of Hellfire to the next generation."

At these words, the murmurs and whispers grew louder, my heart thumping just as loudly against my chest with every second that passed. There was no way. There was no way that he was about to say what I thought he was going to say.

"He's really going to do it." Laurie leaned over the railing. "The old bastard is really going to do it."

Before the words sank in and I could process what I was seeing, the king held up the crown.

No.

No, he won't.

He can't.

This wasn't at all what we decided.

"The coronation will be in the coming months, but let it be known here and afar that Prince Leo will soon ascend the Hellfire throne as the next demon king."

I had to get down there. Leo had been adamant he wouldn't become king. There had to be something else going on here. What was he thinking? How could he let this happen? I had to find him and talk to him, I had to—I had to—

"Vera."

Below us the king was still talking, saying who knows what because I couldn't think about anything other than the fact that he said Leo was going to be the next king. I pushed my way through the crowd and almost made it to the stairs.

"Vera. Stop!" Laurie's wings enabled him to catch up to me, and he grabbed my arm, holding me tight. "You can't run down there."

"Watch me."

"No." He gripped my arm a little tighter. "I will not watch you get murdered in front of me."

"I have to talk to him, Laurie. This isn't right. This isn't what we talked about. He said... He promised..."

"Are you surprised that a demon is a liar?"

I wrenched my arm away from him. "You don't know him."

"I don't have to know him. Look at him, Vera. Really and truly look at him," he said, pointing down at Leo.

And I did. We both did. From where we stood at the edge of the balcony, we saw the king hold the smaller crown up in the air. The room burst into applause, demons laughing and cheering. I felt tears prick at the corners of my eyes as the crown was lowered onto Leo.

"Something is wrong," Laurie said beside me.

"Everything is wrong!"

"No. Look again." Laurie pointed down to the throne where Leo stood. "Something is wrong with *him*."

Now that the crown was placed on his head, a glow enveloped Leo, a glow not unlike that he had when using my magic. The crowd gasped in shock.

"It's a sign!" someone called out. "A sign that he was chosen to sit on the Hellfire throne!"

"I'm going down there." I turned away, but Laurie grabbed my arm again to stop me.

"You can't."

"Like hell I can't."

The noise from the ballroom below grew louder, and both of us turned sharply to look. All I saw was the end of Leo's long cloak trailing behind him as he hurried from the room.

Where was he going? I had to go find him. I had to talk to him. I had to understand what the hell was happening. Ignoring Laurie, I gathered my dress in my hand so I could move without it dragging on the floor. Hurrying down the hallway and then down the stairs, I lost

Laurie and avoided the ballroom by heading toward a hallway close to where I'd seen Leo go. Other than the click of my shoes on the floor and the faint rustling of my dress, the hall was silent, with no sign of Leo. I peeked into a few of the open rooms, listening for any sound that might be him, but nothing. Just silence.

The whole night seemed like a bad dream.

The Hellfire rubies made from the hearts of fae.

Leo accepting that crown. That revolting crown.

It wasn't going to do any good to wander the hallway all night, but what else was there to do? The distant sound of applause made it seem like the ceremony in the Great Hall was over, but I had no idea where Leo would be now. I could find Laurie and get him to take me home and wait for Leo there. I was imagining all the things I was going to say to him when a female demon appeared by my side.

"Can I help you?"

Her hands folded neatly at her waist, she smiled at me with an over-the-top politeness that I instantly knew was fake. The all-black uniform she wore let me know that she was a servant, like the demons I'd seen scuttling around downstairs earlier.

"No, thank you." I stepped around her to continue down the hall, but she stepped to the side as well, her wings expanding to block my path.

"Please," she said again with that same sickly-sweet smile. "I insist. If you would come with me, his highness has requested your presence."

How had Leo known that I was there? Had he seen me?

"Where is he?"

"Please," she said again, "follow me."

Before I knew it, her wing was around my shoulder, guiding me down the hall. "Right in here." She opened a side door and ushered me in. Leo was sitting in a high-backed chair with his back to me, just the top of his wavy black hair visible.

"What the hell is going on?" I asked, trying to control the anger in my voice. How could he sit there calmly when he knew I just saw him accept the Hellfire throne?

When the chair spun around, I gasped.

It wasn't Leo at all. All my words stuck in my throat, the anger veering sharply in another direction, this time toward fear.

The demon flicked back his cloak and leaned forward in his chair, hands clasping in front of him as his elbows rested on the top of the desk.

"So you're the little bitch who is manipulating my son."

20

LEO

A s soon as the crown was fully placed on my head, I could feel it. I could *hear* it.

The sounds and sensations emanating from the Hell-fire ruby only grew louder the longer I wore it. There was noise. So much noise. It wasn't the noise of the demons gathered in the ball-room though. This was different. Hundreds—no—thousands of voices all speaking on top of each other, a cacophony of chaos, over-whelming me in sound.

I'd never been allowed to go near any of the Hellfire rubies before. Once I was old enough to know what they were and how they were made, I didn't want to. My father had never let me anywhere near them, and now I knew why. Had he known I'd react like this? Or was this a side effect of the drug?

More than anything, when I wore the crown, I felt heat. Heat and pain. A scorching, sharp heat that seemed to take hold of my blood.

I could stand the pain. On some level, it even felt good. The serum had felt like my body was being cut into pieces, but this felt like electricity zapping those pieces until they tingled and twitched.

But the strangest part, over all the noise, two questions kept repeating in my mind, the words oddly clear above the confusion and shouts.

Who are you?

What *are you?*

Rushing out the side entrance, unable to stay in that ballroom for one second longer, I grabbed the crown in my hands as those two questions kept repeating over and over.

Who are you?

What *are you?*

"Shut up!" I yelled into the empty hallway. I grabbed the crown and yanked it off my head. Without hesitation, I threw it down, the gold clattering against the floor. The noise finally stopped, as did the heat, but my head was throbbing. Leaning over with my hands on my knees, I sucked in deep breaths to steady my racing heart.

Now that I had a moment of clarity and the noise was gone, I realized I felt slightly less empty than I had earlier. It was a small change, hardly noticeable, but something had happened. Was the ruby connecting to the fae part of me that was still hanging on? Something pulsed in my pocket, and when I put my hand inside, I remembered the ring.

The golden ring with the tiny red stone. Made from my mother's heart.

Something inside me urged me to put it on. I couldn't resist, and my breathing slowed as I slipped on the ring.

"Leo?"

Rand took long strides directly toward me. His eyes flicked from me to the crown on the floor and back again before he stooped down, picking it up and holding it in one hand. Gone was all his usual mischief; now there was only concern.

"Are you okay?"

"Yeah," I said as he approached quickly. "I think so, at least. I'm not sure—"

My words were cut off when Rand's fist connected with my cheek.

"What the hell?" I yelled at him, rubbing where he'd hit me. "That fucking hurt!"

"Good! That was for keeping me in the dark about tonight. I knew you had something planned, but *this*? What the fuck, Leo? Don't you think you should have told me? You vanish and then show up doing something like this? When were you going to tell me that you were going to accept the throne?"

As much as I wanted to, I couldn't tell Rand everything right then. The fewer demons who knew, the better. My father had eyes and ears all over the palace, spies disguised as servants, and hidden cameras in every nook and cranny. Glancing around the hall, I knew there was no way to know who was listening to us right then.

"I need you to have some faith in me, Rand."

Rand let out a hollow laugh. "I've had faith in you for years, Leo, but right now I'm having a hard time after what I just saw. We are business partners, but more than that, we are friends. Or at least I thought so. And if you think I'm pissed, then you have no idea what you are in for once she finds out."

There was no need to say her name. I knew exactly who he meant. There was no doubt Vera would be angry; I'd known that before the party started, but this had to happen tonight. If my plan was going to work, I needed every demon to think that I was going to be the next king, including the old bastard. *Especially* the old bastard. She wouldn't hear the news until morning, but I'd be able to tell her myself first.

Rand tilted his head as he stared at me, brow furrowed. "You look awful."

I was starting to feel awful as well. I couldn't take my eyes off the crown in Rand's hand. I could have sworn that ruby was pulsing red, but no, that wasn't possible. I wanted to touch it again, I wanted to break it. I felt like *I* might break if I didn't have the crown, but I felt like I might break the crown into pieces if I did.

Without thinking, my thumb rubbed against the ring on my finger.

"Leo?"

Rand's voice sounded like it was a million miles away.

A servant flew down the hall toward us, casting a confused glance at the crown now in Rand's hands before bowing his head. "Your Highness," he said, "you are needed by the king's councilors. They wish to speak with you immediately."

Just as I knew they would.

"Tomorrow," I told Rand. "I'll find you and we'll talk."

"Damn right we will. Hey!" he called out after me, but I was already walking away down the hall following the servant. "You forgot something," Rand said, holding out the crown.

"You keep it. For now."

21

VERA

There he was. The king of the demons.

There sat the demon who ruled over a vast empire, the monster who had the rest of the world trembling in fear. He oversaw an empire whose most profitable product was created from the blood of fairies. Standing in front of him a few feet away, I could understand the reputation; the demon king's mere presence emanated a palpable, threatening aura. It wasn't like the glow that surrounded a person when they took Dust, but I could feel it, a thickness in the air that shed off him in waves.

There was no word for it other than *evil*.

But he was also Leo's father. The demon he had crossed an ocean to escape.

With painstaking slowness, the king rose from his desk, his mammoth body taking unhurried steps around to stand directly in front of it, directly in front of me.

"Come closer, girl."

For just a moment, I considered staying where I was by the door. First, it felt safer to remain there in case I needed to get away quickly, and second, I didn't want to do one damn thing this old demon asked me to do. But under his glare all my resolve melted away, and I walked toward him, stopping a foot or two away. I'd watched him from the upper balcony earlier, but that was nothing compared to being face-to-face with the demon king himself.

It was a strange thing to look up into eyes so similar to those I loved, eyes whose gaze conveyed love for me as well.

There was no love here. Leo's eyes and the king's might have been shaped similarly, but those staring at me now were unfamiliar. The silver in Leo's eyes burned bright with passion, but the king's glare was cold and crystalline.

Suppressing a shiver, I forced myself to stand still under his examination. There was a darkness there, too. A darkness in his eyes that I hadn't seen in any demon before. He didn't seem angry or upset to see me; in fact, he stood completely motionless, his stoic demeanor that much scarier. I was used to Leo's passion and energy, but his father seemed completely devoid of those feelings. If Leo was fire, this demon was nothing but ice.

"A slave who doesn't kneel to a king?" His deep voice rumbled in his chest, and standing this close to him, I wasn't sure if I was shaking myself or feeling the vibrations from his words.

"I'm..." I swallowed; the words stuck in my throat. "I'm not a slave," I finally said. "Leo freed me."

"Meaningless." If the king noticed I didn't address him by his honorific, he didn't show it. It was a small rebellion, but it felt good to not address him as a king. Small rebellions might be all I had now that I was faced with the king's full power and intensity.

His long cape draping onto the floor, the king folded his large arms over his chest as he stood tall, looming over me. "What does your freedom mean? Do you think you could stop me if I took you right now and wrapped a new collar around your throat? Or if I squeezed that pale neck in my hands until it snapped? I've done worse for smaller crimes."

"No," I admitted, making myself maintain eye contact even when I felt like trembling at the truth of his words. "I couldn't stop you if you wanted to hurt me, but you haven't done it yet, so there must be some reason I'm still here."

"Still here for now." The king clicked his tongue, his eyes never leaving mine. "A fae who doesn't have wings. At your age. How has such a pathetic insect bewitched my son? He was willing to sacrifice his rightful place as the next king for a *slave*." He hissed the word in obvious disgust. "Does he dress you like this to pretend you're more than the insect that you are?"

"You're giving me too much credit." I felt braver now that I'd adjusted to being this close to him. "Leo has never wanted to be the next king. I don't understand how you convinced him to put on that disgusting crown in front of everyone, but he had to have had a reason."

"A reason? Other than taking what is rightfully his? I know about your kind," he huffed. "Your plan is to stick to him like a leech, isn't it? It won't work. Fae are used and thrown away here. That's just how it is. I don't care if you call yourself free or not. Your fate in this kingdom will be the same as the rest."

"No. That's not true. He loves me, and I love him."

The king threw his head back, and his loud laugh echoed off the stone walls. "Love? Since when did that matter? My son is going to become king and marry a demon, not an insect like you."

As he spoke, I noticed that the stoic exterior he'd projected earlier seemed to crack, letting the slightest irritation sneak into his voice. What had changed? Why now? Was it because we were talking about love and marriage? I thought about what Leo had told me of his parent's own marriage, of his stepmother and his father's relationship. Suddenly, it clicked.

It was my turn to laugh. "Wow. Just... wow. I can't believe it."

The king's eyes narrowed.

"You're jealous." When he didn't say anything, I kept going. "That's why you're mad now. It's because you're jealous."

"Of a *slave*?"

"No. Of your son." Knowing I was right, the words started pouring out of me as it all became clear. "He's happy, or at least he was before we came here, but you can't stand him being happy when you're so miserable, can you? It's all about you and what you want. You don't really give a shit about him at all."

"But I do. I care about him so much that I should kill you right now and save him the trouble of doing it later."

"Would that make you feel powerful? Does the mighty king of the demons need to threaten a wingless fae to prove his own strength?"

"Maybe I will kill you after all."

Blood boiling in my chest, my hands clenched into fists by my side. "Like you killed his real mother?"

And then he broke. My words were finally enough to completely fracture the king's composure. Black wings spreading out wide, he took full demon form for the first time.

It all happened so fast.

The king reached for my arm, but instead of pulling me to him, he bypassed himself completely and slammed my chest down against the top of his shining wooden desk. All my breath knocked out of me, I gasped and tried to stand up, but a large hand pressed down between my shoulders while the other twisted my arm behind me, pinning me in place.

"You know nothing."

"I know enough," I spit back. "Let go of me, you sick bastard!"

"You're the one who is sick. All fae are sick. But I have a cure."

I didn't know what the hell he was talking about, and I didn't care. All I knew was that I had to get out of there immediately. With my suppression bracelet still on, I couldn't use my full strength against him, and without my magic, there was no way to defend myself against a monster like this.

"I don't give a shit about your cure. Let me go!"

"You're all the same," he said, yanking my arm back tighter. "I knew suppression of your magic wasn't enough. But don't worry, I have a permanent solution—"

The door creaked open. The king didn't relax his hold on my wrist, but he was silent as someone came into the room.

Wrenching my head to the side, I saw Zell kneeling on one knee, his head bowed. *Of all the demons in this palace,* I groaned internally, *the one who might save me from this bastard is* this *guy?*

"Zell!" I called out, even though I knew how pathetic and desperate I sounded. The hand on my back pushed down, smushing my face against the desk, my word coming out as a grunt.

"What is it?" the king asked him, ignoring me completely.

The redheaded demon stood up from where he knelt, his eyes only briefly flicking to me before meeting those of the king. Seemingly unbothered by Zell's appearance, the king didn't relax his hold at all, keeping me pressed against the wooden desk.

"I apologize for interrupting, Your Majesty," Zell said, and I couldn't help but hear the slight lilt in his voice that bordered on amusement.

With a shove that sent me forward on the desk, the king withdrew his hand from my back and let go of my wrist. "Don't let it leave," he said.

I jumped up, not wasting a second, and took off for the door. The second Zell stepped in front of me, there would be no way I was leaving that easily.

"Caught ya." Zell smirked and wrapped a wing around me effortlessly, as if catching me was the simplest task he'd done today while I struggled against him. "Missed you, you little shit."

"Let me go!" Throwing an elbow back to hit him, I tried shoving him off me, but Zell's hand gripped my shoulder firmly.

"I don't think so. Not letting those elbows get near me this time."

The king was rounding his desk, looking for something in the drawers. "Bring it here. You'll get to watch its death firsthand."

In a panic, I twisted and scrambled every way I could, but Zell's wing covered my mouth, my shouts coming out as muffled noises.

Zell didn't move. "I was thinking, Your Majesty, that maybe she'd be worth more alive."

The king closed his desk drawer. "Why is that?"

"Well, once she's dead, we lose that leverage over Leo. She's a pretty cute bargaining chip, don't you think?"

"Perhaps." The king seemed to be considering this idea, but then finally nodded. "Take it away."

Before I could shout or scream or do anything at all, Zell hoisted me up and over his shoulder. I kicked his chest and hit against his wings as hard as I could, but he stood firm as a wall of rock, not moving in the slightest.

Even though I couldn't see him, I could hear the disgust and dismissiveness in the king's deep voice. "You're responsible for it until I decide what I'm going to do."

"Looks like we finally get some quality time together then," Zell said to me, turning to go and taking me with him. From my place over his shoulder, I could now see the king clearly even as Zell carried me out of the room.

"Leo is going to beat the shit out of you when he finds out you're doing this!" I screamed at the king as Zell opened the heavy wooden door.

My last view as the door closed was of the king, still standing in the middle of the room, his long cloak pooled on the floor.

"*King* Leo?" the king asked. "Let him try."

22

LEO

It was early morning by the time the councilors were finished with me. Thankfully none of them asked where the crown was. I didn't know and didn't want to know. Demons still gathered in the Grand Hall, their voices louder now that alcohol had been flowing for the past few hours. After I finally got my phone back, I'd tried calling Vera, but no one answered. She was probably asleep already, which meant that I'd need to find her first thing in the morning.

With the ring on my finger, I felt more like myself, as if the hole created by that serum was now partially filled. I could think more clearly, and my heart didn't feel like it was going to explode at any moment.

While I started another text to Vera, Elise appeared at my side, her hand looping through my arm to hold on as she swayed slightly.

"Leo." Her voice slurred, making me wonder how many drinks she'd had. "Or should I say Your Majesty? Oh, I like the sound of that. Or is it *My* Majesty? Can I start calling you that?"

"No," I said without looking up from my phone. Why wasn't Vera answering my texts?

"You really are cruel, aren't you? Making your little fae watch all this tonight was something I didn't expect from you. But I suppose she isn't yours anymore, is she?"

"What?" Elise suddenly had my full attention. She stared up at me with big eyes, still holding on to my arm for support.

"Can I kick her out now that you've moved on?"

"What?" I said again, shaking her off me as my heart started to thump against my chest, a panic quickly rising through my veins. "Did you say Vera's here? Where?"

"How should I know?" Elise wrinkled her nose. "I'm shocked you invited her."

"I didn't. When did you see her?" I grabbed hold of her shoulders to keep her standing up straight. "Where is she?"

"Is this how you treat your fiancée?"

"This is not the moment to test me, Elise. Tell me."

"She was up in the balcony watching with the press and all the other lowlifes."

Fuck.

Fuck. Fuck. *Fuck.*

"Be specific. With who? When? Where exactly? I need to know everything."

"I saw her with Zell a couple of hours ago, so I assumed you'd cut her loose if she was hanging out with that manwhore. He hardly even talked to me tonight, can you believe that? Who the hell does he think he is? Just because he's got that gorgeous red hair, and those big hands that look like they could snap me in half, and—"

"Zell? Where is he?"

"Who cares?" Elise slurred, drawing out the words. "Probably hooking up with whichever bimbo he chose as his victim tonight. He texted me that he'd brought that stupid little fae of yours up there to his rooms and that I should come join them, but if he thinks it's that easy to get me—"

I was gone before she could say more.

Eyeing Zell's doorway once I flew upstairs to his suite, I wondered if he still had the NCS installed to hide whatever shady fucking thing he was doing. The first real invention Zell and I worked on together was a noise canceling system, a series of devices that vibrated in response to sound waves coming in and out, neutralizing them instantly. As teens, I used it to hide from my parents while Zell used it to hide girls from his. From where I stood in the hallway, I couldn't hear anything, but if he was using the NCS, I wouldn't have been able to.

When the door opened and a couple stepped out, giggling as they stumbled into the hallway, I heard the party inside. So he still used it. It seemed like tonight Zell was using it to block the noise of the party from the rest of the palace.

Elise had been right. The crowd downstairs in the Great Hall might have dispersed, but it looked like most of them had come up to Zell's set of rooms, or at least the younger set had followed Zell up here to his makeshift after-party.

Any illusions I'd had of going unnoticed vanished the second I stepped into the room. A cheer went up at the sight of me, demons shouting and congratulating me, offering drinks and Dust, some women offering more than that.

With no sign of Zell or Vera anywhere, I pushed through the room past their congratulations. Demons deep in conversation lounged on black leather couches positioned all over the room while a few others danced to a stereo near the floor-to-ceiling windows. The room was dim overall, but the city lights shone through the huge windows, casting shadows on the floor. There were demons I recognized from the ceremony earlier but also many others who must have arrived afterward to party at the palace.

Dread formed in the pit of my stomach as I followed the noise down the hall, past demons in a side room snorting Dust off silver plates toward the bedrooms in the back. Zell's room.

The door wasn't even locked. When I pushed it open, there was a shuffling of bodies and high-pitched yelps of surprise. Two human girls grabbed blankets to cover themselves before they rushed past me out of the room.

But did he make any effort to move? Of course not. Even though I'd come into his bedroom, the red-haired demon still held a blond human girl on top of him firmly in place, his fingers digging into the skin of her hips. Zell lifted his head up from the bed, craning around the girl to see me.

"Here to join?" he smirked.

"Fuck you. Where is she?"

"No? You just want to watch? I didn't take you for the type, Your Highness. I can get you a blond one of your own if you want," Zell said as he smacked her ass and she yelped. "But no. You prefer girls with dark hair, don't you?"

This son of a bitch.

"Where is she?"

"I might even be able to find you one without wings."

"If you don't want to die naked, Zell, tell me where she is."

"Wouldn't be the worst way to go," he said, rolling his hips up, the girl letting out an obscene moan. He seemed perfectly happy engaging in this spectacle with me standing there. "But fine."

With no further warning, he pushed her off him, and she fell onto the bed. Zell wiped the sweat off his face before throwing a look of disgust her way.

"Get lost," he said to her.

"But sir—"

"I said get lost." Slowly, he got up from the bed and took his time finding a robe to slip on as the blond girl scampered away. "You're handed a kingdom, yet you come here looking for your whore. Your mother—my aunt, rest her soul—would have been embarrassed to see you now, you know."

Visions of my stepmother tossing my actual mother on the ground like a piece of trash flooded my brain. I didn't give a shit what that demon thought of me, not now, not ever.

"And your parents would be proud of you for using women like this, Zell?"

"At least I know it's just sex. Unlike you, the crowned demon prince, who prefers a fae over his own kind. You make me sick, you know."

"The feeling is mutual. Get dressed."

"It's fine to have favorites, cousin, but you have to draw the line at having slaves think they're your equal."

"She isn't a slave. I freed her. Now tell me where she is."

"You did no such thing. Where's the documentation? The proof? I've never heard of a freed slave. There are fae we haven't caught yet, and there are fae slaves. There is nothing between."

"You're wrong. She is free."

"Is that how you got her to sleep with you? Really, Leo, there's no need to persuade a girl when you can just take what you want. This kind of shitty decision-making is exactly why—"

My fist connected with his jaw in one solid punch, and Zell's head jerked back from the impact. He shook his head, and his silver eyes seemed shocked for the briefest of seconds, but then the corner of his lips turned up in a smirk and the bastard *laughed*.

"Is her pussy that good, Leo? Might have to try it myself."

I was on him in seconds. Tackling him to the floor, my brain swam with the dull buzz of rage. I don't know how many times I rained down blows against his face, but he hardly fought back.

Noises behind me made me pause. A quick glance revealed a group of demons standing by the door, watching us. Damn it. How much had they heard?

"There he is, everyone," Zell coughed where he lay on his back on the floor, spitting out droplets of blood. "There's our prince. There's the heir to the Hellfire throne. A demon who defends the honor of a slave. I can't wait for everyone to stop seeing you as the chosen one and see you for who you really are."

Hovering over him, my chest heaving, I reared back my fist to hit him again, but that look on his face told me hitting him was exactly what he wanted me to do.

"Shut up," I said, backing off. "They should be glad to know I finally put you in your place."

"And what place is that? Beneath you like I am now? You don't get to take the moral high road and act like you're so much better than all of us, Leo. There's a monster inside you too, and you know it."

"You're right. And this monster will murder anyone who hurts Vera."

"Hurts your *slave*. I knew all that moral outrage was bullshit." He coughed another laugh, sitting up on his elbows. "You're just as depraved as me."

"I'm nothing like you. Where is she, Zell? Tell me right fucking now. I won't ask again."

"Everyone out!" Zell shouted.

I hadn't realized how many demons were crowding around the door watching the two of us, but when I looked behind me, there they were, straining to see into the room.

Of course. I'm sure putting on a show for his adoring fans had been his part of his plan all along. How much had all of them heard? Had they heard what Zell said about Vera? Judging by the shocked looks on their faces, they'd all at least seen me hit him, which meant they'd probably also heard me defend someone they would see as a slave.

Zell got up off the floor as the room slowly cleared out. He went to the door to close it and pressed a button on the frame. "Now we can talk in private."

"Enough. I've been patient long enough. If you don't give me an answer in the next ten seconds, I'm going to tear your suite apart, room by room, until I find her."

"Wait." He put a hand out in front of the door. "She's fine, by the way, not that you asked. She'd have heard your yelling just now if it wasn't for the sound barrier."

I breathed a sigh of relief. "The barrier I made."

"*We* made," he said, and I snorted at the memory of him doing absolutely nothing while I worked on it. "It served us well as teenagers, I have to admit."

"Served *you* well. I wasn't the one convincing the servant girls to come back here every night."

"Right," he nodded. "You were too busy being the golden child. So, golden child, I need something from you. And then I'll take you straight to your girlfriend."

"You want to bargain with me? When you admit that you kidnapped her?"

"Was it really kidnapping? I mean, maybe? That's such a tough word to define."

"Spit it out. Now."

Zell straightened up, adjusting his shirt and taking a deep breath. "I want you to call off your engagement to Elise. You have your fairy bitch anyway. Why do you need to keep stringing Elise along?"

I struggled to understand what he'd just said. Why did he care who I was engaged to? It wasn't like Elise and I were a real couple. Why was he standing up for her?

"That engagement is a farce," I told him. "And even if I did end it, do you think she'd all of a sudden jump to join your little harem that fawns all over you?"

"No. I have this little harem to fawn over me, Leo, because I can't have *her*."

I blinked. "What?"

"These girls are fun, but they're a distraction. All I hear is 'you have the best dick ever, Lord Zell' or 'I love the way you fuck me, Lord Zell.' They're all so dumb and easy, always looking at me with their big dumb eyes. It's gotten old."

"Are you serious right now?"

"Deadly. I want wit, I want spark, I want *Elise*."

"I'm done here. I don't give a shit who you fuck, Zell, as long as you stay away from Vera." I headed for the door. I'd find her myself.

"Wait!" Zell jumped between me and the door. "I don't want to just fuck her. I want Elise." His voice softened. "All of her. All these girls do is kiss my ass all day, and believe me, I enjoy that kind of thing, but what I'd enjoy even more is someone to kick my ass instead of kiss it and tell me I'm an idiot every now and then."

"Then take that up with Elise!"

"How? How exactly?"

"I don't care!"

"Then let her go! How can I ever have Elise to myself if you're going to marry her, you pompous, oblivious asshole!"

"I'm never going to marry her!" I shouted back. "I only want Vera! Where the hell is she?"

"I'll tell you when you agree to call it off."

"I can't call off something that doesn't exist!"

I'd stayed long enough. Wrenching the door open, both of us froze. A timid-looking demon stood wringing his hands in the doorway. Seeing me, he instantly bowed his head. "I'm so sorry, Your Highness, I had no idea. I apologize. But sir..."

"What is it?" Zell snapped, pushing past me into the hall.

"The... uh... girl..." He kept his head bowed, stumbling over his words. "She... The... She's *gone*."

Zell exhaled loudly. "Shit."

"Gone?" I roared, already flying down the hallway, pushing through the demons still crowding around Zell's room.

23

LEO

I f these demons didn't get out of my way, I was going to knock them down myself. I rounded the corner out of Zell's bedroom and pushed past the demons crowding the hallway, flinging open each door, but all the rooms were empty or occupied by surprised demons caught with little to no clothes on. I was already plotting all the ways I was going to dismember and destroy Zell when I opened the very last door.

The last thing I expected to see was Elise and Vera, standing together.

Vera wore a long blue dress I'd never seen before. The fabric hugged her perfectly, and she looked like a beautiful, sad angel. Like a princess.

My princess.

"Leo!" Vera's eyes lit up when she saw me, and she ran, leaping into my arms and burying her head in my neck. I breathed in her scent, allowing myself to indulge in the warmth that came from her touch. It was difficult to not take it all right then, to soak in that feeling of her magic, of *her*, now that she was back in my arms. When she pulled back and I placed her gently on the floor, I could see the tears wetting her face.

"Where have you been?" she asked. My thumb wiped away a tear from her cheek.

"Did Zell hurt you?"

"No. He didn't. But your father..." I felt my own heart stop as I saw the terror in her eyes.

"The king?" I asked, heart racing at the idea of him seeing her. "What did he do?"

"Leo, he..."

"Why focus on the past?" Zell interjected from behind me. "Everything is all right now, right?"

"I will deal with you later. Come on, we're leaving this place," I told Vera.

"Leo. Wait a sec."

Reluctantly I let her untangle herself from my hold, and she spun around in my arms to face Zell. I hooked my head over hers, keeping her close.

She said, "You brought me to your rooms on purpose, didn't you, Zell?"

Zell crossed his arms over his chest as he leaned back against the wall. "Yeah, because the old demon told me to."

"No, that's not true. It was your idea to bring me here."

The sight of Vera unharmed had helped me calm down, but hearing that, my tail twitching on the floor, a surge of heat started to rise back to the surface. "You bastard—"

"No, Leo, it's not like that." Vera tilted her head up to look at me. "Let me explain. I think I understand now. He's gross, but I'm pretty sure he was trying to help me get away from your father in some kind of messed up way. Once I was here, Zell texted Elise."

"Yeah," Zell shrugged, "because I wanted to get laid."

"No, Elise said that you texted her that I was here."

"He wanted to flaunt the fact that he can get whoever he wants," Elise said, rolling her eyes. "I ignored that idiot's texts because I know he only wants one thing, but then it made me mad this stupid fae of yours was with him now too. Not that I care who Zell sleeps with, but

I knew you would be upset about it, Leo. When you rushed off, I just followed you. To help."

"I don't know what the king's intentions were," Vera said. "But he... He said I was sick, Leo. I think if I had stayed there, if Zell hadn't walked in... I'm not sure what would have happened." The small tremble in her voice made me want to rip the world apart.

"Yeah? Yeah! That's right!" A smug smile broke out across Zell's face. "In other words," he said, "you owe me, Leo, for saving your girl."

"I don't owe you shit."

"Yes, you do. If I hadn't intervened, I'm not sure your toy here would still be around for you to play with. Not after what I saw the old demon about to do."

"You want me to thank you for kidnapping Vera?"

"No, dumbass, for saving her life."

"It is almost morning, and I'm sick of all of you," Elise interjected. "Fairy girl, I'll see you at work."

"Elise, I didn't text you because I wanted to fuck."

"You didn't?"

"Okay, well, honestly, yeah, I did, but I also—"

"Bye, Zell. I'm out," Elise waved as she walked away.

Zell cleared his throat.

"Oh for fuck's sake," I groaned. "Elise!"

She stopped, looking over her shoulder at me. "Yeah?"

"Zell wants you to call him an idiot."

"What?"

"He's right," Zell chimed in. "I do! That's true."

Elise paused, squinting at all of us. "Everybody already knows that he's an idiot."

Beside me, Zell actually fucking sighed. "Gods, that's so sexy," he whispered.

"He wants something official between the two of you," I told her. "He told me he will be faithful only to you if you agree to date him."

"Huh?" both Elise and Zell said at the same time.

"And she likes you too, Zell. She keeps your magazine covers in her office."

"Leo!" Elise screeched.

"There. I'm done. Vera and I are leaving." I gave Zell a shove forward toward Elise. "Go after her, you idiot."

"It's not as sexy when you say it." He grinned, following after Elise all the same.

Not wanting to stay one second longer while they figured that out, I scooped Vera into my arms and left the palace as quickly as possible. I didn't care if I was being followed. I didn't care about any of that anymore. She was in my arms, and that was all that mattered.

SHE SPENT the night in my arms as well. I brought her back to her room at the club, and she told me everything that had happened. How she had looked for me. How she'd watched me walk into the ballroom. How the king had...

I couldn't even let myself think about it. I held her to close and breathed in her scent, hoping it would be enough to stop the guilt I felt over leaving her alone.

The next morning, after closing the door quietly so as not to wake Vera, I turned around to see blue eyes glaring at me from where the fae sat on the floor in the hallway, his back against the wall. He made no effort to stand or bow, seemingly comfortable scowling at me from the floor. I'd seen him before, that night Vera fought the girl at Elise's club, and I knew it was no coincidence that he was here tonight, waiting outside her room.

"Laurie, was it?"

The fae stood up right in front of me, blue wings extended behind him. We were almost the same height, and I wondered from the tense expression on his face if he was about to try to fight me.

"Have you been out here all night?"

Instead of answering, he simply brushed past me, his large wings hitting my shoulder as he passed and headed down the hall.

"Hey!" I called out. "Where are you going?"

Stopping halfway down the hall, the fae turned only his head of white hair around to answer. "I was here to make sure Vera was okay. Now that I know she is, I can go."

"Were you the one who brought her to the palace tonight?"

"Yes."

"I see. Then fuck you for bringing her in the first place. She never should have been there."

That made the fae finally turn around. "Wait just a second," he said, pointing a finger at me. "I only brought her to the palace because she wanted to see *you*. You're the one who lied to her about your intentions, who betrayed her trust, who—"

"Keep your voice down," I snapped, knowing that Vera was in the room right behind me.

"No. Someone needs to tell you the truth. She spent the whole night defending you. A fae defending a demon. How insane is that? Until you put that gross crown on your head."

"Something is wrong with that crown."

"No shit. Like the fact that fae were murdered to make that big ruby you demons are so proud of. You disgust me. Vera is kind and genuine, and for some reason I can't figure out, she doesn't think that you're a piece of shit."

"You're right."

"Huh?"

"I said you're right. I know I don't deserve her, that I've failed her, but I will do everything in my power to protect her."

"You didn't protect her last night."

"I know."

The fae laughed a laugh that didn't sound like it had an ounce of happiness behind it. "You're only borrowing her," he said. "You know that, right? Eventually she'll see that she belongs with me, with us, with other fae. Not here, not with demons."

The fae's face suddenly looked incredibly punchable. If he took one more step forward, I wasn't sure I could hold back. It took every bit of my self-control to avoid knocking him to the ground right there in the hallway.

"Vera gets to decide where she goes and who she goes with. That's what freedom is. I'm not making her do anything."

"Oh yeah? You really think you're not? You're even more selfish than I realized."

I'd heard enough from him. I flew forward, slamming into him and knocking him onto the floor, my tail wrapping around both his legs to keep him from kicking me. I kept one knee grounded into his stomach, my hands holding his arms down. Despite all this, the fae only seemed amused.

"She will never truly be yours," he smirked.

"And she'll certainly never be yours."

"We'll see about that."

"What's going on here?"

At the sound of her voice, both our heads turned toward the door. The door I hadn't heard open. There she was, staring at the two of us while I held the fae down.

Vera.

Giving him a final shove back onto the floor, I left him there, going immediately to Vera. She backed up into her room as I approached, and I let the door slam behind me. I hoped that was enough to send a message to that white-haired asshole. This girl was mine.

Vera hadn't even bothered to turn on the lights in her room.

"He was right. I am a selfish bastard," I whispered into the darkness as I followed her to the bed. "But I can't seem to let you go."

24

LEO

Rand came in and closed the door behind him, but he stayed there by the door, crossing his arms over his chest. As I sat behind Elise's desk in her office, I swirled the drink in my hand. There was no amount of whiskey that was going to make this easier.

Putting down the drink, I reached into my pocket, taking out the gold ring again. I hated what it was, but there was also something calming about the way the smooth metal felt against my skin. The tiny Hellfire ruby appeared to glow when I touched it, and when I put the ring on, I could breathe easier, I could think more clearly, and some of that rage I'd felt inside quieted down.

I'd felt the same way as a child when Aurora would sit with me at night and read me books until I fell asleep.

"I don't like this," Rand said, pulling me out of my memories.

"It's the right decision." I put the ring back in my pocket. I'd tried everything to keep Vera safe, and there was only one option left. If Aurora had left Vestia instead of staying with me, would she still be alive today?

Rand propped himself up on the corner of the desk, his tail angrily swatting the floor. "He just has such a smug face. I'm the only one allowed to have a smug face. Before calling for him, I asked around to see if I could dig up any dirt, and you know what? Everyone only says nice things about the blue-winged fae. How annoying is that?"

"What else did you find out?"

"Elise told me that he meets in secret with several other fae. They think they're smooth, but she has cameras and sees them together. That's probably when they're planning their escape."

"What else?"

"Unless you want to hear about how hot everyone thinks he is, there's not much else. Surprisingly, not much else. He's hiding something. We've met fae with wings like his and his sister's before, and all of them had been wild their entire lives. So how did they get caught? The way Elise describes it, they basically showed up on her doorstep. I don't know what the real story is, but something's missing there."

I touched the ring in my pocket again, the heat from the ruby calming me. "Everyone has their secrets. If he can do what I want, he can keep his to himself. You were able to get the information about the bracelet from Zell?"

"Yes, it seems these new ones, like the one you found, can take away not just fae magic, but also affect the wearer's regular energy as well. He's sending me the details this afternoon."

"Good. Then it's settled."

"I still think this is the wrong move."

"It's not."

"You won't even let me talk with her first?"

"No, Rand. She'll see right through you. This is the best plan."

As if on cue, the door to the office opened slightly, and the white-haired fae walked into the office before flinching at the sight of us. "Must be the wrong room," he muttered, turning to leave.

"Nope." Rand was already across the room, closing the door behind the fae. "You're in the right place."

The fae exhaled loudly and crossed his arms over his chest. "Is this an ambush?" he asked, eyeing both of us.

I held up my hands as if surrendering. "Sit down."

"No, thanks."

"Fine. I want you to know that I thought about what you said."

"The part where I called you a piece of shit?"

"Leo, do we really have to do this?" Rand asked from where he stood. "I already can't stand this guy."

The fae snorted. "I'm not a fan of demons either, yet here we are."

"Enough. Both of you. Look. Laurie, right? I know you're planning an escape."

There was a long pause where the fae didn't say anything, only continued glaring at me from the door. "Are you going to stop it?" he finally said.

"No. I'm going to help."

The fae stared at me in disbelief. "I don't believe you. What's in it for you?"

"I hear there are multiple fae involved." I ignored his question. "But I will only help you and your sister."

"Why help us at all?"

"Because I want..." I swallowed, unsure if I could force myself to say what I needed to say. But no, I had to say it. For her. I got up and came around the front of the desk so we could see each other eye to eye. "I want you to take Vera with you when you go."

He stared at me, face blank. "Why would you want that?"

"I don't have to explain myself to you."

"Yes, you do. Especially if you're asking for a favor. Especially a favor like this. Pardon me, *Your Highness*, but I'm going to savor this moment—the demon prince lowering himself to ask a pitiful little slave like me to do something. So tell me. Why?"

Every question he asked made my tail twitch that much faster.

"You know why," I said between clenched teeth. "You saw it yourself. It's not safe for her here. It's never been safe for her here. I've heard that the fae of Rowan never leave their city, that they live peaceful lives. Humans and demons cannot enter the fae city. Does that satisfy you?"

"No."

A low growl of frustration rumbled deep in my chest. I didn't give a shit if my answers made him happy, but I also needed him to agree with me. "You might not believe me, but my goals align with yours more than you know. Rowan is the only place where she can be safe right now. That is why... That's why I need..." I had to force myself to say it, no matter how hard it was. "I need you to take her with you."

He didn't move from where he was, watching my reaction.

"She won't want to leave," he said after what felt like minutes had passed. "She's free, remember? Weren't you the one who said that freedom means that Vera gets to decide what she does and where she goes?"

"I'll make her leave."

"How do you plan on doing that, exactly? The only way you'll get her to leave is to make her so mad that— Oh *shit*. That's exactly what you're going to do, isn't it? You're going to make her so mad that she leaves on her own." Laurie let out a hollow laugh and shook his head with disdain. "You damn idiot. For some reason I can't figure out, she loves you, and you're about to break her heart, aren't you?"

"It's for the best. Rand will go over the details with you and fill you in on the rendezvous point."

"You just have it all figured out, don't you?"

"If by that you mean I have a plan for you to successfully escape to freedom, then yes, I do."

"Unless you somehow have a lot of experience with escapes that we don't know about?" Rand added. For just a second, the fae flinched, and I saw a tiny break in his expression. Rand was right. There was more to this fae than he was telling us.

"If I want Vera to get out of here, I need this to be done right. That means you will do what I say."

"You really are such a selfish prick, Leo." The fae shook his head. "Can't you stop and think about her for even one second?"

"How dare you?" I seethed, flying straight toward him. The bastard didn't even bother to move, letting me grab him by the shirt. He didn't fight or try to fly away as I lifted him into the air a few feet. "All I do is think about her! She can get over a broken heart. A few days of sadness is nothing compared to being tortured or killed for the crime of knowing me."

"Are you even listening to yourself? You really think she'll magically get over you in a few days? What is wrong with you?"

I stared back at the fae, forcing myself to hold eye contact. "Nothing. I know how to make hard decisions. In this case, it means choosing what is right over what I want."

I let go of him, and Laurie stumbled back once his feet hit the floor, rolling his eyes. "So self-sacrificing. Look, do what you want, but this is going to crush her. I'll do it though. I'll take her with me, but now you know that *I'm* going to be the one by her side picking up the pieces."

With that he stormed out, and Rand followed to give him the details of the plan.

No matter how hard getting Vera to leave the demon kingdom was going to be, it was the right thing to do. Touching the ring in my pocket, I knew she couldn't stay here. If she was with this fae asshole, at least I knew he'd watch over and protect her. If she stayed here with me, there was no way that I could be with Vera all day, every day. Even if I managed to hide her in some other spot, they found her once before, and they could find her again.

Laurie would pick up the pieces. That's what he'd said.

"Good. I'm counting on it."

25

VERA

Leo had been quiet all afternoon, the kind of sullen quiet that was typical for him when he was working through a new project or frustrated by an experiment. When I heard him call my name from the bedroom, I thought for a moment that maybe his mood had changed, but when I walked in, he was sitting on the bed, holding something in his hand.

A ring. A gold ring with a red stone that I could see glowing from across the room. I didn't want to go anywhere near it.

"Is that what I think it is?" I pointed to the red stone set in the ring as I stayed near the door. He didn't look up at me, continuing to roll the ring in his fingers.

"It's a Hellfire ruby."

"Leo, aren't those made of…" I couldn't bring myself to continue. The idea was too terrible to say out loud.

"They're made from the hearts of fae," he said quietly. "The more hearts, the larger the stone. This one was made from a single heart."

I was speechless, but I couldn't take my eyes off the tiny stone as he twirled the ring.

He closed his fist and sighed, his eyes still focused on his hand. "We should have talked sooner. If I could have, I would have, but you know the outcome. I accepted the crown, Vera. I don't have to tell you what that means."

Forgetting the ring entirely, I rushed over to the bed, kneeling at his feet and taking his hands in mine.

"It means you agreed to be king," I said, looking up at him even as he wouldn't look at me. "But I know there's more to it than that. Talk to me. Were you threatened? Does this have something to do with me?"

Leo looked up, silver eyes staring at me with more sadness than I'd seen in a long time.

"Be the king, Leo, if that's what you want," I told him, "but I'll be here with you."

"No." He took a deep breath, his eyes on the hand that held the ring. "We have to end this. You and I..."

"No," I said simply.

"What?" His face wrinkled.

"No, Leo. I said no."

"No to what?"

I stood up in front of him, wanting him to see all of me right then, wanting him to look at me when I told him what I thought. "No to everything you just said. No to ending things between us just because you're scared of how they will play out in the future. I'm telling you, I'm not letting you break up with me."

"It's not that I'm scared. Fuck," he said, standing up as well and running a hand through his hair. "That's not true. I'm fucking terri-fied. I'm just not sure we have a choice. Once I'm king..."

"Well, I have a choice. This is my relationship too. And I say no."

"That's not how this works."

"Leo. You know I'm stubborn. I've always been stubborn. Wasn't that what made you want to buy me in the first place all those months ago?"

"Vera, look at this ring. Really look at it," he said, opening up his hand and holding it up. "This is all that's left of her. All that's left of my *mother*." I gasped when the word left his mouth. "I think my father made it himself after she died. I can't let that happen to you too."

"Your mother... Her *heart* is in that ring? No." I shook my head and grabbed his hand, closing mine over his and encasing the ring inside. "I'm not going anywhere. I don't care how much you push me away. We are not your parents. I thought leaving you was the right thing to do months ago, and now I know I was wrong. We belong together."

"I belong here. As king."

"With me by your side."

"As what? My queen? That will never happen here."

"Why not? If you're in charge, just change the rules."

"My father tried to keep a fae close before, and you know how that ended. This," he said, unlatching my hand and holding up the ring again, "is how it ended. She died. I can't be the reason you die. I won't survive it."

He was trembling, I realized, and a new sense of fear shook me as I watched this incredible, strong demon tremble before me. Leo placed the ring on the bedside table before coming back to me, wrapping his arms around me, and burying his head in my hair.

I reached up and gently touched his face, and he leaned into my palm. "You love me, Leo."

"I can't."

"But you do. Or else you wouldn't be pushing me away. Trying to make me leave you proves that you love me."

"Do you hear how fucked up that sounds?" Suddenly Leo pushed me away, grabbing my wrists, and shoving me back against the wall. "Don't you get it?" Leo's voice was a growl, his mouth so close to mine that our lips were barely brushing each other's. "I'm killing you."

"No," I shook my head. "You're not."

"I am," he whispered. "I will."

"Leo—" All words left me when his mouth latched on to my neck. I groaned with pleasure from the feel of his hot lips on my skin, tossing my head back against the wall as he sucked on my flesh. There would be marks left behind to find in the morning, I knew, and

I wanted more of them. I wanted proof that Leo was mine, that I was his, that this happened, no matter how dark and deep the bruise was.

His tail circled my ankle, coiling around it and pulling my legs apart. Then he released my ankle, his tail curling up my leg instead until it found the tender flesh of my inner thigh.

"What are you—?"

But his hand clamped over my mouth, muffling my words while he continued to suck purple bruises into my neck and shoulder. His other hand wrenched open my shirt, ripping it down the middle, and as soon as that skin was exposed, his mouth was on it as well. My brain was slowly turning to mush with all the stimulation.

Behind his hand still covering my mouth, I yelped when I felt the tip of his tail snake into my panties, the arrow-shaped tip rubbing back and forth between my folds.

Leo's mouth left my nipple with an obscene *pop*. "You're so fucking wet."

"Mm-hmm," I mumbled behind his hand.

"Wet enough for this?"

Even though I sensed what was coming, there was no way to prepare for it. I tensed as the end of his tail pushed up slightly, the tip beginning to enter me. The end wasn't sharp; it was firm like a finger, but bigger than Leo's fingers, and I yelped again as it pressed into me more, breaching my walls and pushing in.

Leo took his hand off my mouth, and for a brief moment I wondered if he was going to let me talk, but then he shoved his fingers between my lips, roughly swirling them in my mouth as I gagged around them. His tail hit a sensitive spot inside, making my body flinch back against the wall, and I moaned around his fingers.

"Can't handle it? If you can't take my tail, how are you going to take my cock tonight? Hm?"

I *will*, I wanted to tell him. *I can and I will take all of you, Leo. I want all of you. I want nothing more than you and me, tangled in each other forever, no matter how much it hurts.*

Tears sprang to my eyes as drool started to leak out around his fingers.

Removing his mouth from my chest, he smirked. "Do you like being hurt? Is that it? Is that why you insist on being with me?"

I shook my head, even as his fingers jammed toward the back of my throat.

All I could do was moan around his fingers, trying desperately to run my tongue around them as I struggled not to gag. But Leo was relentless. Even though his fingers were jammed down my throat, his tail continued to thrust in and out, going further than I thought possible and stretching me out with each push.

"I can feel you pulsing around me, little one. Are you getting off on just my tail?" I couldn't answer, so he took his fingers out, a string of drool following them as they left my mouth.

"I want you," I sputtered, swallowing back my own spit. "Oh fuck," I moaned as his tail pulled out of me, leaving me aching and empty.

"Then get on all fours. Now."

That tone meant there was no room for argument. The second I was on the bed, I heard him taking off his clothes, but before I had a chance to enjoy the sight of his naked body, Leo's hand shoved my head down into the pillow while his other rubbed my thighs.

"You like it when I'm mean to you?" His tail smacked the flesh of my ass. "I asked you a question."

"You're not mean," I mumbled into the pillow. "You're not."

Another smack. My ass had to be bright red from the spanking, no doubt turning an even brighter shade with each smack of his tail against my sensitive skin.

"But I am. I'm a demon. I'm going to be the king of the demons."

And another. I jolted forward from the sting.

He flipped me over, climbing on top of me and shoving my knees up toward my elbows.

Body trembling, tears wetting my cheeks, I wrapped my arms around Leo's neck as he sank into me.

"This little fairy pussy belongs to me, doesn't it?" he groaned, thrusting all the way in, going deeper than it seemed possible.

"To you. Yes, to you. Only to you."

"Fuck. I love you," he moaned, burying his head in my neck as his thrusts became more and more wild by the second. "I love you, I love you, I love you." The words were like a chant, the phrase building in volume with the brutal pace of his thrusts.

Finally, he came with a deep groan, collapsing on top of me, our sweat slick between us. Not wanting it to end, I clenched around him, keeping him inside me, even if it only meant that he was there for a moment longer.

"I love you too," I sobbed into his neck, pulling him as close as I could. "So much."

I'm not sure how long we stayed like that, the two of us clutching each other. Later, after we both showered and slipped back into bed, he held me close, closer than he ever had before, as if he wanted every part of our bodies to be touching for as long as possible. I did too, and I let him press me against him.

His hand played with my wrist, rubbing the spot where there was normally a suppression bracelet. He was gentle and loving, softly caressing the skin where the bracelet typically rubbed.

"I am so sorry, Vera," he whispered in the dark.

"For what?"

"For everything. For everything I've put you through."

"If it means being with you, it's worth it."

Beside me, he sighed. "I wish that were true."

"It is," I insisted. "That's what loving someone means. I love you, Leo. I love you more than I've ever loved anyone or anything."

He squeezed me against him. "And I love you. Vera, everything I do, I do to create a better world for you. I hope that one day you understand."

"Of course I understand," I said as he reached over me to the table beside the bed. Then he leaned back, taking my wrist in his hand once again. Gently, he snapped a suppression bracelet around my wrist.

"What is this?" I asked, but my words were muffled as his lips met mine. I pushed him back, wanting this to make sense. "Why do you want me to wear this? I thought I didn't need these around you anymore?"

Even though the room was dark, I could feel him tense next to me.

"Leo?"

This bracelet was different. It was like the one I'd worn the day I'd almost collapsed. Why did Leo have one of these? I felt my eyelids start to droop. I knew I was tired, but this, this was something else. Why wasn't he saying anything?

"I don't feel right," I told him, trying to fight it, but I had to close my eyes to stop the room from spinning. What was happening?

"I'm so sorry, Vera," I heard Leo say again, but his voice sounded distant.

And then everything went black.

26

LEO

Would Vera ever forgive me?

Did I deserve her forgiveness?

Watching her sleeping form on my bed, I already knew the answer to that. All I could hope was that one day she'd understand; one day after she had put some distance between the two of us, she'd understand I had to make her leave to save her life.

I threw a cloak over my head, a long black one that would hide my hair and wings, hopefully making me unrecognizable in the event that we were caught. After getting her dressed as well, I scooped up Vera in my arms and walked her quietly through the dark apartment. No one else was awake, and the only sounds were my shoes on the floor. A small part of me secretly hoped we would be seen; then I'd have an excuse to go back to our room and pretend like this night never happened.

I kept an eye out for anyone who might spot us while memorizing the feeling of her in my arms, the soft sounds of her breathing, the smell of her hair inches from my head. Forcing myself to take each step, I trudged down the hall and up the back stairs.

On the roof, the two fae were waiting for me like they said they'd be. The girl had a bag on her back, a bag I recognized as Vera's. This was it. I knew I had to hand her over to them, but all I could do was grip her tighter. She stirred slightly in her sleep, nuzzling her head against my chest, and I wondered if I would be able to give her to them.

"I wasn't sure you would really do it." Laurie flew toward me, landing a few feet away. "I didn't know if you'd be able to let her go." He walked closer, arms outstretched, but I turned away sharply. Like hell I was going to hand her to him.

"You're going straight there," I demanded. "No detours. Stop for no one."

"We know what we're doing, Your Highness. Give her here."

The murderous look in my eyes must have made him take a step back.

The fae girl flew over to me then and held out her arms, indicating for me to pass Vera to her instead. "I packed all her things," she said, gesturing to the bag on her back. "It should only take us a couple of days to get home." When I didn't move, unwilling to let go of Vera, the girl smiled sadly. "We'll take good care of her."

It felt like an invisible chain had been anchored to my heart, and when the fae girl took her from me, the entire organ was tugged out of my body, leaving my chest hollow and cold.

That was it. The two took off, and from where I stood on the roof, I watched their blue wings fly away into the darkness.

Until one of them started to fall.

Son of a bitch.

Immediately I flew into the air, stopping short of the edge of the roof. The blue bastard lay on a lower roof, arrows protruding from his body and wings bent at all angles.

What the fuck had just happened?

My eyes darted around the skyline, trying to find the source. There. A pair of demons, crossbows in hand, standing on a lower balcony of the building across the street. They searched the sky, then ducked inside the building. From where they had been standing, it was unlikely they could have seen where Laurie had fallen, but they might be able to figure it out and could be on their way to get him right now.

Someone knew. Someone had known these fae were trying to escape, which meant those arrows were likely suppression arrows, and as long as they were stuck in that fae bastard, he wouldn't be able to fly. Worst-case scenario, they were also poisoned, and he would never get up at all.

I was confident the girls would get away without him, and if he managed to live until morning undetected, I could try to find him then.

So why was the fae girl not flying away?

She was frozen, with Vera in her arms, three roofs away. The building they were on was taller than the one where Laurie had fallen, so they were dangerously exposed. I needed to get them moving regardless of what happened to the fae, and that meant I needed to get him out of there.

"Damn it!" I yelled at no one, at everyone, at the whole situation as I flew down to the fallen fae. "If this asshole is dead, I swear to all the gods I'm going to kill him."

"Laurie!" the girl called out. When I looked up, the fae girl was standing on the edge of the roof a few feet away from me.

My heart lurched at the sight of Vera, slumped over in the fae girl's arms, her eyes closed as she slept. But no, as much as my entire body told me to go to her, I'd already said goodbye, and I wasn't sure if I would survive it a second time.

"What the hell are you waiting for? Go!" I shouted at her. "Now!"

But the damned girl didn't move. She was waiting for her brother, but where he'd fallen was hidden, and she couldn't see him lying on the roof. If she flew back to him, she'd risk being seen.

Cursing under my breath, I knelt beside where his body lay unmoving on the concrete, multiple arrows stuck in his wing and torso. My stomach turned as my mind flashed back to Vera months ago, bleeding in my arms. She had had more stab wounds, but his injuries were just as severe.

The fae was still breathing at least, even if the breaths were shallow. Luck was on his side it seemed; if the arrows had been poisoned, he would already be dead. Still, as long as the arrows stayed inside him, he would be unable to fly. If he didn't fly, someone would find him eventually. Whether he would have any blood left by that point was hard to tell.

Seconds ticked away, and I considered letting him die.

I could.

Vera would be able to get away with the help of just the fairy girl. I'd seen that girl fight in the arena; I knew she could hold her own, and Vera was strong too.

I wasn't confident I could heal him anyway. Were those fae parts of me gone forever? I hadn't tried to link with anyone since the day I was injected with the serum. But if I let him die, Vera would be furious, and like hell I was going to be responsible for making her cry any more than she was already going to.

"Stupid." I yanked an arrow out from his wing. "Fucking." Another from his shoulder, tossing it behind me. "Fairy." I wrenched the final arrow from his abdomen, his body flinching and eyelids fluttering.

I reached into my pocket, pulling out the small, gold ring. Concentrating, I felt some of that spark—it was small but there, nonetheless.

Here goes nothing.

I pressed down on the wound on his stomach, fae blood soaking my hands. Thanks to Teddy's instructions, I had plenty of practice absorbing Vera's magic without letting it send me into a frenzy, but this was different. Vera's power felt like electricity coursing through my veins, like an addictive high that made every hair on my body stand on end, every inch of my skin sensitive, like an inferno was burning inside me, a blaze threatening to jump out and consume the world.

Being with Vera every day, touching her, touching every part of her, I'd learned how to burn *with* her flame without letting it completely devour me, but his blood wasn't like that at all. That fire was still there, but it wasn't a blaze. Was that because he was almost dead? Or was his natural magic less than hers? Or was it because the serum had destroyed parts of me that reacted to fae magic?

I didn't have time to think about it as I closed my eyes and poured everything into linking with him, visualizing the magic coming from the ring, flowing through me and into him. This bastard was going to live whether he wanted to or not.

I took a deep breath, drawing in as much power as I could before exhaling, letting it flow into this stupid fae who couldn't even escape properly.

When I opened my eyes, fae blood was splattered all over my clothes and hands, but the wound on his shoulder and wing had closed, and blood had stopped oozing out of the wound on his stomach. It would have to be enough. Sitting back, my hands sparkling from the link, I was thankful for the cloak that would hide most of me in case anyone saw me before it wore off.

The fae's eyes were wide open, staring back at me in shock.

"'Bout damn time you woke up," I muttered.

"My wing..." His voice trailed off as he tried to sit up, his body shaking as he looked at the mostly healed spots where he'd been hit.

I was surprised it had worked so well. I could still feel the warmth of the ring on my hand.

"It'll still work. Get the hell up and get out of here before you have a hundred more demons after you."

"But they shot me. And you—"

As I watched his eyes rake over me, I knew what he was thinking. I knew he saw the way my skin was changing, my face undoubtedly taking on that slight sparkle that comes from linking. I knew he was about to ask how I'd healed him, but there was no way in hell we were going to have that conversation right then.

"Get up. If you don't get the fuck out of here right now, I'm going to rip off those ugly blue wings and throw you off this roof."

The stupid bastard didn't move. "I don't understand. You're *fae*? But you're a demon. How is this possible? Why...? And Vera, does she know?"

"Worry about that later when you aren't about to be murdered.

There are two demons with bows down there." I pointed to the building across the street. "I saw them go back in the building, but if you can stay low and try to stay between buildings, you should be able to stay off their radar."

"The others," he said, voice shaking as he struggled to get to his feet. "If guards have been tipped off, they're all in danger, we have to—"

Instead of standing, he stumbled, and I had to catch him, wrapping my arm around his shoulder to keep him upright. "Listen to me right now," I insisted. "The only thing you have to do is get Vera the hell away from here. Do you understand me?"

The fae finally seemed to understand, because when I took my arm away, he took a few unsteady steps before giving his wings an experimental flutter. Seemingly satisfied, he was up, flying off the roof, gone. Or at least I thought he was until he landed on the edge of the railing, facing me.

"Why did you do this?" he called out, and even at this distance I could see his blue wings sparkling in the night sky. "Why did you help me?"

I met his stare, refusing to look away.

"Because you have a promise to keep."

After a moment's hesitation, the fae nodded once before he really was gone, the blue wings of the twins vanishing into the night sky, taking my entire heart with them.

27

VERA

The fresh scent of dewy grass and damp dirt. A cool breeze gliding across my face. A bird chirping somewhere in the distance. The natural sounds and smells were all so lovely, like a perfect dream after the noise and chaos of Vestia.

But this wasn't a dream.

I sat straight up, then immediately clutched my head, a dizzy feeling taking over like all my energy had been drained away. Slowly, I opened my eyes, becoming more and more aware of my surroundings by the second.

Grass.

Dirt.

Birds.

A field. I was in a field.

I wasn't wearing any suppression tech, and this field certainly wasn't in Vestia.

What. The. Fuck?

The last thing I remembered was being in my room with Leo. Now I was here, wherever the hell here was. I felt my pockets and didn't find my phone anywhere. And my clothes... The last thing I remember was wearing a T-shirt and shorts because I was headed to bed, but now I had on a tank top and pants paired with low boots.

Someone had dressed me.

Leo. I needed to call him. I needed to let him know I was okay.

"You're awake," said a familiar voice. "How do you feel?" And then Laurie was there, crouching in the grass in front of me. Lips parted slightly like he was about to say something, his blue eyes searched mine.

"What's going on?"

He reached for me, but I jerked away from him.

"Are you feeling any side effects?" He said. "We could link—"

"Where are we? Why are we here? And where is my phone?"

Laurie sighed and sat down in the grass. "Mia!" he shouted over my head.

"Are you okay?" she called out to her brother, flying over to us. "Are the spots bothering you or— Oh." She landed with a thud when she saw me awake.

So they were both with me, but it seemed like no one else was there. Did Leo know I was with them? They weren't wearing suppression devices either, so did that mean they had escaped?

"We can explain everything," Laurie said.

"Good. Start now."

"I know this is probably very confusing," Mia said.

"You're damn right it is."

"But everything is going to be okay."

"It will be when I tell Leo where I am. Where is my phone?"

Laurie cleared his throat. "Leo knows where you are."

I blinked. "What? How?"

"He gave you to us," Mia said, leaning forward to take one of my hands in hers. "To take you home."

"Gave me to you?" I yanked my hand away and wrinkled my nose in disgust at those words. "And what home? His home? I don't understand."

"No," Laurie said, drawing the word out as he exchanged a glance with Mia that made my stomach churn. "Our home. Rowan. We're taking you to home to be with other fae."

A tingle started in my fingers, just the smallest vibration, but then it moved up my arms until the anxiety spread all over me, my whole body shaking with rage, with fear, with confusion.

"How...?" I didn't know what to say or what to ask. I had so many questions, but none of them seemed right, none of them made sense at all, just like everything Laurie and Mia had told me.

Laurie reached into his pocket, taking out several pieces of metal. A bracelet. Suppression tech. "Leo modified this to do slightly more than suppress."

"Holy shit. He put that on me last night. It knocked me out."

"I'm not completely sure how it worked, and thankfully it won't work ever again," he said, holding up the pieces, "but it seems it like it suppressed not only your magic but also your basic energy. You fell asleep, and then he—"

"He gave me away like... like I was a slave," I said, not attempting to hide the bitterness and anger in my voice.

"Would you have ever left if he hadn't?"

"No! I wouldn't have left him at all. I need to go back," I said, standing up, but Mia grabbed my hand again to stop me.

"We're about half a day away from the palace on the edge of Vestia, and we should be close to Rowan by tomorrow night. We aren't going back, Vera," she said. "We can't go back."

"So that's it then? I'm kidnapped by the two of you?"

"Please don't think of it like that."

"Can I at least call him to let him know I'm okay?"

"We don't have phones," she admitted. "They don't work in Rowan anyway. The intensity of fae magic in Rowan prevents most technology from working inside the veil covering the city."

"This is bullshit. I can't believe you agreed to this. I trusted you. I thought you were my friends, not my kidnappers."

"Vera." Laurie's face was serious. "I'm going to be very blunt. There was no way for you to remain in Vestia."

"What? That's not true, I—"

"Let me finish, okay? You know you were being used as a pawn, as a way to get to him, and there are demons there who would like nothing more than to see you hurt or dead. Am I right?"

"Yes," I said reluctantly.

"If you went back home to Leo's estate, you would still be at risk."

"I know."

"Sending you with us was the only way to keep you safe. Only fae can enter Rowan, which means you will be away from the plots of the Vestian court, and one day, I hope, you'll be happy."

I would be happy if I was with Leo.

Turning away from them so they wouldn't see I was barely holding back tears, I closed my eyes, forcing myself to speak calmly when all I felt like doing was raging. "I need time to process everything you just told me."

"That is completely understandable," Laurie said.

"Time *alone*."

"Oh."

When I could no longer hear the sound of their wings, I sat down again, gripping some grass in my hands in the hopes it would ground me. I was so mad at Leo. So incredibly mad. But was he the only one to blame? It had been my decision to come to the demon kingdom, knowing full well I would be hated and misunderstood by everyone who knew Leo.

He was a prince. The demon prince. The future king.

But me? I was no one.

Of course he had responsibilities that came with his role, and some part of me had known he wouldn't be able to escape them if he came back to Vestia no matter how much he wanted to. I'm sure that was why he had avoided the demon kingdom all this time. But now that he was back home, *of course* the other demons would expect things of him.

Things like becoming the next king.

Like marriage to a demon noble.

My heart clenching, tears streamed down my face even faster at the idea of Leo getting married one day. Once he became king, Leo would marry Elise. I was sure of it. They'd probably get married in a big, gorgeous wedding and have gorgeous demon babies with gorgeous blond hair and soft demon wings. But he'd be king, and once he was king, all the fae in the demon kingdom would be freed. The changes Leo would make in Vestia were amazing and wonderful. If he left Vestia, and some other member of his family became king instead, there was no way his dream, our dream, would ever be fulfilled.

So why was I so fucking sad?

Was I really that selfish? Would I really choose the two of us being together over the freedom of every fae in the demon kingdom?

I was scared of my answer.

"I hate him," I sobbed into my hands.

I felt a hand smooth down my hair, and when I opened my eyes, it was Laurie, holding the long brown strands of my hair in his fingers. He dropped them when he saw me looking and sighed. Burying my face in my hands, I couldn't look at his blue eyes for another second, knowing they were filled with pity as he watched me cry. I didn't want his pity or anyone's pity.

"No, you don't," he said.

"Yes, I do! I hate him. I hate him so much. How, Laurie? How could he flat out lie about his feelings when he knows we are better together than apart? Please make this make sense, because right now I want to hit him in his stupid handsome face."

"As much as it pains me to say this, Vera, he sent you away because he loves you."

"Ha." I choked out a dry sob that came out more as a gasp for air. "Then he should have had the courage to tell me instead of being a coward. He didn't... I didn't..." I couldn't finish the sentence as sobs racked my body, and I buried my face in my hands again. "I didn't even get to say goodbye."

"If it makes you feel any better, he snarled at me like a feral wolf when I tried to take you from his arms."

I huffed out a laugh behind my tears. "Sounds about right. You must think I'm pretty pathetic, crying over a guy you hate, huh?"

"I don't hate him. Okay," he said when he saw me give him a suspicious look. "I strongly dislike him." Laurie's face suddenly turned serious, and he stared down at his shoulder and touched a place on his stomach. "Or at least I used to."

"I love him. I still love him even after this. I hate that I love him. Why did he do this to me?"

Laurie lay back in the grass beside me. "We all do crazy things for the ones we love. I'm not defending how he went about it, but I do think he was thinking of what was best for you."

"What's best for me would have been to stay with him. He's such a fucking hypocrite. I'm sorry. I'm venting. You have no reason to sit here and listen to me cry about a demon who doesn't even want me around him."

"Just so you know, when he brought you to us, he was all *grrrr*." Mia made a mean face to imitate Leo. "And I was all *awwww*." She placed a hand over her heart, pretending to swoon. "I know it wasn't right how it all went down, but I saw the way he looked at you. I saw how hard it was for him to let you go."

"Couldn't have been too hard!" I shouted, letting out some of the anger and frustration I'd been feeling. "He gave me away like old clothes being passed on to the next person."

"Actually, I have an idea," Laurie chimed in.

"You do?"

"Yeah. Just hang on, okay?"

"Hang on to what— Oh!" I yelped as Laurie scooped me into his arms, flying straight up. Higher and higher we flew, and he hadn't been kidding about hanging on; we were going so fast I had to squeeze my arms around his neck. "What are we doing?"

"Scream!" he shouted over the wind rushing past us.

"Huh?"

"Let it out! Scream as loud as you want to!"

So I did. We soared into the sky, the wind rushing past my ears just as loudly as I screamed. It felt good to let out the anger and sadness and frustration, all of it vanishing into the wind. When I'd exhausted my lungs, my voice hoarse from yelling, we landed in silence. Tears now mostly dried, I sat down in the grass and hugged my knees to my chest.

"Feel better?" He watched me, studying my reaction.

"A little." Letting go of my knees, I flopped onto my back in the grass, watching the clouds roll by but not really watching anything, my mind still swimming with the mixture of sadness and anger that made my entire body feel tense and shaken.

Laurie sat down a few feet away. "Is it all right if I just lie here in the grass near you? I won't say a word unless you want me to. Sometimes you just need a friend to sit beside you."

At that moment, I didn't have the emotional strength to care whether Laurie was near me in the grass or across the universe. The only thing I knew and felt was the deep, deep ache in my chest from the pain of losing Leo, of being forced to lose him, of him sending me away. With a shiver, my tears returned, even as I desperately wanted them to stop. It was like my body wouldn't let me stop grieving the loss.

True to his word, Laurie lay down in silence, folding his arms behind his head and staring at the sky.

"I know I said I wasn't going to talk," he said a few seconds later, "but it's killing me to listen to you cry."

"I'm okay." I sniffed. As much as I would have welcomed comfort, something about the idea of him hugging me made the tears flow even harder.

"You're not okay."

"You're right," I admitted.

"Do you need a hug?"

"No." I shook my head. "I mean yes, but no. That doesn't feel right. It wouldn't be fair to you."

He didn't say anything for a long moment, both of us sitting in silence. Until finally he said, "Stay there."

He got up and walked away but then a few seconds later sat down on the log next to me. He wrapped an arm around my shoulders, but something was off. The hand gripping my shoulder was too small, the arm too light.

It wasn't Laurie.

"Mia?" I opened my eyes to see her bright blue eyes smiling sadly at me. Behind her I could see Laurie, down by the lake where Mia had been a few minutes earlier.

"Hope this is okay. Laurie said you needed a hug."

Choking on my own breath, I felt all the tears I'd been trying to hold back flood my eyes. He had been right. I did need a hug. I didn't even try to fight Mia as she pulled me to her, enveloping me in her arms as my head fell against her shoulder.

And I cried.

FINALLY, it was time. Once we were over the river, we'd no longer be within the boundaries of Vestia. In no time, the skyscrapers and cars and heat of the city would be far behind us.

"It's amazing how different things are just on the other side." Laurie gestured to the far side of the river. Even from where we stood, I knew he was right. It looked like a different planet on the other bank. We'd been traveling through fields and low grasses, but the other side of the river was all lush forest, dense and deep. Tall trees swayed in the wind, and yellow light from the sun filtered through their branches to highlight green leaves rustling against each other and falling to the ground.

"It's not all bad over here though," Mia said, pointing to the water's edge on the side where we stood. "Looks like some parts of nature are making do."

My eyes followed her finger, landing on the yellow flowers that grew in little clumps right along the water's edge. When I saw them, I closed my eyes.

Of course.

I turned back to Mia and Laurie. "Can I have a minute before we go?"

"Sure," Mia nodded. Then she nudged her brother.

"Of course," Laurie said. "Take as much time as you need."

The two siblings exchanged a look, but I didn't stay to see more. I needed to do something before I left the demon kingdom for good. After walking down to the water, I crouched at the edge. Daffodils, delicate and yellow, grew all along the bank.

"You've done well, little guys. Sorry for doing this." I picked two from the dirt and held their stems in my hands. This was it. This was the moment when I would leave all Vestia behind. The city and the noise I was grateful to leave behind, but the rest?

A piece of my heart would always live in the demon kingdom.

With that piece gone, would I ever feel whole again?

Leo was going to be king here. He'd marry Elise and hopefully use his power to free all the fae in Vestia. I clenched my eyes shut, trying to block out the images of the two of them together.

Was he with her right now? Or was he thinking about me like I was thinking about him? Would we run into each other one day? When fae were all free, when the world wasn't in chaos? Would we see each other and talk like friends? Or would we avoid the awkward small talk altogether and remember how well we fit together? Or would that only bring both of us more pain?

Did we fit together, though? Or were we two puzzle pieces that were never meant to connect, and no matter how much we tried to force it, we'd never line up?

Recognizing that I'd never have the right answer, I relaxed my hand, only then realizing how hard I'd been gripping the delicate daffodil stems. Gently, I tossed the flowers into the water, watching them as they briefly floated before they sank below the surface, never to be seen again.

"Goodbye," I whispered into the wind.

I'm not sure how much time passed while I stood there at the edge. The flowers were long gone, most likely at the bottom of the river, their delicate petals destroyed by the water. When I finally turned around, Mia and Laurie were watching me from the top of the hill, their beautiful blue wings sparkling in the sunlight.

When my eyes met Laurie's, it seemed like he finally understood. With his help and Mia's, maybe I could put it all behind me. I could go to the capital. Maybe I could start over. Maybe one day this pain wouldn't feel like it was about to swallow me whole.

"I'm ready," I told them when I made it up to the top of the hill. "Laurie, would you carry me? So we can go faster. I don't want to slow us down."

His blue eyes lit up, all pity and sadness gone in an instant.

"It would be an honor."

28

LEO

"Why did you want to meet me here in my new lab?"

While I waited on Zell to answer me, I picked up a couple of the bottles off the lab table, turning them over in my hands. I knew the names, potions that we'd been forbidden to touch as kids.

"It's only yours once you're officially crowned."

"Which will be soon. Remember when we were little," I asked him, "and we would sneak down to this lab when our parents weren't paying attention? Rand too."

"Yeah, he was never far behind," Zell agreed. "I see he's still following your every footstep. Does he spend more time getting you out of trouble or getting you into it?"

"Like you can talk. I was grounded for a month when you gave the night guard a sleeping potion so you could sneak out with his daughter."

Zell smirked. "Oh yeah. I did do that, didn't I?"

"And then you blamed it on me."

"You were down here more than me anyway. It was more believable."

"Not *that* believable since you got caught."

"You probably ratted me out."

"I didn't," I told him. "But I know who did."

"Oh yeah? It had to have been you."

"It wasn't. Elise must have been tired of us ignoring her because she's the one who told the guards that you were gone."

For a second Zell's expression faltered, his brow furrowed, but then the grin was back. "Whatever. I should have known better than to blame you. It's not like the golden child could ever do anything wrong."

"That's not fucking true, and you know it. If anything, you were the one who always got away with everything."

"I got away with everything because all eyes were on the little prince."

"Only the eyes of my father's guards."

"Aw," Zell mocked me. "Did the poor little prince not get enough attention? How awful for you. Your life of luxury must have been so hard."

"Don't talk to me about hardship. You said fuck the rules and did whatever you wanted with whomever you wanted whenever you wanted."

"While you were praised simply because you are the crowned prince," Zell said. "Everyone kissed your ass from sunrise to sunset, so forgive me if I don't feel bad for you."

"I wasn't asking you to feel bad for me."

"Good, because I don't. You left for years, and the old bastard still welcomed you home with open arms. Everyone still fawns over you."

"Is that what this is about?" I asked. "You're jealous of me?"

"Like I'd be jealous of some spoiled loser who comes crying back to Daddy when things don't go his way. If anything, you're jealous of me."

"As if I'd ever be jealous of a demon who pretends to be the kingdom's bad boy to get attention but is really just an insecure womanizer."

"Not all of us have cute little fairy fuck toys of our own, Leo."

"You bastard." I reared my fist back but froze when I heard a muffled noise in the back of the lab. "What the hell was that?"

A smile broke out on Zell's face. "I was wondering when you'd notice. That's why I asked you to meet me here. I figured you needed to be cheered up, so I found a gift for you."

I was already moving toward the noise. "I don't want anything from you. What is it?"

In the back of the lab was an alcove hidden behind a wall, a small room filled with a row of patient chairs, designed for taking blood. In one chair was one of the last humans I ever wanted to see.

Instantly, I spread my wings as far out as possible, my blood boiling with rage. "You."

There, tied to the chair, was the same human who had attacked Vera all those weeks ago. The human she'd thought was her friend but was really just the king's pawn. Henry's eyes were wide open as he squirmed in his seat, mumbling something behind the tape covering his mouth. I remembered the maniacal way he'd looked when he stabbed Vera, the insane glee he'd had while hurting her.

"I told you that if I saw you again, I'd murder you."

I moved to choke him with both my hands, but Zell got in front of me. "Murder him later, okay?" Turning to Henry, Zell ripped off the tape over his mouth, and the human gasped for air. "Or not. I don't really care. What I do care about is what this pathetic excuse for a human has created. Go on. Tell his royal highness what you made."

"I don't want to hear anything he has to say." I punched Henry in the face. His head jerked to the side, eyes closed, completely unconscious.

"Well. All right then." Zell rolled his eyes, digging into his pocket. "I'll tell you myself." He held out a vial in front of him, and reluctantly I took it. The color of the powder was slightly more purple than the pink of most Dust, but otherwise it seemed like regular Dust.

"Looks like Dust," I said, popping the top on the vial.

"No shit, genius. Open it, smell it— Wait. Don't—" At his words, I stopped before touching any of it. "Don't use it, moron. You don't even know what it is."

"It's not Dust?"

Zell snatched the vial from me. "It is and it isn't. Since our dear friend here can't talk anymore, let me skip to the good part. This vial contains regular Dust with an undetectable amount of a special poison developed by this slimy little weasel of a human."

"That explains the color difference... Wait. Poison? What the fuck, Zell? Why didn't you tell me that in the first place?"

He shrugged. "Then there'd be one less prince in the palace? That would have been your fault, really, for being an idiot who would take something when you didn't know what it was." Before I could tell him who the real idiot was, Zell continued. "And you don't use Dust anyway, right?"

"True. I don't."

"Didn't think so. You have morals or something. Anyway, touching it won't actually do anything to you more than regular Dust does. You'd have to ingest it. Snort it, eat it, something like that. I haven't even told you the best part. This particular poison is completely untraceable. No scent. No taste. No resonance in the body or blood. No matter what types of tests they run after you die, it won't show up."

"How do you know?"

Zell's lips turned up in a sickly grin. "Do you really want the answer to that?"

"On second thought, no. No, I don't."

"I didn't think his highness would want to dirty his own hands right away, but I could show you right now if you really want to see," Zell said, nodding in the unconscious human's direction.

The human's mere presence was making me want to force him to take the poison myself. "No. He doesn't deserve to die in his sleep."

"That's the spirit. I could use him as a test subject for a few other projects anyway."

"Why are you showing me this? How does giving me a poison benefit you?"

"You really have been out of the game too long, Leo. You have a meeting with the Ignitors soon, don't you?"

"You know I do."

"All I'm saying is you'll never have what you want as long as those old bastards are still lurking around. The general could probably be persuaded, but the other two? Never. They end every meeting by taking Dust. I'm sure they'd be happy to taste test your new version. It would be a shame if it wasn't Syn at all. I'll let you use your imagination for the rest."

I didn't have to imagine much. He was suggesting that I kill the Ignitors of the Flame, the king's chief advisors.

The bastards who had murdered my mother.

"I see." I took the vial, holding it up to get a better look. "Why give me this information?"

"Because you obviously can't do anything on your own. And..." Zell mumbled something I couldn't hear.

"What was that?" I asked him.

"I *said* Elise spent the night last night. So thanks or whatever." He clapped me on the back as he walked past me out of the lab. "Now go get some revenge."

Aside from the king himself, the Ignitors were the most feared demons in Vestia. These three demons, named the Ignitors of the Flame for their role in tending to the kingdom's metaphorical flame of knowledge and progress, met with my father regularly and would be my first obstacle to any true and lasting change. If I wanted to protect Vera and create a kingdom where she could one day be safe, I had to start here.

The three demons of the council sat at a long table, their scowling faces watching me with interest, no doubt wondering why we were meeting.

Good. Let them wonder.

In the chair closest to me was Ignitor Veller, Master of Commerce, a salesman at heart, his words always oozed a revolting mix of sweetness and slime. He'd made the kingdom a lot of money through the exporting of Dust and the gods only knew what other methods, and I knew he saw me as a threat to the entire Dust industry. I imagined Elise in his seat instead; she would handle his role with ease and more skill than Veller could ever have.

Beside him sat Ignitor Cassum, Master of Research and Development. Cassum was old as dirt, his droopy eyes damaged from years of staring into microscopes as he worked in my father's labs. He was Veller's opposite in every way; I'd probably heard Cassum say ten words my entire life. He ruled the labs with his glare alone. Zell already knew most of his work, and with his popularity, he would do a better job managing the creative and collaborative aspects of research.

And finally Ignitor Balthazar, or as I knew him, *General* Balthazar, retired General of Vestia, sat directly to my right, his stoic gaze just as unsettling now as it was when I was a child training under him. He'd left the military when the Blood War ended, only coming out of retirement when my father asked him to be on the council. A gnarly, jagged slash ran down his left cheek; the scar, now purple and wrinkled, had terrified me as a young demon, and it was no less intimidating now.

He was also Rand's father.

He'd never had a slave, never touched Dust, never touched a drop of alcohol either. Aloof where Rand was charming, silent where Rand was gregarious, cruel where Rand was empathetic, the two were like oil and water. I don't think the general was surprised when Rand chose to move with me away from Vestia. He might have even been relieved to no longer have to fend off questions from the press about his son's latest escapades. It seemed like Zell had stepped into Rand's old role as the resident royal celebrity anyway.

As the Ignitors waited for me to speak, smug in their seats around a long table with me at the end, I imagined they must have discussed my mother at this same table before her death. No one kept secrets from the Ignitors; the general hadn't been part of the council at the time, but I had no doubt Veller and Cassum knew who she was to my father.

Did the two of them encourage my father to murder her?

Was it their idea?

Had she been discussed like a piece of property at this very table?

Had Vera been discussed in the same way?

No matter what, I knew they had known what was happening and hadn't stopped it.

"Gentlemen," I said, standing up at the end of the table. "We have much to discuss."

"Indeed, we do." Ignitor Veller chuckled. "It seems the king has taken a much needed vacation since the announcement."

No one had seen the king since that night. I wasn't sure what he was planning, but it couldn't be good. Regardless, I planned on taking advantage of his absence.

"While he's gone, I am in charge."

"Of course! I have to admit that we heard news of your... indiscretion with a slave. Believe me, my boy, we've all been there. They're wicked little things."

"We certainly have not all been there," General Balthazar's deep voice interjected, his gaze intense and unforgiving. "Let's get to the point. Why have you summoned us? It was my understanding your coronation was set for a few weeks from now. Until then, I don't see why we need to meet."

"I wanted to get a head start. With the king on... vacation... I am speaking with his voice. But I understand you are all very busy, so I won't keep you long. We are all in agreement that we want Vestia to be a beacon of progress and innovation, yes?"

The three nodded.

"Vestia is seen the world over as the premier place for advancement in technology and science. I have a plan to honor that great legacy and push the kingdom as a whole forward into a new era."

"This sounds wonderful, Your Highness," Veller said, clapping his hands in front of him. "We cannot wait to hear your ideas. Do you have a new invention to show us?"

I thought of the poison Zell had given me earlier. If the Ignitors didn't agree to this proposal, then yes. Yes, I did.

"We cannot move forward until we begin to right the wrongs of the past. I want to give you a preview of what is to come for Vestia. Your screens, please." I nodded toward the small holo-screen in front of each of them, the text of my decrees appearing in front of them.

"The first new decree is that slavery will be outlawed."

"What?" Veller turned off his screen. "You can't possibly expect us to—"

"It's not a question of expecting. It's what will be."

"How?" All politeness vanishing, Veller's voice was now full of exasperation and disbelief. "What are you planning to do, Leo?"

"I'm doing what my father should have done a long time ago."

"You're not the king yet, Your Highness," he said, rising from his seat. "It would do you well to—"

"It would do you well to stop there." The room was suddenly silent at the tone of my voice. "You heard my father at the ceremony. I'm the next king, and if you think for a second that the old demon won't back me up, you're wrong."

"I don't understand," Veller said. "Your Syn may eliminate our desire for Dust, Leo, but some of us enjoy our slaves for *other* purposes."

I glared at him; the implications of his words not lost on me at all. He was notorious for the harem of fae slaves he kept at his mansion. "I am well aware."

"And the last thing Vestia needs is civil war." Balthazar spoke up, his face giving away no emotion. "Once their magic is no longer suppressed, freed slaves will seek retribution against their former owners, and soon there will be blood in the streets. This kingdom needs peace. How will you keep the peace while also freeing the slaves?"

"I'll give the fae the chance to return to their homes, if they can, or set up temporary residences for those who wish to stay here, although I doubt any will. While we can never right the wrongs committed against the fae, we can end slavery now. I also hope to rely on the good counsel of demons much wiser than myself moving forward. Can I count on you, General?"

Balthazar stared at me for a long time, the room silent. Finally, seemingly satisfied with my answer, he nodded.

"We could use any remaining fae to make new Hellfire stones."

My head snapped to Ignitor Cassum, his words bringing to mind the sensation of the voices from the crown, the pain.

I slammed my fist down on the table. "I will destroy those stones."

Cassum's tired eyes didn't blink. "The work. The time it took with those fae insects. You would destroy it all?"

I felt my hand gripping my chair. "I'll destroy anything reminiscent of fae slavery, especially those stones. Starting with those stones."

"I'm sorry, Your Highness, but this simply cannot be. Perhaps one day this could be discussed, but the ramifications are too great at this time. Surely you understand that." Veller smiled that fake smile once again.

As I had expected, they hadn't agreed. While I had hoped that they would, ultimately, it didn't matter if they agreed with me to free the slaves or not. It was time for plan B.

Veller was still prattling on. "We know you wish an end to slavery for the sake of your little fae indiscretion, Your Highness. They are little temptresses. Trust me, I know. Your father tried something similar in his youth."

Without even knowing it, my hand had strayed to the ring in my pocket, slipping it on.

Cassum tapped his finger on the table as if all this talk bored him. "We put an end to that."

"That's why we're here, Your Highness, to be your council and make sure you don't fall into a similar trap. It would be a shame if your slave met a similar end."

I swallowed back the bile coming up my throat. If I'd had any doubts about what I was about to do, they were all gone now.

"I move that we end this meeting," the general said.

"Seconded," Cassum grunted from his seat.

"Great. Now did you bring us any of that new Dust of yours to try?" Veller clapped his hands, eagerly watching the two silver boxes in front of me. "I hear only good things about it, which is no surprise since it was developed by you, of course."

"Of course," I said, forcing myself to return his smug smile. Veller and Cassum each took one of the silver boxes while the general refrained, as I knew he would. When I'd spoken with him earlier in the day, he'd listened to my proposal but had correctly predicted the outcome of this meeting. He wouldn't stop me, but he wouldn't help either.

"It's such a small amount," Veller pouted when he opened it up.

"Small," I agreed, "but potent."

"We'll see about that. If this is more powerful than the Dust made here in the Crown's lab, as they say, should we use all of it?" Cassum asked as he eyed the contents. He shook the box in his hand and smelled it.

Odorless and tasteless, Zell had said.

"Yes," I told them. "It's best used all in one dose."

I watched as Veller and Cassum tipped the silver boxes to their mouths, downing all the contents in a single gulp.

It was done.

An overdose, they would say later. Tainted Dust. Dust they'd received from the king's own stash. How could any Dust be trusted after such an incident? I hoped it wouldn't be. If demons wanted to make sure to avoid any possibility of poison laced Dust, their only option now was Syn.

As he walked out, leaving the bodies of the former Ignitors behind him, General Balthazar stopped at the doorway beside me. Jaw tense, he placed a hand on my shoulder, his large hand clamping down with the same chilling force I remembered as a child.

"You bring change, Your Highness," he said solemnly, his words deep and gruff. "Slavery is a scourge on our kingdom that must end. But when you bring this change, don't let it end in war."

With that, he released my shoulder, continuing out the door. Letting the door slam behind me, I kept walking without looking back.

Two threats to Vera had been eliminated, but the king remained.

This was only the beginning.

29

VERA

We arrived at Rowan at dawn.

We had alternated walking and flying until finally we made it to the top of a long, sloping hill. The hillside looked like any other, lush and green, with thick, tall grass we had to wade through as it swayed in the breeze.

As we stood there, Laurie reached out to me and to his sister. "Are you ready?" he asked. "We're here."

Swallowing back my anxiety, I put on a brave face. "I think so?"

This was it. Mia had explained the process of opening the gate to Rowan as we traveled. First, we would link, and then the Willow Gate would appear. Recognizing fae magic, the veil would sense the presence of fae and allow its gate to be seen. The gate would allow us access to Rowan; only when fae were linked together could the magical veil that protected the city be lifted. As a safeguard to prevent outside forces from manipulating a fae into accessing the city, it took more than one fae to open the gate.

"Better question, Laurie, is whether *you're* ready. Mom and dad are going to be pissed that we left."

"They'll be happy that we're back."

Mia looked doubtful. "Keep telling yourself that."

"Enough." Laurie steeled his face, looking off into the distance at what appeared to me like just more field and hillside. "Let's do this. Just follow our lead, Vera. Close your eyes."

Mia and Laurie bowed their heads, so I did the same.

"Of many leaves, one tree," they said in unison, and at first, I felt nothing. I was tempted to peek and see if anything was happening in front of us, but then slowly, starting with my fingers, I felt those familiar zaps of energy, tingling and tickling my wrist, up my arm, and then all over. Laurie squeezed my hand as the warmth of our combined magic spread out over my body as if we had been suddenly placed directly in the sun.

"Now look," Laurie said.

I gasped when I opened my eyes. In front of us, two golden trees slowly took form, their thick trunks materializing first, then growing up, up, up to an impossible height. As the name of the gate implied, they looked like willow trees but much, much larger, rising to the sky high over our heads and full of golden branches of equally golden leaves. The branches hung long, weighed down by the multitude of heavy gilded leaves. At first glance, the trees looked like they were made of actual gold, but as I stared, I realized the trees were alive. The leaves rustled in the breeze even as the massive tree trunks stayed firm.

Beside me, Laurie smiled and squeezed my hand again. "We're not done yet."

As I watched in awe, a gate took shape between the two trees. The two sides of the gate were bracketed by the trees, the doors meeting in the middle with a heavy lock. The gate itself was easily two stories tall, its color matching that of the trees, with vertical golden bars. Tiny delicate leaves on branches adorned the top of the gate, the branches dancing and twisting along the bars.

"That happened a lot faster than when we left," Laurie said, and when I looked over at him, his brow was knit in confusion as he stared at the gate.

"Maybe because there are three of us now?" Mia offered.

I didn't care how fast it had materialized. "It's beautiful," I whispered, mesmerized by the sight in front of me.

"Hell yeah, it is." Mia laughed beside me. "We told you those demons didn't know anything about art or beauty. This is only the beginning. I can't wait until you see the palace."

"We'll go there?" I asked her.

"Mia." Laurie said her name sharply, drawing our attention back to the gate. "Let's take this one step at a time."

"Sorry," she said. "Looks like it's time to unlock it. I don't see any guards on the other side though."

"Does that surprise you?" Laurie asked her. "It's not like anyone is going in or out. Now let's link again to open the lock and get on with it."

But I pulled away and walked toward the golden gate as if my feet were moving on their own. I was drawn in by the beautiful shining gold in front of me. It was as if I was being pulled forward, and I couldn't take my eyes off the massive lock that held the gates together.

"Vera, come back," Mia called after me. "We have to link in order to open it."

Even though I heard her, I couldn't help myself. As soon as I was close enough, I reached up, my hand barely able to graze the metal of the lock. Instantly, I felt a shock and yanked my hand back, checking to make sure my skin hadn't been burned. I was fine, and when I looked up, I saw that the lock had completely vanished. As I watched in awe, I heard the slow creak of the gates as they started to open.

Mia and Laurie were beside me. "That isn't supposed to happen," Mia said. "It's not supposed to open unless we're linked, but when you touched the lock, it went *poof*." She flung her hands apart to emphasize the word. "Laurie, what does this mean?"

"I don't know." He inspected my hand. "It seems Vera was able to open the gate without being linked with us." He laced his fingers through my own. "You're full of surprises, aren't you?"

I shook my head. "I just did what felt natural."

I didn't miss the look Mia and Laurie shared, but then it was time. Time to enter Rowan.

As we stepped through, it seemed like we had been transported into a completely different space. I took a deep breath, inhaling the air of Rowan. Although I'd only walked a few feet, everything felt clearer, a sense of peace washing over me.

The world behind us vanished, and there was no sign of the hill where we had just stood. Instead, a winding gravel road was laid out before us, and I could see forests in the distance. I expected to hear the gate clank shut behind us once we were through, but even it was gone, as if it had never existed.

Mia darted up into the air, spinning in glee before landing back on the road. "We're home!" she shouted. "I can't wait to show you everything, Vera!"

"I can't wait to see everything."

And see everything we did. Riding on Laurie's back so we could fly, the three of us took off, following the road. Tiny butterflies seemed to chase us as we passed small cottages and expansive farms, a river that had the clearest water I'd ever seen, and trees taller than any I could have imagined. We stopped flying at what looked like the outskirts of a village; if we continued following this road, it seemed like it would take us right through the center of town, but the road also forked off toward the river we'd seen.

"How many fae live here?" I asked, pointing to the village while we debated which way to go.

"In this village?" Mia asked. "I don't know, but probably not that many."

"What about in all of Rowan?"

Mia and Laurie exchanged a look. "Fewer than before the war," Mia offered.

"But if you had to guess, how many do you think?"

"Maybe... half a million?"

I froze where I was, unable to process what Mia had just said. "What?"

"I guess it could be closer to a quarter of a million?"

That number didn't make it any better.

"Quarter of a million fae," I said, unable to hide my shock. "And they don't leave here? How? With that many fae, with the amount of power that many fae have... How have that many fae stayed ignorant to what's happened to the rest of us outside that gate? Surely someone has been bringing information back to them."

"So about that..." Mia's voice trailed off as she looked to her brother for help.

"What?" I asked them. "What about that? What am I missing?"

"Vera," Laurie said softly, and I didn't at all like the way I could hear the pity in his voice. "They all know."

"Excuse me?"

"They know. They know what's going on in the rest of the world."

I shook my head, unable to believe that. "No. There's no way. Because if they knew... If they knew and just didn't *care*..."

"They think it is best to keep the gate closed and focus on our own people instead of getting involved in conflict with outsiders."

I heard what Laurie was saying, but I couldn't process it. It didn't make sense, or I didn't want it to make sense. I was unable to believe that thousands of fae knew the rest of us were living in slavery or being bled in labs or bred for the next generation of slave owners. No. It wasn't possible this many fae knew how horrible our lives were outside that gate and chose to do *nothing*.

Laurie was right in front of me. "Breathe, okay? Just breathe."

But I was too angry to breathe. I shoved past him and pointed at the houses we could see from the road. "That many. That *many*. And they're all here? Just going about their lives, living in their pretty houses and flying around with no suppression tech and *what the actual fuck*?"

"It sounds bad," Mia admitted, "but we're trying—"

"No," Laurie cut her off. "There are no excuses for this. Vera is right. The fae can no longer wall themselves up in Rowan and pretend like the outside world doesn't exist."

"The fae king and queen. Where do they live?" I asked them. "When we get there, we need to tell them what's going on."

"We will," Mia insisted. "We will tell them."

Laurie sighed. "But getting them to actually take action isn't as simple, unfortunately."

"Yes, it is. I'll tell them the truth of what I've experienced. We need to tell them about Leo, that there's an opportunity for a possible alliance with him in the demon kingdom one day. We need to tell them about Syn and what's happening with the auctions and—"

"We'll get there, I promise," Laurie insisted. "We agree with you that they haven't handled any of this well, that the fae of Rowan should be doing more."

"That's the understatement of the year!"

"And Mia and I both agree that the king and queen need to be convinced of the need for action." By Laurie's side, Mia nodded eagerly.

"Convinced? Fae are *enslaved*. What else is there to say?" I could hear the pitch of my voice rising the longer I thought through what I'd just learned. Anger was pouring out of me in waves, but I couldn't stop it. "What the hell kind of king and queen are they if they don't want to protect their own people, no matter where they are? Those royal assholes have to be convinced to actually do something instead of sitting here in this beautiful place pretending like the world is fine? This is insane."

The whole time I ranted, a small smile appeared on Laurie's face. "You are... so hot when you're angry."

"This is not the time, Laurie!"

"You're right. I'm sorry. Vera. We're not disagreeing with you. Trust me—"

"Laurie." Mia pointed behind me. "Look." When I spun around, I saw six fae in long blue robes flying toward us.

"A welcoming crew from the town?" I asked hopefully, even though their speed and focus were ominous. Too ominous. "This isn't a welcoming crew."

"Shit," Laurie muttered. "I knew we shouldn't have followed the road."

Beside me, Mia threw up her hands in defeat. "Well, that didn't take long. Here we go."

"What didn't? Who are they?"

Laurie ignored my question, turning to Mia instead. "I thought we'd make it a little farther at least."

"We should have gone toward the river instead of following the road."

Laurie shook his head. "The woods are too thick there."

"We could have flown."

I held up my hand to stop them. "Can one of you please explain what the hell is going on because I am *this* close to finding that golden gate on my own and getting the hell out of here."

Instead of answering, Laurie was right in front of me, taking my hands in his. "I'm sorry I didn't tell you sooner, Vera. I really am. You have nothing to worry about. I'll explain everything later, I promise."

I dropped his hands and took a step back. "No. Tell me now."

"I agree with Vera," Mia said. "We should have told her sooner!"

"This is not the time, Mia!"

"Yes!" I shouted at him. "Yes, it is the time!"

Over Laurie's shoulder I could see the group of fae rapidly approaching. Their wings were larger than any I'd ever seen before, their colors vibrant in the sun. Their robes flew out behind them as they came closer, and within seconds they landed directly in front of us, forming a semicircle around the three of us.

"Are we about to be arrested?" I whispered to Mia.

"Uh... kind of? Hey, guys!" Mia smiled and gave a little wave. "Nice to see everyone!"

Immediately all six fae knelt on the road, their heads bowed, their long flowy robes pooling in the dirt.

"This really isn't necessary," Laurie said, gesturing for them to stand up, but one of the fae in the middle of the semicircle, an older man with a stern, sharp face, lifted his head and Laurie immediately stopped speaking. He eyed the three of us, his grim expression indicating that he was obviously displeased by what he saw.

"Welcome home, Your Highnesses. The king and queen have eagerly awaited your return."

30

VERA

"You're a prince, and you're a princess. The prince and princess of the entire fairy realm. Fuck, I'm such an idiot."

Sitting on the bed in the room I'd been given in the palace, I grabbed a pillow, holding it tight over my face so they wouldn't see the embarrassment written all over me, or maybe so I wouldn't see them.

Once the royal guard had intercepted us, they'd flown with us to the palace, but it had felt less like a royal escort and more like a prison march with the way they kept their eyes on us, not allowing anyone to stop for any reason.

The fae palace was immense, with tall towers of stone rising into the sky. Every eye was on our procession as we flew in, with many of the fae waving and cheering when they caught a glimpse of the twins. I'd never seen so many fae in one place, so many smiling, happy faces, going about their day, living normal lives. I wasn't sure if I should be thrilled or disgusted.

Guards let us in, and once we were through the palace gates, Laurie and Mia had been shuffled away from me while I'd been taken to a bedroom in one of the towers, left alone but with a fae guard placed outside the room. He hadn't been thrilled when I tried to leave the room to go explore, so I'd gone back to waiting patiently to talk to Laurie and Mia, whenever that might happen.

As the hours passed while I waited, servants brought food and drinks, extra clothes, and pretty much anything I might need. Just when I thought I wasn't going to get a chance to talk to them that night about everything that had happened, just when I'd finally decided to go to bed, Mia and Laurie showed up at my room. Mia had flown in right away after only the briefest of knocks, not caring that I was about to go to bed or that I might not be properly dressed. Laurie, however, had held back and only finally came in once Mia gave him the all clear.

Now that Mia was home, suppression bracelet long gone, she'd changed into a long, flowy white dress, the skirt divided in the middle at her waist to reveal white trousers underneath. The fabric looked soft and elegant, perfectly complimenting her white hair. With her makeup done to perfection, her hair softly curled, wearing a dazzling blue stone at the end of a silver chain around her neck, she looked every bit like a princess.

Even though Mia sat beside me, Laurie stayed standing at the foot of the bed, holding on to one of the wooden bedposts. He too wore white, a crisp white button-down shirt that had once been tucked into the gray pants he wore. The sleeves were rolled up, exposing his muscular forearms, and he'd unbuttoned a few of the top buttons as well.

"I called your parents *assholes*," I said behind the pillow covering my face. "Oh gods, I called the *king* and *queen* assholes."

"To be fair," Mia said from where she sat on the bed beside me, "we agree with you on that one."

"I can't believe you two kept this from me. You could have said something once we left Vestia, at least. And at those meetings back in the demon kingdom, all those fae knew? Everyone knew you were royalty except me?"

"With your connection to the demon prince, we couldn't risk telling you. Everyone understood the risk."

"I wanted to tell you so many times," Laurie said. "You have no idea how much I wanted to tell you. But then we were leaving, and I figured it could wait until we got here. I didn't expect the royal guard to find us quite that quickly though."

I threw the pillow as hard as I could at him, and he caught it.

"What other secrets do I need to know about? Any other secret identities that you're hiding? Is it going to turn out that Laurie is actually a god in fae form mingling with us common folk?"

Laurie stood up a little straighter. "You think I look like a god?"

It was Mia's turn to throw my other pillow, but he deflected it with the one he already held. "Get over yourself," she told him. "Servants start reminding him that he's the next king, and suddenly his ego is big enough to explode."

"The next king?" I groaned, flopping back on my bed. "Wait." I sat up quickly and pointed at Mia. "You're twins. Why aren't you going to be queen instead?"

"Don't look at me!" Mia said, holding up a hand. "I don't want to be in charge!"

"Why not?"

"Being in charge sounds boring," she shrugged. "I want to kick ass and do what I want. I'll have infinitely more freedom by not being on the throne. I've seen how it changed our parents. That's one reason Laurie and I left, to do something on our own, to see what we could do to make a difference before coming back."

"I need a captain of the guard, after all," Laurie added.

Mia nodded in agreement. "Hell yeah, you do. With as much trouble as you get us into, you need several."

"What did your parents say when they saw you two?"

"They didn't," Laurie snorted. "They were 'too busy' to see us. What a joke. It's not even a believable lie. They're just dragging it out to punish us. They made us get all dressed up and then wait for them but then never called for us."

"See, Vera! It was okay for you to call them assholes!" Mia smiled. "They weren't always this bad, but these past few years have really changed them."

"What were they like before?"

"Our family came to power relatively recently, not long after we were born," Laurie explained. "The previous king and queen died, and since they didn't have any living children, the council decided on my family. The crown is not something that is inherited anymore if there are no heirs. So many fae were killed in the Blood War that lineages and genealogies are all screwed up."

"There's a lot that's screwed up because of the war."

"You're right. I think initially our parents' intentions were good. They wanted to protect the fae here. I truly believe they think they are doing the right thing by not getting involved in conflicts outside Rowan. We're hidden here, and I think they believe if we can simply shut the Willow Gate and keep the rest of the world out, we'll be safe."

"And all the enslaved fae?" I asked. "They're just unlucky?"

"Collateral damage in their eyes. The consequences of war. The wild fae who choose to remain outside Rowan do so at their own peril, knowing the risks. Most of the fae who purposely live elsewhere are part of a group of exiles, and most of those are militant, bent on getting revenge on slave owners."

"The Black Guard."

"Yes. You've heard of them?"

"I've heard they're dangerous."

"Of course that's what your demon would tell you. The Black Guard wants change. They're the only ones brave enough to actually do something about the enslaved fae. The fae here are taught that they're rebels, loose cannons, eccentric weirdos, but that's not it at all."

The door to my room opened, and four guards walked in, all of them instantly bowing. It was a strange sight, one that would take some getting used to, to see fae bowing on their knees at Laurie's feet.

"Your Highness, we need to speak with you."

"I'll be right there," Laurie told them.

"Oh. Um. No, your highness, we mean the princess. His and Her Majesty wish to see Princess Mia at this time."

With a look of surprise, Mia jumped up from my bed. "Not both of us?"

The guard kept his head bowed. "Not right now, Your Highness. They will call for you later."

After an apologetic look, Mia followed the guards out of my room. Then it was just the two of us. Laurie seemed tense as he watched the door, and he tapped his fingers against the wooden bedpost.

"So," I finally said, not sure what I was going to say next, but feeling like something needed to be said to save us from this awkward silence.

At the sound of my voice, his expression changed, the irritation vanishing as he turned his attention back to me.

"I'm assuming we'll be next," he said.

"You mean you, right? Not me."

"No, after I speak with them, they'll most likely want to talk to you as well. Maybe not tonight, but eventually they'll want to meet you. I want them to hear what you've experienced. They need to hear it."

"And you're sure they'll want to meet some stranger?"

"You're not just some stranger. Some stranger wouldn't have been given a room in the palace and guards outside her door." Suddenly Laurie grinned and sat down next to me on the bed, his sparkling blue eyes watching me for a reaction. "Some stranger wouldn't have the Prince of Rowan sitting on her bed."

"I guess... you're right." It was hard to focus with him this close, this close on a bed of all places, this close with those large dazzling wings behind him. His wings were remarkable from any distance, but when we were only inches apart, the way they shimmered in the light was truly mesmerizing. "I'm sure they'll be happy to see you," I managed to say.

Laurie exhaled loudly, his wings drooping behind him. "I'm not so sure. I know asking to see Mia first was a message to let me know they're unhappy. They're always like this with me. It's like I can never—"

"Nope. That's it. I'm going home." I jumped up off the bed and waved my arms in the air with exaggerated frustration. Then I pointed at him. "I'm done with royalty. I'm done with princes who have trouble with their parents. I don't want any part of this."

His look of alarm switched sharply to one of mischief.

"Too bad. You can't get away that easily." Laurie chuckled, reaching for me. "Get back here." He grabbed my arm, pulling me back onto the bed. I fell forward, tumbling right into him, right onto his lap.

Both of us froze, realizing the awkward position.

I swallowed. He was close. So close. Laurie immediately released his hands.

"I'm sorry," I muttered, backing up off him.

"No. That was my fault." Laurie stood up from the bed too, smoothing down his clothes and clearing his throat. "I'm sorry if I made you uncomfortable just now."

At the moment, it seemed like both of us were uncomfortable. "It's pretty late, and we've been traveling all day so…"

"You're right." He nodded. "I should probably go. They might be looking for me."

"Right. Sounds good."

"Right," he repeated, walking to the door. He stopped before leaving, looking back at me. "And Vera?"

"Yes?"

Laurie's mouth opened as if he were about to speak, but then closed again and he smiled. "Sleep well."

MIA AND LAURIE were busy for the next few days, and as each day passed, I seemed to have more and more time alone. What was I doing here? Would I stay here forever?

Feeling restless one morning, I let my nose lead me through the palace toward the kitchens, hoping to find a snack, but I heard noises outside that sounded like a woman shouting. I ran out the closest door, but all I saw in the distance was Mia, far away underneath a large tree, the largest tree on the palace grounds, pacing back and forth in front of a line of fae.

Even at this distance, Mia was loud, certainly louder than I'd ever heard her. I walked through the garden and out into the field, getting closer so I could see what was going on. The fae in front of her wore lightweight blue jackets, a blue that matched Mia's wings, each embroidered with swirls of white thread on the shoulders. Underneath the jacket, they wore stiff white shirts combined with black pants tucked into high black boots. All of them were standing at attention but sweating and breathing heavily from whatever they'd been doing.

I sat down against a much smaller tree, keeping my distance but still close enough that I could hear them.

This was the palace guard, I realized, and Mia was their captain. Mia seemed to be in her element commanding them, confidently flying up and down the line of fae, emphatically talking with her hands while her white hair flew behind her. She had them all lined up in the grass, and another fae stood in front of the group with her. He had a matching scowl, but that's where the similarities stopped. With his black hair tied in a low knot at the base of his head, the fae man stood with his large, muscular arms crossed over his chest as he glared at the guard. He wasn't wearing an embroidered jacket like the others. Instead, he wore a simple black tunic and loose black pants in a simple style that seemed like it was from another time. Much taller than Mia, with broad shoulders, he towered over the fae in front of him, his dark purple wings twitching with obvious irritation behind him.

"What the hell kind of training have you been doing while I've been gone?" Mia was shouting at her guard. I'd never seen her angry like this. Normally Mia was a bouncing bundle of joy, but right now she looked ready to attack any of them the moment one dared to speak. "Whatever the lieutenant had you doing, it wasn't enough. You're out of shape and lazy. Now that the prince has returned, we can't have a lazy guard. Do you understand?"

"Yes, Your Highness," they said in unison.

It made sense that her troops had grown lazy in her absence. The veil shielded Rowan from all intruders, allowing only fae in, so there was no need to be prepared for outside threats. Within Rowan itself, it seemed as if crime was nonexistent, so the guard was mostly just used for the basic protection of the royal family.

"We need to brush up on hand-to-hand combat. Lieutenant." Mia signaled to the tall fae. "Come stand behind me." With a curt nod, he approached Mia, stopping a few inches away from her. "I'm an intruder, and the lieutenant must remove me from the premises. What does he do first?"

"Disable!" the group shouted.

"Good." Mia glanced over her shoulder to where the tall fae stood looming over her. "Lieutenant? Proceed."

"As you wish, Your Highness." His huge arms slammed around Mia, one around her waist, the other holding tight in the middle of her chest. I wasn't sure if it was the closeness of his hold or if she simply couldn't breathe, but Mia's eyes were wider than I'd ever seen. "Is this all right, Your Highness?"

"Of course it is," she snapped, her composure returning. "You'll notice my arms are still free, so if I had a knife, I could still throw it or stab someone with it. So what's next?"

"Disarm!" the group called out.

"Precisely. Lieutenant?"

In a flash, he had Mia's arms wrapped behind her in one of his big hands. She twisted around in his hold, but he swept her ankles with one of his feet. Seconds later, Mia was flat on her back, the lieutenant straddling her waist and pinning her hands above her head on each side.

But of course she wasn't going to let him win in front of her own guard. Mia wrapped both her arms around one of his and rolled, flipping both of them over so that she was on top of him. I knew Mia wasn't paying attention to them, but her guards were exchanging looks and giggling at the sight of their captain panting on top of the lieutenant.

As if she only then realized the position they were in, Mia let go, and she flew back off him. "Yep. Just like that. Excellent work, Lieutenant," she said, avoiding his gaze.

"It was my pleasure, Your Highness," his deep voice replied.

"Um... right." She cleared her throat before turning her attention to the group. "Anyway. As I was saying. After disarming the intruder, what do you do next?"

"Detain," the fae replied.

"How?"

"You could use wing clamps to prevent them from flying off," one chimed in.

"What if your opponent doesn't have wings?" I shouted over to the group.

For a moment Mia's brow furrowed, but when she saw me, her scowl turned into a smile. "Vera! How long have you been out here?" The fae behind her began to murmur as I walked over to the group, but the snap of Mia's fingers put an end to that quickly. "Vera has a point. What if you were up against someone like her?"

Several of the fae frowned, obviously confused by Mia's question. A few snickered, most likely assuming that taking on a wingless fae like me would be no problem at all.

"She doesn't appear to be a threat," one fae said. "She doesn't even have wings. It's not like she can fly away."

Mia shook her head. "Never underestimate your opponent. You should know that by now."

"Forgive me, Your Highness," a fae guard with red wings said. He might have been apologizing, but the smug look on his face seemed anything but apologetic. "Since when are outsiders allowed on palace grounds?"

At his words, the others again started talking to each other in hushed tones, and I heard a few whispered comments about my lack of wings.

"Silence!" Mia shouted at the group. "This 'outsider' is fae just like you are, Damon. You up for a rematch, Vera? We could show these lazy fae a thing or two."

Before she finished speaking, the lieutenant was at Mia's side, a hand on her arm. "Is this wise, Your Highness? Isn't this lady a guest of the prince?"

Mia brushed him off. "She's my guest too. Come on, Vera. Let's do this."

Was she joking? I'd just seen her flip over her monster of a lieutenant, and from my own experience, I knew firsthand how strong she was.

"No, thanks," I said, holding up a hand. "I'm fine watching."

"Weak," I heard the red mutter.

"Do you have something to say?" I asked him. "If so, say it instead of mumbling it to yourself."

The fae crossed his arms over his chest, smiling smugly. "Fine, I will. Rowan doesn't need trouble from outside the gate. You should go back where you came from."

Before the red had even finished talking, Mia's lieutenant strode forward toward him with big, menacing steps. Mia put out a hand to stop him.

"You're right. There is trouble outside our gates," Mia told him calmly, "but Vera is not part of that. I already said that she's my guest, Damon, and she should be treated as such."

He wrinkled his nose, glaring at me. "What kind of fae doesn't even have wings?"

"That's it," Mia snapped. "You," she said, pointing to the fae with red wings. "Spar with Vera. If she lands one hit, you're on dish duty for a week."

"Fine." His fingers interlaced, the fae stretched his arms out in front of him, cracking his wrists. "It would be my pleasure."

"Vera," Mia said, turning to me, "please kick his ass."

"It will be my pleasure as well."

He was probably stronger than I was, since he was a palace guard after all, but I wanted to wipe that smug look off his face, even if it meant getting a little beat up in the process. Moving closer in the grass, I readied myself while the other fae guards took a step back to give us space under the big tree. Luckily, I had on a pair of loose pants and a tank top, so I wouldn't be constrained when I kicked his ass.

I would be able to do that, right? I suddenly wasn't as sure. I'd held my own against Mia when we first met, at least for a little while, and she'd already said that the guards were out of shape. He was taller than me, true, and could fly, but I could be fast if I concentrated my magic in my legs.

At first it was like we were doing a little dance. He'd move forward, and I'd move back. I'd move toward him, and Damon would fly into the air, easily getting away. I was used to dodging feints from my time spent with Leo in the pit. With Leo I had to watch out for not only his hands but also his tail. Going up against this fae seemed easier than those training sessions since I didn't have to worry about a thick tail smacking me or wrapping around an ankle.

Thinking of Leo, I was too distracted and barely avoided a fist to my stomach.

"Are you even trying?" Damon sneered as he hovered a few feet off the ground. "You keep running from me like a scared rabbit. Are you afraid because you don't have wings?"

I rolled my eyes. What a dick.

"You're the one flying away when threatened."

"Threatened?" He cocked an eyebrow and landed in front of me. "Yeah right. I'll stay on the ground if it makes you feel better, freak."

"Do whatever you want."

A sadistic grin spread across the fae's face.

Oh, I wanted to kick his ass so badly.

Damon lunged forward, and to dodge, I jerked back. My sudden movement caused me to stumble against the tree, my back hitting the bark.

A crowd had formed around us, I realized as I collected myself. Not just the guards, but several palace servants stood nearby, watching from a distance as we sparred under the giant tree.

What would they all think if they saw me, a wingless fae, the guest of the prince and princess, so easily overpowered? Would they think me weak as well? Or would they begin to agree with him, that I was different, a freak, an outsider?

Damon was spouting more bullshit taunts, but I wasn't listening. With my hand against the tree trunk as I steadied myself, I took a deep breath. But instead of air, it felt like I inhaled something sharp. Acidic.

My whole body shook in a single tremor, a jolt not unlike the feeling I'd experienced when I touched the lock of the Willow Gate. Instantly, every part of me tingled, as if I'd suddenly been filled with electricity.

Power. I was breathing in *power*.

I didn't know where it was coming from, and I didn't care. I sucked the feeling in deeply, willing it to fill my lungs and body.

Meanwhile, Damon was right in front of me, and when he swung a punch, I was sure it would hit me at such close range. But it didn't. Instead, his fist appeared to hit something solid in midair less than an inch from my face. He bounced back, his mouth dropped open in shock.

"What the hell?" Damon asked, face twisting in confusion. "What did you just do?"

I didn't know what had happened myself, but what I did know, somehow, was that he wouldn't be able to hit me. Not when I was feeling like this. Instead of defending, I walked toward him, one slow step at a time. Damon stumbled backward as I approached, and though he continued to swing, each time he was met with the same invisible resistance.

Finally I grabbed his wrist, stopping a punch midair. With a simple twist of my arm, Damon flipped over, landing on his back in the grass. He didn't jump up; the fae lay there staring up at me in shock.

Looming over him, I breathed in and out, then in and out again, that rush of energy slowly leaving me. In its place, however, was pride. I'd bested a palace guard.

Me.

A wingless fae.

"Your Highness, is that enough?" I asked Mia. Below me, Damon still grimaced from the impact and clutched at his back.

"Doesn't look like he's getting up anytime soon, so yep. Game over."

I let out a breath. Holy shit. I did that. I really did that. I'd held my own against a palace guard. An obnoxious palace guard, sure, but still he was a fae with more training and inherent strength than me. For the briefest of seconds, Leo's face appeared in my mind, and I wondered what he would have said if he'd been watching.

"Yahoo!" Mia shouted, clapping and fluttering up into the air, before she seemed to realize what she was doing and landed, straightening her clothes. "I mean, well done, Vera. Damon, no linking. I want you to feel that pain for a while. Oh, and you're on dish duty for the next week."

All I could do was stare at my hand, the hand I'd used to flip a full grown fae over onto the ground. I'd never felt strength like that, and I'd certainly never put up a shield like that either. The fae stood up and brushed off his tunic, his wings shaking off dirt and grass as he scowled. "I don't know what the hell kind of trick that was." He spit.

I didn't know either. Scanning my body for signs of anything weird and finding none, I truly had no explanation for what had just happened. If I could be that strong and prevent attacks, why had I never put up a shield like that before? When Henry had stabbed me at Leo's house, my body hadn't put up any kind of barrier to protect me, so why now, why here?

If only Leo was here, he could run some tests, or he would know—

No. Leo wasn't here. He'd sent me away. I was going to have to figure this out myself.

I tried remembering what I had felt moments before, when I'd experienced that surge of power. But no matter how long I stared at my hands, nothing happened.

"Darach Tor," I heard a deep voice say. When I looked up, Mia's lieutenant's head was bowed as he faced the giant tree we stood under, his hands clasped in front of him as if in prayer. "Of many leaves, one tree," he said, raising his head, his dark eyes meeting my own. "It is the ancient magic."

At his words, the whole group was quiet. Even Damon was speechless.

"Um, well, I don't know about all that," I said to break the awkward silence. I scratched the back of my neck. "I mean, I don't even have wings, so..."

Without another word I turned away, heading back the way I'd come, wanting to be alone to think through what all this might mean.

"Vera, wait! I'll walk with you. The rest of you—five laps around the palace!" she barked at the group as I stopped. "No flying." Their faces fell, but after a mumbled "yes, Your Highness," they were off, jogging away from us.

"Lieutenant, you can take it from here? I'm headed back," she called over to him, and the fae nodded, his dark eyes watching us.

"Is Your Highness in need of assistance?"

"No, no!" Mia shook her head vigorously, white hair bouncing side to side. "No, thank you."

"I could assist you later," he said, putting particular emphasis on that last word. "If you wish."

"No, thank you, Lieutenant. You're good. I mean I'm good. No! I mean, I'm going. I'm— Bye."

Did Mia even realize how quickly her wings were fluttering behind her every time he spoke?

Watching the two of them, I chuckled as Mia flew over to me. She slung an arm around my shoulder as we walked away. "He's the one who needs assistance. With the way they've been training, those guys wouldn't last a second in the arena," she said, hooking a thumb back at the guards. "Victor's too soft with them."

"I'm not sure anything about Victor is soft," I mused, nudging her in the side and gauging her reaction. Just as I'd expected, Mia's face flushed, her pale cheeks turning a bright shade of pink.

"I meant... That's not what I meant. I was trying to say..." I couldn't help but laugh as she stammered and covered her face with her hands. "You're just trying to keep me from asking about what happened back there. What was that? Where was that energy when you fought me back at the arena?"

"I don't know." I shook my head, wondering the same thing. "All I know is that right when I thought he was about to hit me, I felt like I was breathing in... *something*."

Mia scrunched up her nose, and I could tell that she was thinking it over. "I've never seen magic like that myself. I've known fae with fast reflexes or fae who were experts at anticipating moves and dodging them, but never one who actually created a barrier like you did just now. That's never happened before?"

"No, never. I have a friend who has the ability to lessen the impact of blows," I said, thinking of Lydia and what I'd seen her do when we practiced together at Leo's mansion, "but she didn't create a physical barrier between herself and someone else."

"Well, whatever it was, I enjoyed seeing that look on Damon's face." She smirked. "He needed to be taken down a peg or three. I should get back. Victor is probably letting them walk instead of run. Are you okay being alone? I could go get Laurie, or...?"

"No. I'll be okay. Some time alone to figure this out might actually be for the best."

She clapped me on the back as we got closer to the palace. "Let me know if you need anything."

I peered over her shoulder back into the garden behind us, and there I saw the tall fae with the dark hair and dark eyes staring back at us. "I'm not the one who needs something, I think," I said, nodding behind her.

Mia's eyes went wide when she saw him before she quickly looked away. "I don't know what you're talking about," she said, sticking her chin out as if to show me how serious she was.

"Keep telling yourself that." I grinned, waving goodbye as Mia flew back to him.

THE NEXT DAY WAS A WHIRLWIND. A messenger let me know that the king and queen requested my presence at their evening meal, and from that moment until Mia showed up at my door to escort me, the day was a blur of activity. As the guest of the prince and princess, the maids assigned to me insisted I dress the part, and they'd chosen a simple long dress made of a light green fabric. They fussed over my hair and makeup longer than what I felt was necessary, and I had almost reached my limit in their game of dress-up when it was finally time.

As I waited for Mia to arrive to escort me to the dinner, I looked at myself in the mirror and thought about another time when I dressed up before going out to meet Mia. Tonight was not going to be anything like that night at the arena when the two of us had fought, or at least I hoped that was the case, but from what I'd been told, it sounded like it might be a fight of a different kind.

I would be polite of course, but I also knew how important it was that the king and queen understood the importance of helping the fae who were enslaved in the rest of the world. With the power of the fae of Rowan, the possibilities were endless, and if they managed an alliance with someone like Leo—

I suddenly felt like I couldn't breathe.

My legs felt weak under me, and I stumbled, thankfully being caught by one of the maids nearby. As she helped me back up, the door swung open and Mia flew into the room. Seeing the maids surrounding me, she rushed over. "Vera, are you okay? What happened?"

"I'm fine. I think," I said, trying to smile and feeling more embarrassed than anything else. "Just nerves, maybe?"

Mia smiled gently and took my hand. "You have nothing to be nervous about. My parents are the ones who should be nervous once they hear what you have to say."

It was then that I finally was able to see her outfit. Instead of a dress, she wore a formfitting blue top with a small white coat over it, gold accents swirling around the sleeves and cuffs. With her matching blue pants and black boots, Mia looked more suited to standing guard herself than eating dinner with her royal parents.

"I'm loving the look," I told her.

"You like it?" she asked, her eyes lighting up as she fluttered a few feet off the ground, spinning in the air. "No offense to pretty dresses like yours, but I feel more comfortable like this."

"I do like it. It suits you. What does your lieutenant think?"

Mia landed in front of me with a thud. "Why would Victor care what I wore?"

"No reason."

She eyed me suspiciously. "Right. That dress looks great on you too, although selfishly I wish it was blue instead."

"Mia..."

She held her hands up in surrender. "I know, I know. Let's go."

Together the two of us walked to the back of the palace and out into the yard. The dinner was set up in a small pavilion near the stream that ran near the back of the estate, so we followed a cobblestone path through their carefully manicured gardens, each one filled with an even more colorful flower than the one before it.

For some reason, I thought of the park on Alliance Island, the one place the humans allowed us fae to go while we waited for the auction. Rob and I used to take care of the few tiny patches of flowers that somehow survived, and together we'd celebrate when our meager efforts actually led to pretty blossoms. Those victories had been so small, but they felt huge at the time.

Thinking of Rob made me smile. He would like it here. If only there was a way to get in touch with him, to call him and find out how things were going back home.

Home.

Did I even have a home? Or was I back to where I had started months ago, shifted yet again to a new place that I couldn't call my own?

Could Rowan be my new home? Or did they all see me as an outsider, like that fae guard had?

"Vera, we're here," Mia whispered, and I realized I'd been lost in thought, not realizing we were approaching the pavilion. Laurie was already there, and he stood as we came closer. He wore a crisp white suit, and he adjusted the jacket as we came closer. The king and queen looked very much like their children, both with hair just as white with blue wings as well. The queen wore a long gown of a deep blue, and the king wore a suit in a similar color with the same gold accents that were on Mia's jacket. They smiled kindly when Mia introduced me, and some of my nerves went away.

"Our children have filled us in on your story, my dear," the queen said. "We want you to know you are welcome within the walls of Rowan now and always."

I bowed my head. "Thank you, Your Majesties."

"We are thankful for your friendship with our children, and we welcome you here as our guest. Our children seem to hope you will come to think of Rowan as home."

"I appreciate that deeply, and I thank you for letting me stay at the palace."

Conversation was easy and light, and all of us laughed at the stories of the twins when they were little. But despite how easy the conversation flowed, the dinner felt strange. I couldn't quite put my finger on it, but it felt like something was off. On the outside it looked like five fae enjoying an evening meal together, but the more I watched Mia and Laurie's parents, the more I felt a pang in my heart.

Parents.

That was it. I had never seen fae my age with their parents before. Every fae on Alliance Island was an orphan; the humans made sure to split up families immediately to break our spirits more than they already were. Yet here was a mother and father with two children, all existing in the same household. Children who had been raised living with their parents.

No matter how Laurie and Mia felt about their parents, to me it was a miraculous, beautiful thing, and I couldn't help but be jealous that they had grown up like this, the four of them, together.

While the rest of the family was engrossed in conversation, Laurie nudged my shoulder, grinning. "Are we all that boring? You seem to be spacing out on me."

"I'm sorry, no. That's not it at all," I said, keeping my voice low so the others wouldn't hear us. "I was just thinking about how lucky you are to have a family."

"Vera." Laurie's smiling face turned somber as my words sank in. "You could have a family too," he whispered. Underneath the table, I felt his hand touch mine, looping his pinky finger around my own. "If you wanted that."

"I've always wanted that," I whispered back.

"Lawrence." The queen's voice rang out, drawing our attention back to the group, and Laurie dropped his hand away. "Why don't we discuss the preparations for the party?"

"I think that can wait," he said. "I'd rather talk about what is happening on the human continent. You've heard what we had to say about what's happening in Vestia, but Vera can explain how awful—"

"First, let's discuss your homecoming party," the queen said. "There will be plenty of time for chitchat later, Lawrence."

"Discussing the enslavement of our people is not chitchat, Mother. If you would let Vera tell you about the dorms and the auction and—"

"That's enough." His father's sharp tone made even me sit up a little straighter, shocked by how stern he suddenly seemed.

"No, it's not," Laurie continued. "Mia and I risked our lives to gather information to bring back here. Vera's life has been on the line for years. But all you want to do is talk about a party?"

The queen put down her glass and stared at Laurie. "You're being very selfish, Lawrence."

"Selfish? Me? If you want to talk about selfish, then look at everyone here who is only thinking about themselves and not the rest of the fae in the world."

The king's glare was equally as severe as the queen's. "Rowan wants to celebrate the two of you. Our people want to enjoy life and forget the atrocities of the war, not be reminded of them."

"How nice for them!"

"Yes, it is nice. Our fae are happy and safe," the queen said, "and we will not be the reason their happiness ends."

Laurie slammed his fist down on the table, and Mia and I both flinched. "How can any fae be happy when other fae are enslaved?"

In an instant he was up from the table, flying away. After an awkward silence, the conversation shifted to talk of the party, the food, the music, anything and everything that avoided the earlier topics completely. When dinner was finally over, Mia walked with me back to my room, but instead of going straight there, we took a detour down a hall I hadn't seen before.

"I'll leave you here," she said, nodding to the door in front of us. "He can walk you back."

"Laurie's in there?"

"This is his studio, so I'm fairly confident that he is. Laurie could probably use a friendly face right about now." She smiled and squeezed my hand before knocking. No one answered. "He's so stubborn. Your turn," she said, and then with a wave she was off down the hall.

Opening the door to his studio just a crack, I saw Laurie's blue wings and white hair. He was hunched over a desk, furiously drawing with a pencil. I'd hoped there might be a chance to get his input on how my magic seemed to be changing, but after that dinner, and now seeing him like this, I knew tonight wasn't about me.

"Mia thought you might be in here." I crept in, keeping my voice low as I shut the door behind me. "We don't have to talk. You know, a good friend once told me that sometimes you just need someone to sit beside you."

Laurie put down the pencil but still didn't turn around in his chair. "I'm sorry you had to see that. I thought things would be different when we came back, that my parents would be so happy to see us that they'd actually listen for once. But no, of course not. They want to stick their heads in the sand and forget about the outside world completely."

"I don't agree with them, but I understand that your parents want to protect the fae here."

"They want to live in ignorance. They don't want to do anything at all to disrupt their own peace. Why can't they see what they're doing is wrong?"

"Because if they admit that, the next step could mean war for the fae here. Not everyone is as brave as you, Laurie."

He spun around in his chair, and before I could breathe, he took one of my hands in his. "You are."

I took my hand away. "Because I've had to be. Your parents have never been slaves. To them it's still an abstract thing because they haven't seen what life is like for young fae growing up, knowing their lives are not their own. Your parents want to spare their fae from ever experiencing that kind of pain. There's something noble in that, I think, even if it's misguided."

"Don't defend them. Please."

"I'm not. I'm on your side."

"Are you? Vera, when I become king, I am gathering the strength of an army. I'd do it now if I thought I'd have enough fae to follow me."

"But that would mean war."

"Then so be it," he said, standing up and pacing around his studio as he talked. "Why are we hesitating? Why is this taking so long?"

Those were questions I'd asked Leo a hundred times, and each time he'd told me that there were steps that had to be taken, procedures we needed to follow, strategies to stick to.

"I want to do whatever I have to do to end slavery," Laurie said. "Maybe that's war, maybe it's not. I don't know, but I do know we can't sit here and do nothing. We will take back our people and punish those who have wronged us. That includes those who have wronged *you*." Laurie stopped pacing, his blue eyes on me. "I want to punish them most of all."

Those who have wronged me. Did he want the whole list? Because if he did, it was going to take me a while to write out the names. But no, revenge wouldn't give me another chance at a childhood, revenge wouldn't erase the night I was stabbed by a man I thought was a friend, and revenge certainly wouldn't bring back—

"Vera. You're doing it again."

I blinked. "Doing what?"

"That thing you do sometimes. You go quiet and get that faraway look in your eyes." Laurie ran his hand through his white hair and sighed. "You're thinking about him, aren't you?"

There was no reason to say his name. We both knew he meant Leo.

"I was thinking about this homecoming party," I lied. "It seems I completely forgot to bring any dresses with me when I was given away like a sack of potatoes against my will. The one the servants gave me today is nice and all, but..."

Suddenly his whole expression changed, and his eyes lit up, just as I'd hoped. In an instant, he was across the room thumbing through dresses on the rack.

"I know it's been a while since you've been home, so I'm sure you couldn't possibly have anything that would be in style." I grinned.

"Oh, just you wait. If we have to go to this stupid party, we are going to find you something that will make everyone at court fall in love with you just like I—" he stopped talking abruptly. "Um. What color would you want?"

"I was really only teasing. I can wear anything. Everything you make is impressive."

"Damn right it is." Laurie snorted and grabbed one linen dress, obviously unfinished, and held it up so he could see the whole thing. "I could finish this one this week."

"You don't have to do that. It looks lovely, but if you don't have time, I can borrow a dress from your sister."

"No! That's not it. Vera, I'll make time." He placed it on his table on top of the piles and piles of fabrics so I could look at it with him. "This is just the underlayer, but what do you think? Imagine more volume to the skirt, and I'll probably change the neckline." Laurie already had out a pencil, making marks on the linen dress.

"Maybe not quite that low?" I suggested when I saw where he'd drawn the dip in the front.

"Can't blame me for trying." He smiled, erasing all the same. "You still need to tell me a color."

"I don't know, but maybe something other than blue this time?"

Laurie blinked, the hint of a blush appearing on his face at the memory of the dress he'd made me before. "Oh. Sure. Of course. What color were you thinking?"

My fingers grazed the fabrics on the table until one in particular caught my eye. "I'm thinking silver."

31

―――――

VERA

The palace ballroom buzzed with the murmurs of beautiful fae eating and drinking, the rustling of sparkling dresses and wings, and the faint tones of music in the air. This party made me think of the one we'd attended in Vestia, except now I wasn't watching from the balcony.

The balcony might have been preferable, because at this party, in this room full of happy fae dressed in their finest, I was the center of attention. It seemed that everywhere I turned, fae wanted to know why I didn't have wings (*I just don't*) and if my parents also didn't have wings (*I don't know*) followed by an uncomfortable silence when I told them that I didn't even know my parents. The mere mention of having once been a slave was enough for most of them to leave me alone, briskly flying away with a polite smile, but a few still stuck around, asking questions about the royal family and wanting to gossip about them more than me.

"Are you staying at the palace?" one fae asked me, a middle-aged woman whose brown hair was piled high on her head with tightly curled ringlets framing her face. Her eye shadow was about four shades brighter than any I'd ever seen before, and either alcohol or an insane amount of blush made her cheeks outlandishly rosy. Even her bright yellow wings seemed over the top and simply too yellow if such a thing existed.

"Yes," I told her. "For now."

"For now?" chirped the lady's friend, a blond fae with an identical hairstyle who was standing way too close to me. "You won't be staying here permanently?"

"I'm not sure. There's a lot to figure out."

"If you plan on leaving," asked the brunette, "why did you come at all?"

"What?"

"She's right," her friend agreed. "We don't need outsiders coming here, stirring up trouble, and then reporting on us once they leave."

"I'll be surprised if they'll let you leave," the brunette added.

"Let me? I'm not a prisoner."

"Of course not, darling, but why would you want to leave? Especially when you know what it's like out there."

"That's exactly why I *would* leave," I said, growing more and more irritated by the second with both these women.

The brunette sighed dramatically. "I really don't know what you're thinking, but if you think—"

"I'm about to tell you precisely what I think," I said, and I would have too if I hadn't heard the fae around me start to murmur.

"If you'll excuse me," I heard a voice say, and the fae that had been surrounding me immediately parted to make room for their prince to come through. Laurie gave me a crooked smile and raised one eyebrow when he saw me. "Everything okay here?"

Before I could answer, the brunette fairy with the yellow wings stepped in front of me. "Oh yes, just fine, Your Highness. We were getting to know Miss... Miss... What was your name again, dear?"

"Sounds like you still had a long way to go. Vera," Laurie said, emphasizing my name, "would you do me the honor?"

Laurie held out his arm, and I leaped at the chance to get away from those women. "Perfect timing," I told him. "One second later and I might have done something that would have gotten me kicked out of your palace."

"Don't let them get to you. You're the shiny new object in their eyes, so of course everyone wants to play with you."

"Play with me?"

"Or at least I do."

I was trying to convince my brain that I needed to respond, but no words came to mind, probably because Laurie had walked us out to the middle of the room where other fae were dancing to the light music being played. Some fluttered effortlessly just off the ground, twirling and flying together in a beautiful sea of wings and color.

Not surprisingly, Laurie was a good dancer, making it easy for me to follow his lead since I didn't know any of the dances that everyone there knew. When I glanced around to see how other couples were dancing, I noticed something.

"Everyone is staring at us," I whispered to him.

"I should hope so." Laurie's lips quirked up in a grin. "You're probably making your fans jealous."

"Fans? No way. You are the one with fans. They see me more as an interesting creature they want to study. Those ladies were about two minutes away from asking if I could prove I was fae."

"You wouldn't be able to be in Rowan if you weren't fae. The veil's magic won't allow it."

"Try telling them that."

"Maybe I will."

The longer we danced, the more confident I felt. Was this the moment to talk to him about the changes I was noticing with my magic? However, every time I tried to catch Laurie's eyes, he wasn't looking back at me at all. His eyes kept straying to my body, lingering on my waist.

"Stop staring at me like that," I told him.

"What? I'm watching how the fabric moves. For... research purposes."

"Oh, I'm sure. You're awfully flirty tonight."

"Forgive me for flirting with the beautiful woman currently dancing in my arms."

I sighed, realizing that no matter what I said, it wouldn't make a difference.

With a dramatic swing of his arm, Laurie spun me away from him before pulling me back, the force of his pull causing me to land against his chest. I gasped, my hands grabbing on to the lapel of his jacket as he used his other hand to grip my waist, keeping me firmly against him. Suddenly we were airborne, Laurie's wings taking us into the air above the other fae dancing below. I grabbed my dress to hold it tight against me, and before I could complain that everyone was no doubt watching us, Laurie spun us around in swift little spins, his blue wings fluttering gracefully behind him.

"You're causing a scene," I hissed, forcing my eyes to look only at his so I didn't have to see how high above the floor we were.

"I hope so," he said, slowing the spins but keeping us hovering in the air. "I want to show you off a little. But you're uncomfortable?" Noticing the pained look on my face, he frowned.

"A little," I admitted. "You, dancing, flying around, everyone watching. It's a lot to take in, this feeling of having nowhere to hide from everyone's eyes."

"I won't ever hide you, Vera."

Instead of waiting for a response, Laurie's wings slowly swayed in the air as he lowered us down onto the dance floor. The fae parted as we landed softly, and Laurie placed me down next to him.

"Vera, what's next?" he asked, blue eyes focused on mine. "For us."

There it was. The question I had known was coming. Even though I'd expected it, I still froze, dropping my hand from Laurie's and taking a step back away from him. I couldn't look at his beautiful, hopeful eyes, so close to mine, so I looked away only to see something much worse: almost all the fae in attendance were still watching the two of us. Knowing their eyes were all on us made it even more difficult to speak.

"Well." I tried to choose my words wisely, but that only made me stumble over them more. "I'm not sure. It's obvious that you—No, I don't mean you. It's obvious that I—No, it's not obvious at all. What I mean is that—"

"I meant are we going to dance the next song as well?" Laurie asked.

It was then I realized the music had already ended, yet there we were, still in the middle of the dance floor.

"Oh gods. I'm so sorry," I blurted out, wishing I could melt into the wooden floor and disappear right then and there. "I didn't mean to imply that you meant something else."

Laurie only chuckled. "Who's to say I didn't?"

"Oh. Well, did you? Or didn't you? You know what? I should... I'm going to... I'm going to go find Mia," I finally was able to squeak out, walking as quickly as I could in the other direction.

Why did I feel so flustered around him? This was Laurie, after all. *Laurie*. Sure, he was objectively gorgeous—that was just stating a fact —and extremely charismatic, but again, anyone who met him would think the same. He was just Laurie, nothing else.

Right. Just Laurie. The Prince of the Fae.

The same prince who was suddenly at my side.

"Damn wings," I muttered, not stopping for him, my eyes searching for Mia, for anyone. Hell, I would have even settled for those two crazy fae ladies from earlier if it meant not having this awkward conversation right then. "It's not fair that you can fly that fast."

"I wouldn't have to fly this fast if you weren't rushing away from me. Can I at least walk with you wherever you're running away to?"

"I'm not running away."

"Good, because the Vera I know doesn't run from anything."

That was enough to get me to stop.

"Come with me." Laurie gestured toward the doors leading out to the back garden, and I followed behind him. I'd walked in this garden with Mia before, but now that the sun was setting, the colors were all different and it seemed like a completely new place. The sunset sent shadows over the flowers and bushes, deepening their reds and greens, and the gravel walkway was lined with tiny, twinkling lights. No, not lights, I realized. The lights were actually fireflies, hundreds of fireflies flitting about, their soft yellow glow blinking and illuminating the path.

Laurie held his arm out, indicating for me to take it, just like he'd done earlier before we danced. This time I hesitated, even more unsure about everything in front of me than I had been moments ago.

"There's something I need to say to you," he said. "Walk with me?"

That made me hesitate even more. "We should get back to your party. You're the guest of honor, so I'm pretty sure they'll notice that you're gone. Or they'll notice you followed me out here, and I'm not sure which is worse. Shouldn't you go back in?"

"I'd rather be here with you. I only need a few minutes. Can you at least give me that? Then we'll go back to the fancy party with all the fancy people."

Maybe it was the eager and adorable look in his bright blue eyes, or maybe it was the influence of the dreamy twilight evening, but I took his arm, letting him lead me down the path. Even though he had said he wanted to say something, we walked in silence, the only sound the gravel crunching beneath our shoes.

"What is it you wanted to say?" I finally asked him.

"Hold that thought. First, I need to fix something."

"What's that?"

Turning to face me, in one fluid motion Laurie slipped a hand around my waist, moving my other hand in his so that we were back in the position we'd been in earlier when we were dancing.

"We didn't get to finish our dance."

"There's no music," I protested, as he started leading me in the steps right there on the gravel path.

"I'll take care of that."

Bringing me closer, his head beside mine, he began to hum a low tune. It was slow and simple, and I felt silly at first, but Laurie moved us so smoothly and gracefully that soon it didn't feel silly at all. Eventually the song ended, and he took a step back, bowing slightly as I did the same.

"There," he said. "That was even better than dancing in front of all those nosy fae inside, wasn't it?"

I didn't remember my heart pounding like this when we were back in the ballroom. While it was true that everyone had been watching us inside, somehow being alone with him out here in the garden was making me more nervous.

"Can we talk now?" I asked.

"Yes. Yes, we can. Vera," he swallowed, his wings lightly fluttering behind him. "I thought I was brave, running off to spy on the demons, but you showed me what bravery really was from the moment I met you. I can't imagine what your life has been like, yet you still face every challenge with courage and kindness."

"You're being too nice," I said, turning my head away from him and hoping he couldn't see the blush creeping over my cheeks.

"No," he said, his hand gently moving my cheek back to face him. "I want you to look at me. Really look at me, Vera. I'm right here in front of you, I've been here in front of you, and I'm not going anywhere. I want—no—I *need* you by my side."

"Laurie…" I took a step back, putting some distance between the two of us as he dropped his hand.

"Will you at least think about it? You and me. We'll bring freedom to the fae and justice to the world. Together."

"I don't think now is the time—"

"Now is exactly the time. The world is going to change, very soon, and we're going to be at the forefront of this change. I can't imagine taking this on without you." He held out his hand, palm up, waiting for me to put my hand in his. "Be with me."

Why was I being so stubborn? Laurie was kind and smart, genuine and creative, handsome and strong. Like me, he saw the injustices of the world, and he wanted to fix them. He had been willing to become a slave if it meant helping other fae.

On top of everything else, Laurie was a prince. A brave, caring, undeniably attractive prince. A prince who wanted me. Who wanted me to be a part of his family. A prince with his hand outstretched. A prince who wanted me by his side, not one who sent me away.

Laurie was the definition of perfect, so why was I hesitating?

Was it because when I stared into his blue eyes, sometimes I imagined that they were silver instead? That instead of blue wings, at night I still dreamed of black?

I'd been thinking too long, and Laurie's hand was still waiting for mine.

I knew what I needed to say.

"Laurie..."

A loud noise followed by a distant shout interrupted me, both of us looking around to try to figure out what the noise was.

"What's going on?" I asked, but Laurie only shook his head. He seemed just as confused as I was. I ran after him as he flew toward the commotion. He saw me following him and scooped me into the air, flying swiftly around the outside of the palace in the direction of the noise. Soon we saw it, dozens of fae surrounding the front gate of the palace, and Laurie and I landed on the terrace at the front of the palace.

And then I saw him, my body freezing in place as I tried to process the sight in front of me. The dark wavy hair. The wings, black as night, the ends tipped with silver.

Leo.

He was here.

Wings expanding, Leo was airborne, flying over the heads of the fae even as they tried to stop him.

There was so much I wanted to say to him. But there was also nothing I wanted to say to him. Anger and pain I hadn't felt in weeks suddenly rolled over me in massive waves, but there was also something *else*, something I wanted to shove down and never think about again, an emotion I thought I had already pushed down and away from me.

Beside me Laurie tensed, but I stood frozen as Leo landed in front of us, the fae guard rapidly approaching from behind him. His silver eyes shone bright from beneath the hood of a long black cloak that danced in the night air behind him.

"Vera. I'm taking you home."

. . .

To FIND out what happens next for Leo and Vera, be sure to read *Saved by the Demon Prince*, Book Three in the Sins of the Blood War series.

If you enjoyed this book, please leave a review. These reviews help new readers find my stories.

Want to receive updates on new books and sneak peeks? Sign up for my newsletter at http://www.laurencrowne.com.

THE END

ALSO BY LAUREN CROWNE

Saved by the Demon Prince

Book 3 in the *Sins of the Blood War* series

ACKNOWLEDGMENTS

I cannot thank you, my readers, enough. Thank you for taking a chance on this story of Leo and Vera, and thank you for all of the amazing reviews and emails you've sent me! Of course, this page would not be complete with out a huge thank you to my husband. He's my biggest cheerleader, and without him I never would have been able to chase my dream of being an author. This book would not be possible without Victory Editing, Heather at Book Cover Artistry, and Book Witch Author Services.

ABOUT THE AUTHOR

Lauren Crowne writes sexy, funny, action-packed fantasy and paranormal romance, transporting readers into a world of fae, demons, wolf shifters, and more. She always dreamed of being a writer, and she is delighted and honored to share the stories that have been bouncing around in her head for years. When she isn't writing, Lauren is addicted to drinking iced coffee and traveling with her husband and kids.

9 798986 291048